ALERT THE MEDIA

MIA FOX

Evatopia Press

Chapter 1

I didn't flinch when I read my husband's Facebook profile and learned Orlando Bloom is his all time fav actor. After all, Ryan is an actor and Orlando Bloom has a good body of work. I even remained calm when Ryan wrote about that body, citing Orlando's hotness in pirate wear. Okay, maybe this was a warning sign, but one could argue that Ryan appreciates how costume design impacts a film.

Sure, there were other signs...all ignored. In fact, it wasn't until I found his porn stash, with not so much as one breast in the mix, that I realized my rationalizations ceased to be rational. If only I had discovered Ryan in bed with a leggy blonde, even two, I could have managed. His revelation, on the other hand, gave me reason to doubt the existence of a higher being.

"April, we need to talk," he said gravely.

Talk. When people mention four-letter words that one rarely comes to mind, but in my experience it's just as toxic as the others. Case in point was this particular morning when Ryan sat me down in front of a steamy cappuccino and an obscenely large sticky bun. I regarded the bun with suspicion. I was a week shy of PMS and therefore not in need of carbs, and yet, here I was faced with a definite sign that some serious buttering up, apologizing, or pleading would occur. He obviously assumed (correctly) that artificial support would be needed.

"April, my life, actually...our lives, are about to change," he continued once I had taken a healthy bite.

"You're auditioning for a movie? Oh my gosh, I knew this day would come," I said hopefully, if not a bit naively. What can you expect from a girl voted "Most Gullible" of her high school graduating class?

Ryan treaded lightly, "Honey, it's something different. Call it a change of heart, but I've decided that I'm gay."

"Gay? As in happy?"

"No, not exactly, at least not yet. Here, have some more," he said pinching off a piece of the bun and popping it into my mouth that now hung open.

I swallowed hard. "How is this possible? We just had sex last night?"

"Yeah, I wanted to be sure. You gotta admit, we sure gave it the ol' college try."

"I'd say. We did it twice!"

"Just wanted to be 100%. April, sweetie, don't blame yourself. Listen, we'll talk later. I'm going to be late."

After delivering this verbal right hook, Ryan apologized for the "bad news" and left to start his day. Normally, I would take this opportunity to launch into any one of my workout routines. If you think only actors in Los Angeles have to look good, you're sadly mistaken. This rule applies to the thousands of people who work behind the scenes of the entertainment industry as well. Basically, anyone who comes within sneezing distance of a celebrity must be fit or that celebrity will look at your excess pudge and subconsciously believe that it's contagious and fire you. I have it doubly bad. I'm an entertainment publicist who is married to a celebrity.

This means I don't just work out, I "mix it up." I think it was a celebrity fitness guru who invented the phrase and I swear, if I ever learn their identity, I've got a mind to lock them in a room with nothing, but a seven-layer cake and a hidden camera while I'm armed with TMZ on direct dial.

Mix-it-up is code for trying the latest fitness craze, no matter how fleeting or stupid, just in case you're interviewed and asked how you manage to look so remarkable. So, in spite of owning a stationary bicycle when Ryan and I first married, I donated it to Goodwill in exchange for spinning classes at $20 a pop. Next came endurance training on the treadmill and elliptical, before evolving into pilates classes on the mat followed by pilates classes on a reformer. And now, I'm onto vinyasa flow and bikram yoga. Namaste...or in the words of a seriously hungry woman, even 90-minutes in a 102 degree room, doesn't get my blood pumping the way Ryan just did.

"Go ahead, escape," I said aloud. I wasn't sure if I was yelling the sentiment to Ryan or my heart, which was trying to beat an opening through my chest. It was't supposed to be this way. Ryan had seen enough rom/coms to know that there was a certain etiquette to breaking up. A shopping spree at Tiffany's, for instance, would have been an acceptable precursor to this event. He should know that when you're together for years, break ups aren't supposed to be conveniently dissolved over breakfast, like the pouring of Splenda into coffee.

I wondered if he would even mess up his lines while shooting "Setting Sun," his new web series soap. I started scratching the inside of my arm, a nervous habit that left me looking like a heroin addict, but in reality was the telltale signs of an addiction to unattainable men. This ailment began in fourth grade with kickball hero Jeff Simpson and continued until I met Ryan through my work. The first time he eyed me up I thought no way could someone that gorgeous be into me and yet, I landed him as a husband! Yippee! Except now my giddiness had turned to nausea. He was too good to be true.

An on-the-rise actor, I admired his dedication to his craft, but today I started seeing things a bit differently, even though everything was in its place. Ryan's closet was still organized perfectly with clothes hung in color coordinated order. In the bathroom, his cologne was lined up neatly like glass soldiers. His side of the bed was already made with hospital corners, his pillow fluffed to perfection. Nothing had changed for him. After his shoot he would go to the gym followed by his appointment with the masseur. Finally, it made sense why he was so attached to Masimo and nobody else's hands would do. I should have seen it coming, but Ryan led a very cyclical lifestyle, with one responsibility leading into the next appointment, followed by a meeting and other euphemisms that now equated into I just don't want to come home to you.

I walked back into the kitchen, but rather than put my breakfast dishes in the sink, I plunged my head deep within the porcelain walls. I shook and coughed violently, willing my anguish to leave, along with the sticky bun. My hysteria left my cheeks covered in a black trail, which left me looking like a cross between a rock star and a raccoon, which might be acceptable at some Los Angeles offices, but not mine. Like a zombie, I went into the bathroom to reapply my makeup before returning to the kitchen. I couldn't bring myself to leave it a mess just in case Ryan returned home realizing what an idiot he had been.

Carefully brushing the crumbs from the table onto my

plate, along with the half-eaten bun, made me feel better. Make it neat and tidy just as Ryan always said a home should be. Just one week earlier, I had read in Elle Decor that you could bring luxury into your home simply by sleeping on Egyptian cotton sheets, and dining with linen napkins and china just for the heck of it. But as I reached for the crumpled napkin stained with mascara, I realized that the nosy lady at the dry cleaners would now see my distress. I hurled the napkin at a wedding picture that dared smile at me and realized that no amount of tidying could put everything in its place. With welcome anger, I hurled the dirty napkin, crumbs, and then the china at the happy couple.

The phone's incessant ringing saved the remaining cup and saucer from my destruction. I sniffed hard and answered, a huge mistake since it was my mother.

"April!" she said surprised. "I didn't expect to reach you. I was going to leave a message."

"Well, I'm here," I said trying my best to sound normal.

I'm convinced that once women become mothers they develop "mommy ears," the ability to hear a child crying even above the sound of loud noises; "mommy eyes," a trait that allows them to see what you're doing even when their back is turned; and, "mommy intuition," a condition making it impossible to fool them. "You sound odd, April. Is something wrong?"

I wished this could be one of those times when I sob into the phone, letting all of my hurt wash into that tiny little hole in the mouthpiece, never to be felt or experienced again. "No, Mom. I'm just late for work and I ran my panty hose." I was better equipped to handle Mom's advice regarding torn nylon than a torn heart.

"Just put them on backwards, honey. Then, if anybody

notices, they'll just assume you didn't. Wouldn't want anybody to think you're purposefully slobby."

"No, that would be terrible. I'll just pretend I don't know I'm being slobby."

"Exactly, dear," she said in a pleased tone. "Anyway, I'm calling to coordinate Auntie Brenda's holiday brunch menu. These things take planning. You're green."

"Excuse me?" I asked.

"Green. You know, string beans, broccoli, some kind of veggie. Must have a color-coordinated table or it isn't appetizing."

"I'll bring a salad."

"Excellent, but no carrots. We've got plenty of orange. Lots of yam dishes this year. Bye, darling, we'll see you and Ryan tonight."

"Wait." The brunch wasn't for weeks. I frantically tried to remember what tonight was and how I could get out of it. "Tonight just isn't going to work. I have to work late."

"But, April, we agreed to start weekly family meals."

Weekly meals at my parents' home. I would have tried to get out of it even if Ryan and I weren't in crisis. Escaping parental scrutiny and dinner drama were the pleasures that came with adulthood. I don't know anybody who chooses to relive their teen years, and I was certainly no exception.

"I know, Mom. I promise next week."

"Put it in ink, dear. Now I'll have to break the news to your sister."

Melissa would owe me big for getting her out of this new ritual if only for a week. "Just blame it on me," I said hanging up the phone.

Who would have thought a discussion about panty hose could lead to so much exhaustion? An image of Ryan in garters suddenly flashed in my mind. "He's not gay," I said aloud. "It's just a phase," I told our fur children, Buster and Louie. "Daddy will be all better soon. I'll think of something," I said, leaning over for a much needed slurp and the approval of wagging tails.

AFTER AN ENTIRE MORNING OF CRYING, PACING, AND blowing my nose, I looked as sick as I felt. I had hoped the office would be a place where I could get my mind off my personal life, maybe even gain sympathy for looking so ghastly without having to reveal the true reason why. Yet life, particularly mine, rarely presents itself the way I would like it to. This was certainly no exception, particularly since Ryan was one of my firm's biggest accounts and I was his personal publicist.

I entered the office conference room to find my assistant, Bebe, busily applying a green tea, mud mask to our Creative Director's neck. Thus far, my assistants have either needed extensive training, or have just reached the point where they are well-trained and realize they are too advanced to be an assistant. Bebe was thankfully at the in-between stage, good for at least another six months before the threat of quitting would arise unless given a raise. She had also recently relocated to Los Angeles from Atlanta so hopefully she didn't have enough connections for me to worry about her being poached by another firm. The only obvious health benefit I could discern from Bebe bathing Josh Cohen in this green goo was he couldn't request anything from me for fear of cracking its cakey exterior.

The firm's president, Bruce Lindsay, was the only person senior to Josh. My three years at Cohen & Lindsay Creative revealed that Bruce brought forth the money, while Josh supplied an element of peculiar that the media and our clients interpreted as "genius."

I stepped over Josh's supine figure and leaned down to where Bebe was kneeling amidst bowls of slime. "I don't suppose you could give me a hand?" I asked.

"Of course. Just as soon as Josh has been thoroughly cleansed."

"Send him to church," I whispered. "I need you more."

Another ten minutes passed before Bebe appeared. "What took you? I'm on the verge of a life seizure."

Within the hour I had Bebe retrieve that day's edition of *Hollywood Reporter* and *Daily Variety* before Josh retreated into the bathroom with them. I never liked reading the mags after someone else had folded and fiddled with the different sections, disrupting their natural order and creasing the pages. The thought of going through a paper that had been exposed to Josh's bathroom air was even worse.

"Are they fresh?" I asked.

"Of course, they're pre-prune," she said knowingly.

I grabbed for the papers and began feverishly turning the pages until I found what I wanted.

"Ooh, news about Ryan? Hurry, I wanna see, too," she said leaning over my shoulder.

I fumbled with the papers a minute, turning to the "First Look" and "Talent Watch" sections, trying in vein to find any news about Ryan that might give me a sign as to who or what had brought on this epiphany. "Bebe, I don't think we're in luck this morning."

"Okie dokie, I'll just check on Josh if you don't need me."

I waited until Bebe skipped across the hall to Josh's

office before returning to the section that would really give me an answer...my horoscope.

Aries: Love relationship on tender hooks while moon is in Jupiter; give partner space for personal growth. Focus on quiet solitude to promote healing.

I understand the theory of planetary pull, but in my experience, the planets never pull for me. The realization has forced me to discover my own astrological solution. If I find anything remotely negative with my horoscope, Aries (March 21-April 20 to be exact), I search for another sign more suitable. I figure with rising signs, birth signs, moon signs, and sun signs we're all somehow related to nearly every sign. When the planets are completely ignorant of my needs, I form a sort of horoscope soufflé, gently folding in portions of one reading to add to another.

My mother, a devout horoscope follower and Hints from Heloise reader, is convinced my practice can only lead to heartache and poor investments. My sister, Melissa, fears horoscopes reduce spontaneity by causing unnecessary consideration of one's actions. In the continuum of my family, I fall somewhere in between.

"Give partner space for personal growth." Right. As if I could sit idle and allow Ryan to nab more boyfriends than my life's total. I had to do something to correct this injustice. Ryan was obviously insane, and I was meant to be with him!

Today, I was clearly meant to follow my moon sign (planets, please forgive me). I turned to Taurus for a dose of bull-headedness.

Taurus: Avoid regret by taking action. Domestic issues dominate. Much better.

Time to retrieve Bebe, whom I feared if left alone in Josh's office for too long could be catapulted from my assistant to his girlfriend. Life was already too stressful to risk Bebe getting a promotion and an expense account with just a bat of her mile-long eyelashes. Josh was certainly not above falling for her. What she lacked in brain power, she more than made up for in the care she took with her appearance. Those caterpillar lashes were the result of nightly Latisse applications, her hair shined with an obvious Brazilian blow-out treatment and her bum's lack of panty lines were suspiciously due to a lack of panties. With assets like that, Josh declared that I finally hired a winner. And, he had a point.

"Bebe, could you come back?" I called over the intercom.

"I've already left," she answered cheerily.

Even though I was Bebe's direct supervisor, it was obvious that I could learn a few things from this cup-is-half-full type of girl who didn't have the decency to ever experience a bad hair day. I tried to think for a moment how she would handle the depression, but came up with a loss since that was an emotion that never seemed to invade her psyche. She may have only been in her early twenties, but she was wise in the ways of finding inner peace. Since hiring her, she had never once complained about her personal life. An endless smile always adorned her perfect face. And, she took on mundane tasks with the seriousness of a surgeon tackling a heart transplant. She was the perfect assistant. But today, as I watched her annoyingly petite hips sway toward me, it became obvious why happy people are such miserable company when one is depressed. Bebe wasn't just happy, she was practically effervescent. My contact with men makes them believe they are gay; Bebe's bouncy walk and even bouncier breasts made them swoon.

"Bebe, where do you get something like that?" I asked pointing to her obscenely short skirt.

"Josh says this is fine to wear to the office," she answered defensively. He would.

I forced the corners of my mouth to tilt upward. "Yes, it's lovely. I'd love to get one myself."

"Really? Well, I can take you at lunch. We can shop, and..."

"I'm really not very good company today. I should probably shop alone, if you don't mind."

I might as well have been conversing with a puppy. Her brown eyes grew big and wet, her peppy demeanor vanished. "Oh Bebe, it's not that I don't want your company, I just...here's the deal, I need you to drum up some positive publicity for Ryan immediately."

"Is something wrong?" she uttered from lips that didn't have the decency to require collagen.

"No, not really," I said while contemplating how truly wrong everything was in my life.

Bebe was all too familiar with the cover-up public relations campaigns that our firm often launched. Being known as the P.R. firm to call when a celeb got into a tight spot, needed to promote their charity of choice, or just plain needed to get back into the spotlight, she had seen first-hand how brainstorm sessions launched in our conference room ended up as news stories for the latest blogs and entertainment press.

"Was he caught...doing something? You know, drugs, illicit sex...," she interrupted her own thoughts. "Oh April, I'm so sorry!"

"No, it's nothing like that. It's not a personal matter," I lied. "It's just that Ryan gets tired of doing all those interviews. He's been asking for some effortless promotion."

If Ryan was just going through a phase, a romantic dinner and the promise of a feature story might bring him out of it. Besides, I would definitely earn brownie points with Josh and Bruce for a quick media blitz. It was the ideal approach to keep my husband and avoid my corner office from becoming a love gift from Josh to Bebe.

"Bebe, start calling the fashion editors. It's nearly the end of the year, so we have a four-month lead on the spring issues. Tell them we have a great suggestion for one of those celebrity closet cases...uh, I mean a peak into the closet of a celebrity. Make sure you say it right. Wouldn't want them to get the wrong idea."

"You're okay, right?"

Bebe looked at me as if examining a laboratory experiment gone wrong. It was clear that I had better get a handle on my personal life or my professional one would certainly suffer.

Chapter 2

R yan never said he wasn't coming home, so I planned to be waiting with a scene to put those Hollywood movies to shame. But as I imagined a happy ending, in more ways than one, I realized how overdue I was for a visit to my aesthetician. I popped two Advil and headed to the salon during my lunch hour.

"That kills!" I exclaimed as cloth strips were ripped from my legs.

"The price for beauty," Agnes replied happily. "Your man likes smooth skin, no?"

"Yes, he prefers the just-ripped feel of fresh skin over stubble," I agreed as Agnes removed another strip of cloth from my leg, causing tears to form. My only consolation was realizing that these were the first tears of the day not caused by Ryan, at least not directly.

As Agnes, pronounced "On-yes," continued to inflict more pain, I tried to focus on the fact that I would walk out, or perhaps limp away, looking just a bit sexier, more like Agnes, a five-foot-eight French beauty with long, lean, touchable legs. Or I could just pretend. I was five-foot-two with wavy dark hair typical of my Jewish heritage. Agnes probably didn't even have to go through this as she had super-fine, blonde hair. I held my breath as she ripped away another strip, wondering if it were possible that she had problems with limpness, both on her head and in her bed.

Only one more limb to go. I thanked God that I had no trace of facial hair. Fortunately, none of my elderly, female relatives have begun to sprout either. So I assume I'm safe for the duration of my life.

I returned to the office confident that my skin was touchably ready for Ryan, but worried that my clothes would never entice him to take them off. I glanced out my office door to witness Bebe coming out of Josh's office while adjusting her thigh-high knit stockings. Blocking out my mind to the infinite possible reasons why she appeared in a state of half-dress, I stopped her mid-tug. "Bebe, can you find out Josh's favorite color and fabric?"

"On men or women? Bed linens or clothing?" Bebe asked professionally. When it came to fashion, she was all business.

"*Vanity Fair* is preparing a feature, 'What real men will wear this season,' and I want Ryan included. Frankly, Josh's views are more acceptable, uh, I mean accessible. Be discreet," I said nodding toward Josh's door.

"No need for that," she said smugly. "Earth tones and soft cotton for him. Shades of rose for me...I mean women," she recovered. "He likes to decorate his house in clean whites to create a pure environment. How's that? Anything else?"

"That's plenty. Thanks."

Reconstituted lunch meat would be considered more pure. Right now, my insides were a churning mess of feelings that had once appeared so real and now were just a fabrication. I felt as if my entire being had been turned inside out, like one of the dirty t-shirts Ryan used to throw on the floor, used...discarded...unwanted. I loved him so much. I wondered if he could feel me thinking of him, wishing that everything that had transpired this morning was just a mood swing, a temporary moment of insanity. I could forgive him for the turmoil he had put me through. I would just tell him that he had been under a lot of pressure and these passing moments of insanity happen to the best of us. We would laugh until we fell into each other's arms and then stare into each other's eyes when he would lean in and whisper...

"April, in my office!"

Shit. What did I forget to do? Josh never shouts. It's against his zen beliefs and the fact that he usually can't be bothered to care enough.

"Sure," I said while following behind him like a puppy.

"I just got a call from Ryan. Is there something you want to tell me?"

He couldn't have told Josh about our talk. Why would he get so personal? Unless, he really wanted nothing to do with me, even professionally. Oh double shit. I was losing my husband and my firm's largest account all in the same breath. That's what I get for sleeping with clients, although in all fairness we did get married, so the sex part is kind of expected.

"What do you mean?" I asked innocently.

"He asked if we were including him in this month's press releases. Wasn't he recently mentioned by that celebrity blogger? Why the sudden need for hand-holding?"

"I've no idea," I said with a dose of truth. Ryan couldn't have known that I was scrambling for more press. He wouldn't have even expected it considering recent results on his behalf. "Did he say anything else? Did he mention me?" I couldn't believe that I was asking my boss about my husband.

"Only that he expected you to still be in charge of his account. You haven't taken on any new accounts that would limit your time for Ryan, have you?"

"Of course not. It's still my top priority." My heart did a little bounce as I connected the dots. Ryan had to be having a change of heart about us. He realized how valuable I was to him both personally and professionally and he was making sure I knew it because he was too embarrassed to call me at work and say he had make the biggest mistake of his life. He still loved me.

"Alright, then," Josh said standing up, "get on with it. Go find a cover story."

* * *

Ryan's opinions, albeit from Josh, would appear in the April issue of *Vanity Fair*. The editor of *Us* promised that Ryan would be mentioned in a round-up article about celebrity hair stylists and their coifed clients. I had little success with *GQ*, but decided not to fret since it wouldn't serve my plans to have Ryan turned into a pin-up for its predominantly male readership. It was much better to get him featured in a *People* issue about celebrity weekend getaway preferences and have Ryan describe where he would most like to spend time with his leading lady from "Setting Sun." How I wished at a time like this, that he would admit that he was in a committed relationship, but we had agreed long ago that it didn't serve his public image. Still, he would soon be professing his love to me, at least privately.

In just three months the *Vanity Fair* issue would hit the

stands and Christmas would be upon us. We were going to have the holiday to remember forever. I was counting on Ryan's ego to bring him back to his senses and me.

After all, his chest may have earned him the Calvin Klein underwear ad, but I got him the part on "Setting Sun." At first, Ryan's role of the brooding stable hand was small, but it grew as letters from women offering to saddle up with him arrived. It bothered me at first, but I quickly got used to it and even learned to embrace the fact that I was the one who went home with him, even if nobody knew it.

For a brief moment I thought about running my situation past my family. Maybe Mom could've offered some advice beyond my dressing habits this morning, but then I thought better of it. Everything was going to be okay. Why worry them unnecessarily especially since until now, Melissa was always the one to cause worry lines to form on my mother's forehead. I figured I had enough going wrong that I didn't deserve to relinquish my status as the stress-free child and inherit my parents' renewed interest in my personal life. Besides, Ryan was in love with me, and within a couple of hours he would remember it.

I left the office to pick up dinner and an outfit--both had to be sensational.

"SMELLS GREAT. WHAT ARE YOU MAKING?" RYAN ASKED.

Since I couldn't possibly buy a new dress and have time to cook myself, the gourmet market served as my culinary matchmaker. "You will be amazed," I answered smugly.

"April, you're not kidding," Ryan yelled from the kitchen.

"Good enough to eat, huh?" I called back, not wanting

to disturb my perfect pose on the couch. I was showing just the right amount of leg through the thigh-high slit on my new dress.

Ryan returned to the living room, "What is all that?"

He pronunciation was distinct, a speech pattern that erupted whenever he did. "Dinner," I answered simply.

"That's not dinner," he said pointing towards the kitchen. "That's a seduction."

"Just a little one. Nothing to worry about," I encouraged. "You're an actor, a virtual chameleon of characters. Listen, I've been thinking that it's probably normal that you had these thoughts. You pretend to be so many different people that you've probably just lost sight of the real you."

He stood over me while I tried to channel Megan Fox. I thought of smoldering eyes, long, outstretched legs, and my chest rising with temptation. "I'm gay," he said, completely spoiling my moment.

"No. You are not gay. We are married." I stood up and grabbed his arm. "Come on, let's go have our romantic dinner and talk about the wonderful magazine cover I'm going to get you. I heard you spoke with Josh, you sneaky cuddle monkey. You've got nothing to worry about. I am totally on top of your account as if nothing happened this morning."

That's right. Nothing. Happened. That's my story and I'm sticking to it. I hadn't had my share of good luck during my lifetime and it was about time karma started to smile on me. For God's sake, I couldn't stand the fact that my parents' love life might surpass my own. There couldn't be anything more depressing except Ryan's continued "talk."

"I'm sorry if I spoiled your plans for the evening," he said evenly.

"That's okay," I said reaching to caress his face, that perfect high cheek-boned cheek that I so wanted to kiss. "It could be worse," I joked, "you could've spoiled my plans for our life." I started to move toward the kitchen, relieved that the fighting was over.

"April, I'm sorry. You have to listen. As hard as this is, you need to hear me," Ryan continued.

"Okay. Tell me."

"My intention tonight was just to come over and pack up some stuff. I thought the fact that you were offering me dinner meant you were okay with the whole thing."

"Please, Ryan. This is just a phase," I said quietly. "All couples go through it. Take some time, if that's what you want."

He placed his hands on my shoulders. Finally! We were going to kiss! He was going to tell me how wonderful I was for being so patient. "I want to date," he said.

"That's great," I said with relief. It wasn't a kiss, but that could certainly come with dating. "You mean, the once-a-week, 'date night' sort of thing that will renew our spark?"

"Not exactly. I was thinking more along the lines of going out with *other* people and renewing *my* spark," he answered.

Ryan's words were like a piece of chewing gum that didn't have the decency to rub off my shoe and onto somebody else's sidewalk. It just got stickier.

"April, I've felt this way for a long time, at least two years."

"We've only been together two years," I wailed. "How could I miss all this?"

"It seemed like a good arrangement at first," he admitted. "I wanted to be a star; you were an entertainment publicist. It's hard to make it as a heartthrob if you're gay."

"It works for Rupert Everett," I answered glumly.

"He had Julia Roberts."

"Gee, thanks."

"That's not what I meant. You're great. But I had to wait this out until I got my share of good publicity."

"I was more than just your publicist," I said still trying not to hear his words.

"Of course, we're...," he said struggling for the right words. I thought of a few dozen I wanted to interject. He continued, "We're good companions." Oh my God, it was worse than a "let's just be friends" speech.

"April, I see no reason why our professional relationship shouldn't continue. You're very good at what you do. Besides, my career climb has been good for you too. You can't deny that my account isn't important to your firm."

"I don't think of you as an account," I said barely above a whisper.

"Maybe you should."

I was slow, but not catatonic. When one person breaks up with another and talks about dating, they usually have a head start. "Are you already dating?"

"Just a little," he said quickly.

"A little? As in passing a good-looking stranger on the street, whom you wouldn't dare approach because you're married, but might if your divorce was totally final and a proper amount of mourning had passed?"

He nodded sheepishly. "Something like that."

A sudden pounding had started in my temples and was threatening to move south causing my heart to break even further. "Ryan? Just tell me."

"Matthew has become a part of my life."

"You have a boyfriend?" I said incredulously.

"You would probably call it that," he admitted. "Matthew probably would too."

THAT NIGHT, I GOT READY FOR BED. ALONE. I RECALLED our wedding, a ceremony intended to be the most beautiful of events--the perfect send-off for a lifetime of happiness. Hah! Dad should have saved the $50,000. Five years ago, it covered the cost of my one-time-use gown, the hotel venue, band, photographer, videographer, and even a food designer! We actually hired someone to paint little black and white tuxedos out of white and dark chocolate onto the strawberries that were placed at each table. And the flowers. My lord, I've never seen so many. What was I thinking? Multitudes of white roses cascaded over the huppa, the Jewish canopy, ensuring that their fragrance filled the air. Little girls wearing white lace dresses dropped petals along the aisle's runner. We stood holding each other's hands, our guests watching with anticipation. "Doesn't it look lovely?" one woman exclaimed.

That was my dream. The nightmare that occurred during my first night without Ryan next to me was slightly different.

I SAW MYSELF WALKING DOWN THE AISLE, SMILING TO GUESTS on either side. The woman who complimented me was still there, but that's where the similarities ended. Rather than express her approval, she checked her watch and loudly inquired when this sham was supposed to end. The other guests seemed equally annoyed as they waited in sticky, still, humid air.

The harpist played a love song that was made unrecognizable by the uncontrolled sliding of her sweaty hands. My mother bustled nervously, greeting guests who were properly separated on opposing sides of the aisle. "Stifling," escaped from one man as he took a seat next to my Aunt Brenda and removed his jacket to expose damp, yellow-stained underarms, causing Brenda's eyes to roll upward. A mixture of smells filled the air. The men, the catering, and the scent of fifty women competing with one another for a signature bouquet.

Finally, I reached Ryan at the end of the aisle. He held out his hand and I accepted, but no sooner had our hands clasped around each other when mine slipped away as I plummeted to the ground. Our guests watched in horror as I fainted before God, the rabbi, my family, friends, and husband-to-be, an omen of what was to come.

IT MUST HAVE BEEN ONE OF THOSE INVOLUNTARY MUSCLE spasms that made me feel like I was falling. I was awake, but I didn't dare open my eyes yet. For a split second I thought that maybe it really was all a dream and when I opened my eyes, Ryan would be lying next to me.

Don't open them. Don't do it. But it was time to get ready for work, so I had no choice but to face the fact that Ryan wasn't lying next to me. He was probably lying next to Matthew. I padded into the bathroom, turned on the shower and grabbed my clothes.

My thoughts of what went wrong played in my mind as I fed Buster and Louie, our fur children -- a slightly over-weight Golden Retriever and his companion, a mutt-like Terrier. Then, on the 405 freeway as traffic climbed over the Sepulveda pass, I contemplated if there were signs that Ryan was gay as I replayed the rest of the nightmare in my mind.

AS BEST HE TRIED, RYAN'S KISS COULDN'T HIT ITS TARGET. The wedding vows were declared; the rabbi had done his deed. Now it was Ryan's turn to take the lead, but he kept missing. He thanked me for the stroll down the aisle and then turned to the rabbi, I assumed to thank him as well. Instead, Ryan firmly planted his hand behind the rabbi's neck. They locked eyes and Ryan leaned forward. But he missed! It was like watching a perverse game of pin the tail on the donkey as Ryan's lips landed on the rabbi's cheek. If we were French or Italian the gesture would have been perfectly acceptable. Unfortunately, we weren't and any question about the appropriateness of Ryan's display was awash as he tried again and again. One might say the second kiss was hindered by God as the rabbi released two powerful sneezes directly onto Ryan's face. For the first time, I was pleased that Ryan wasn't trying to smack those sprayed lips onto mine. I suppose the moment had been lost for Ryan as well. With a shrug of his shoulders, he opted to do it doggie-style. He stuck out his tongue and licked our rabbi's face.

A BLARE OF A CAR HORN BROUGHT ME BACK TO MY senses. If fate meant that I had to live through this phase of Ryan's, waiting patiently until he came to his senses, then it also had a hand in jostling me out of my daydream just as a large Catholic church appeared on my left. Without a moment's hesitation, I swerved across the traffic dividing line, accepted the horns and finger flips of the two cars that had to slam on their brakes to avoid me and continued straight into the church's parking lot. Work could wait. My salvation couldn't.

Temple was never really my family's thing. Sure, we celebrated the holidays as much as other Jews, but more in terms of eating our way through the religion. I had a warped sense of my heritage. Hannukah was a religious decree to eat fried food. Passover was the seder dinner and on our table the hard-boiled eggs were dyed in pastel colors so Melissa and I wouldn't be sad that we didn't get Easter eggs. For most Jews, Yom Kippur meant fasting for 24 hours to atone for their sins. For me, Mom didn't want me to get light-headed so she merely cleared the house of anything with chocolate. It's no wonder I lived in fear of my family's sins. So to hedge my bet, every once in awhile I would sneak into Catholic confession. I never went to the same church twice in case the priest recognized me and wondered why it had been some two or three years since my last confession. I took it as a positive sign that a church appeared on my radar just when I needed it most.

"Forgive me Father, it has been a very long time since my last confession," I began once seated in the confessional.

"What's important is that you are here now. Continue, my child."

"Well, I'm having some problems in my marriage."

"Marriage is never easy, but things that are worthwhile, rarely come easily," the priest spoke wisely.

"I agree. But it's my husband who wants to end our relationship." I decided to keep my mouth shut about Ryan's reasons.

"Sometimes these things happen for a reason," he said.

Really? Wasn't that the type of rhetoric that spouts from yogis or people who actually believe in letting life unfold as it may? I have to say that I was a tad disappointed in this new priest. I had expected him to tell me to fight for my man, not the 'leave 'em alone and they'll come home' line.

"So, what do you suggest I do?"

"Focus on yourself...your health, your other relationships. Do you have parents? Siblings, friends? Do you work?"

"Well, yes to all of that."

"Then look at this as a gift," he said.

"A gift?" No wonder my parents had raised me Jewish.

"Yes, it's a time for self-reflection and a chance to improve other aspects of your life."

"But there must be something I can do about Ryan."

"Of course, my child. You can always pray on it."

After a few more questions and observant answers, I walked out of the confessional and back to my car. I didn't know what in the world to pray for. Did I pray that Ryan came back to me? I had a feeling that I wasn't supposed to pray on self-serving things. Should I ask God to make Ryan straight, just in case this wasn't a passing fancy? I had a feeling that request would be shot down as well for maybe it wasn't in everyone's best interest.

As for my nightmare, the priest was kind enough, explaining it away as relationship jitters, but so much time has passed since I received a passionate, wedding-style kiss with all of its hope and promise, that I needed a better use for my overactive imagination.

I hoped the office would be a place to put it to use. Thankfully, only Bebe seemed to notice my late arrival. She already had my mail spread out over my desk. A woman's magazine touted how to keep your man happy. The center seam opened to an ad featuring Ryan in his underwear. I slammed it shut and reached for the stack of envelopes. The first one on the pile was my all too familiar credit card bill, but it was strangely thick this month. I ripped it open and scanned the purchases, holding a yellow highlighter, which out of habit I kept nearby to circle the items that could be expense accounted. Only none of the purchases rang a bell. I went through the numbers more slowly, finding the usual suspects -- the client lunch at Versailles, the morning Starbucks runs, the dry cleaners, but these few items didn't even begin to make a dent in the pages and pages of items listed.

I started to panic that someone had gotten a hold of

my card and quickly checked my wallet, but that little plastic security blanket was still safely tucked in its place. I went back to scanning the bill and found listings for restaurants, salons and stores I had never visited.

"He planned this!" I shouted out loud, staring at the bill. Before having the decency to let me down, Ryan had given himself ample time to vamp up his look and lifestyle, bringing the credit card, the one which remained in my name, to the limit.

I was in debt, humiliated, and alone.

Chapter 3

Two weeks after Ryan moved his toothbrush to its new location, I summoned the courage to admit to my friends that he was not "out of town for an audition." I continued, however, to avoid the subject at the office and around my parents. Bebe was likely to hand me a stack of women's magazines. My mother would call Aunt Brenda for a referral to a psychologist. She had at least five at the ready depending upon the mental malady that was currently plaguing her psyche. Jessica, whom I consider to be my closest friend, the one I will even pee in front of, had her own way of helping. She immediately asked if I saw "the signs."

"What signs?" I asked.

"There must have been signs," she said emphatically. "You probably chose to ignore them. Turned a blind ear."

"It's 'blind eye or deaf ear.' Pick one," I said into the phone, sounding much stronger than I felt.

"You had blind ears, alright. Blinders...like the kind horses wear."

"They weren't there," I insisted.

"Sure," Jessica countered.

"Well, not at first," I admitted while watching out for Bebe.

"Reduced sex drive? Changes in personal grooming?" she inquired clinically.

I attempted to make light of my situation, "Isn't marital sex strictly for reproduction?"

"If you're a rabbit," she said knowingly.

"He did have a thing for fabric," I admitted.

"Details, please."

I felt sick and exposed, as if sitting on cold metal with my bum exposed through the back of a hospital gown. "He wore my bathrobe. The silk one. It continued even after I bought him a terry cloth one last Valentine's."

"I can't imagine," Jessica replied sympathetically.

"Yeah," I answered. "He didn't even look good in lavender."

I closed the door to my office and proceeded to tell her about my nail theory. Ryan's nails were filed square at the tips, extremely clean, no torn cuticles in sight, and were void of overt biting. This used to be a good sign in my book. I took good grooming habits to mean a man was responsible. Lack of biting, chewing, or sucking also meant he was free of neuroses.

As I proceeded to relay accounts of the traits that first attracted me to Ryan, Jessica pointed out that most of them also indicated he was gay. I felt like a human metronome with my emotions undulating between humiliation and horror. I had been intent on proving that I hadn't started dating Ryan strictly because of his looks as my family feared. I insisted that we connected on a higher level and had much in common. It was the truth, but it also ended up proving that I found a male version of my sorority sisters with a weak Y chromosome and an opportunistic streak.

"I don't want to say 'I told you so,' but I hope you remember this the next time a cute client comes your way," Jessica added.

"Point taken. Except there are always exceptions."

"April, haven't you been through enough?"

"I don't know," I admitted. "I don't want to think about being alone forever. No children, except for Buster and Louie. Or worse, I do find a man, but I'm so worried he'll end up like Ryan that I seek out really manly men, the hairy ones with horrible grooming habits."

"I hope that doesn't include a subtle smelliness," Jessica stated with a distinct nasal quality in her voice. I assumed she was holding her nose as if to make her point.

"Oh know! I forgot about Antonio!"

"Interesting leap," Jessica teased. "Don't bring him to any of my parties."

"He's my mechanic. No B.O., just a sort of built-in gasoline scent."

"I stand by my first comment."

"I forgot to pick up my car. Ryan used to handle it for me; he was probably after Antonio," I said as an afterthought. We hung up and I searched out Bebe for a ride to the garage.

It was easy to tune out while Bebe drove. She sang to the radio and talked more to herself than to me. The conversation wasn't about anything in particular, which I welcomed in my state. Bebe described her favorite weekend activities such as rock-climbing and marathon training. It was no wonder that she had a body that defied gravity. Somewhere around Wilshire and Doheny I made the mistake of saying that I had a lot of extra time on my hands these days and maybe I should start running.

"How can you have free time?" Bebe asked, suddenly more interested in my half of the conversation. "You have a full client load and don't you have premieres and things to attend with Ryan? It must be so glamorous," she said wistfully.

"Oh it's not all that. Most of the time, I'm still working those events. You know, making sure that Ryan is photographed from his right side, which is actually the left."

"Wow, that is so confusing. April, you are so good at your job."

I looked over just to make sure she wasn't being sarcastic, but she no sooner stepped on the gas and pointedly said, "I'll stick to toiling the trades for news about our clients. It's much simpler than having to create the news."

I leaned back and thought about how nice it would be to lead a simple life where one's personal and professional lives weren't so intertwined. And yet, if I had to do it all over again, I'd no doubt repeat my mistakes.

In spite of Ryan's deception, both about his sexual preferences and maxing out our credit cards, I was still in love with him. I kept thinking about what I could do to make Ryan realize how amazing I was. I could get him the best P.R. of his career, forgive the spending, and forget about his lover, Matthew. But it wasn't as easy as all that because the whole forgive and forget thingie would take a very adult person and frankly, I'm not sure I was cut out for such maturity.

If I were true to myself, I would have to admit that Ryan never showed me the kind of love he displayed to his co-stars, and I couldn't live my whole life wishing for something that wasn't there. My life had all of the drama of a soap opera without any of the steamy sex. I deserved an adult relationship with all of the things that adults claim they want. You know, someone who respects them, shares the same values, would make an ideal life partner and be great with kids. Blah blah blah. But cut to the chase, what I really wanted was someone who wanted me back.

"You're right," I said to Bebe.

"About what?"

"For once, it would be nice to just be appreciated. How many of our clients do that? No, it's always 'why was the article so short?' and 'why did so and so get top billing?' Never do they say, 'Hey April, I know it's just one eeny weeny paragraph mention on page 10, but it's okay because I know how many hours you spent getting me even that and frankly, who am I to want more?' Hell, it's not like they're finding a cure for cancer!"

Bebe was stopped at a red light that had since gone green, but still she continued to stare at me. "You okay?"

"It's green," I pointed out. And when the car started up again, "yeah, I'm fine."

I remained silent for the rest of the journey, but continued to reflect on the fact that my husband finds other men more attractive than myself. If I'm going to be honest, I'm probably at the top of the needs-to-get-laid list. I can't remember the last time I was hit on by a strapping young male. It's possible that in my married state I just wasn't sending out signals, but you'd think that in the last two years someone would've approached me for a little afternoon delight, a casual no-strings attached hook-up. It's not that I condone having an affair, I just wondered if I was even seen as viable in the sex department. It'd be nice to get a little ego boost now and again.

I looked over at Bebe, once again driving happily along, her skirt inching itself up so that every guy in a monster truck or big rig could get a thrill. She probably gets hit on in the produce aisle.

"Bebe, what's your opinion...do men hit on women they find attractive or women who they think are available?"

"A bit of both, I would think," she answered. "And sometimes neither one."

"What do you mean?"

"Most men like a woman who is approachable. That might translate into a woman who isn't the most attractive one in the room, is in fact, married, but she knows how to flirt."

I thought about what she was saying and realized I didn't know a thing about flirting. How was it that I had passed through my college years without ever taking a course? "What if you're bad at flirting? Will you never get hit on?"

"You should know," she answered with a knowing glance.

"Ouch."

"Sorry, April. Why are you asking?"

What was I doing? I shouldn't be discussing my love life, or lack thereof, with a co-worker let alone a co-worker who worked under me. But, then again, I could probably learn a few things from Bebe.

"Just wanting to renew the spice in my marriage, you know."

"The sexperts says a girl should never get complacent," she agreed. "That's the beauty of harmless flirting. It's like a dress rehearsal for the real thing. Hey, we're here," she pointed to the garage. "Ooh, he's cute," she said seeing Antonio, the mechanic, bent over the hood of a car.

"Yeah." Suddenly I wondered if Ryan had perfected his flirting technique every time he took my car in.

"Maybe you should practice with him," Bebe

suggested. "Then, you see what works and bring that home to Ryan."

"I don't know. What would I say? What do I do?"

"Just tell him that your car was obviously in very capable hands," she said.

"Ooh, I don't know. I can't imagine saying that. You're better at this than I am. Maybe we could try that whole Cyrano routine?"

Bebe pulled into reverse. "I'll see you back at the office. Let me know how it goes."

"Thanks for the ride."

I waited quietly for Antonio to emerge from under the car's hood, thinking about how cute he was, how long it had been since I had sex, and whether Bebe's idea of flirting would actually test my attraction meter. Maybe I should bat my eyes at Antonio, if only to jumpstart Ryan's battery. But as I tried to muster up the courage, my feet remained glued to their place. My imagination, however, had its own idea.

"BE CAREFUL MY DELICATE LITTLE DOVE," ANTONIO SAID IN full on Italian sexiness. It was just like me to slip while wearing white. I landed on my bottom, but Antonio was there to dust it off. I told him it wasn't necessary, but he insisted. "You should remove thees right away," he said running both hands down my waist and along the sides of my thighs. I assume that Ryan was pained with jealousy because he hadn't made an appearance in my dream. "Your pants weel be rueened," Antonio continued.

If Antonio had been a typical American Andrew or say an Adam, I probably would have freaked out and told him under no uncertain terms that he was to remove his hands from my body immediately. How dare he. But, with Antonio's sexy accent and the possibility that it would drive

Ryan back to me, I had no problem (at least my imagination, had no problem) of him touching my thighs without even knowing my name.

"Oh it's okay," I gushed. *"It's nice of you to distract me while I wait for my car. My ride seems to have left me."*

Wait a minute…was it really necessary for my imagination to tell my imaginary flirtation that my ride had left me? He might read too much into it and realize that "waiting for my car" was actually a subconscious euphemism for "waiting for sex" and telling him that "my ride seems to have left me" must really be code for "my husband has walked out." Damn my imagination for trying to tell gorgeous Antonio that Ryan had a better lay and life partner to get to. If I were going to have a steamy imaginary friend in Antonio I was going to do it right, so help me. Okay, I was ready. Take two.

"So, you weel remove your pants for me? I weel take care of thees mess you are in." What a charmer he was! Someone to clean up my mess! By now, the grease spot on my backside didn't look so out of place since an assortment of grimy fingerprints had joined it. Thank you, Antonio.

"I weel take you on the ride of your life," he said.

That sounded right up my alley. Antonio placed me on top of the hydraulic lift. With a flip of a lever I start to move upward, and in one swift jump, he joins me. I shimmy my hips back and forth so as to remove my pants while trying to stay flat and avoid being seen, but my gyrations have lodged a splinter into my left cheek. My luck. Antonio flips me on top of his knee like a child about to receive a spanking. He leans forward and plucks the object from me with his teeth.

"There. Eesn't that better?" he asks and spits out the offensive material. I haven't moved and I'm sure anyone entering the garage will see me, but Antonio quickly dissipates this thought by kissing my

bottom better. I don't care who sees me. We could do it standing up, on this lift, six feet above the ground, and I wouldn't care.

I DIDN'T GET THE CHANCE TO PLAY OUT MY ANTONIO fantasy. He wasn't working, which was probably just as well. I was doomed when it came to flirting and even if I weren't, there was simply no time for it. Bebe, who had already made it back to the office, texted me stating that Ryan was waiting to see me. I had planned to get lunch while I was out, but this news squelched my appetite. So I got behind the wheel, grabbed my headset and immediately called Jessica for a pep talk.

"Do you think...under the circumstances...that Josh would forgive me for having sex with Ryan in my office?"

"Oh my god. You and Ryan had sex in your office?" Jessica screamed, before covering the phone and saying to someone in the room with her, "No, you don't know her. No, she's not single. Well, she sort of is, but no you can't go out with her."

"Who are you talking to?"

"It's no one," Jessica explained. "Just that pervy guy in the office next to mine. I'll keep it down," she said scarcely above a whisper. "Go on, tell me what happened."

"Nothing happened. I'm not even in my office. I'm driving there, but Bebe told me that Ryan is waiting for me. Do you think he wants to make up? Because if he does, I'm thinking it should be a really dramatic moment, like looking into each other's eyes, throwing the papers off the desk and then...you know."

There was no answer from Jessica.

"Jess?"

And then finally... "Yes, I'm still here. I just don't know

what to say, April. I'm worried about you. I say this with love in my heart and the utmost of respect. Okay, here it goes. You are a total wanker loser."

"Well, I'm trying not to be a wanker. I mean, hello, I'm willing to have sex in my office. People who wank don't need to have sex."

Jessica sounded even more impatient as she spoke in even tones. "April, I meant that you and Ryan are over, and even if he comes back with his tail between his legs, you should insist on it being over."

Now it was my turn to be silent. A sniffle escaped me.

"Are you okay?" she asked.

"Yeah. You're right. I'll just tell him that I can't get over this betrayal and that we hadn't been connecting in a long time. Right?"

"Right. Good girl," she said.

"But it hurts so much," I wailed into my headset. "Why can't I just get him back?"

"April, you need to stop crying because your nose will be runny and your eyes will be red and that's just not a good look on you, especially when you want to make the point that you're doing fine."

"Maybe he's been crying too."

"Maybe he has," she said, sounding again like my best friend.

But when I arrived at my office I saw that Ryan had not been crying, moping or staying up nights with insomnia. He looked flawless. Even when his wavy, blond hair dared to dip over his eye, he looked sensational because it instigated a head flipping action that showed off his square jawline. As I walked toward him he flashed his perfect smile and my stomach did a back flip. Damn myself for being so eager.

"Hi. What are you doing here?" I said still hoping that the answer was that he was here for me.

"I came to see you."

"You did?" I said with renewed hope. I couldn't wait to tell Jessica!

"Yeah, I'm just not happy with the amount of coverage I've been getting. I thought we should strategize. Don't take this the wrong way, but you've kinda dropped the ball lately."

"Excuse me? You want to have a client meeting? Now? With me?"

"Well, you are my publicist, until I decide otherwise."

"It seems that's your motto with a lot of things. I'm also your wife, but you've decided we're getting a divorce."

"Come on, April, we don't need that little thing to get in the way."

This wasn't happening. "What do you mean by get in the way? You can't be serious about us still working together."

"Why not? I think you're an amazing publicist...when you have your head in the game." I was about to throw a tantrum, something worthy of an academy award, but that only worked in the movies. Also, my boss, Josh, had just spotted Ryan in my office and decided to join us.

Josh gave Ryan the back-pat followed by the two-handed shake. Very manly. Lots of testosterone thrown in for good measure. "Ryan, how you doing? What do we owe the pleasure?"

"I'm good. Just thought it was time to strategize about my account."

Josh looked worried. Whenever a client wanted to "strategize" it meant they weren't happy with the amount of press they were getting and it was basically a polite way of saying get my mug out there or you won't be seeing it around here.

"By all means," Josh said easily. "Why don't the three of us have a pow-wow in my office? I know April's been cooking something up." Josh gave me a look that implied I should turn my brain on and pop out a creative wonder pronto. He seemed to think I was similar to an electric kettle and in a mere ninety seconds or by the time we all got situated inside his office, I would have brewed up the perfect new campaign idea.

"After you," I smiled sweetly, watching Ryan walk ahead of me down the hall to Josh's office. I turned to follow, all the while contemplating if I should pound my fists into Ryan's back and tell him that he could take his account and you know what, or throw my arms around his waist and reassure him that his precious career was safe with me, just like he would be when he decided to grace me with his presence. Neither option was ideal so I simply grabbed a pad of paper, told Bebe to wait on lunch and then scurried after Ryan and Josh.

THE MEETING ENDED A HALF-HOUR LATER. I HAD SAT staring at Ryan in a daze while he and Josh bantered back and forth about how to launch a new campaign directed at women, which Ryan had taken to calling his "core demographic." While he and Josh discussed market ratios, target audiences and leveraging a four-quadrant approach to publicity. I knew of a much simpler way to get him exposure. It was in fact, to simply expose him. All one had to do was undress Ryan a la David Beckham and voila, a star would be born. However, Ryan was now interested in becoming a "serious" actor, which meant that I was sure to endure more of these tete a tete style meetings. Now that I was back at my own desk, I wondered what the chances were of my being captured by an extremist terrorist group in the next five minutes because that could actually save me from the horror of seeing and talking to Ryan on a regular basis, which was surely the worst thing for me as it would never allow me to move on from my doomed relationship. I stared at a picture of Ryan smiling back at me, although in truth, it seemed to mock me. I remember it being taken right after he had just played an hour-long game of soccer. It was played during the height of a Los Angeles heat-wave in which the temperatures had been pushing one hundred degrees, but Ryan looked completely camera-ready. He must have made a quick dash to the bathroom to freshen up before his photo opp. Who does that?

"Egotistical actor!" I shouted. "After years of marriage, during which you repeatedly convinced me the time was not right for children, having robbed me of my valuable child-bearing years, you decide you're..."

"April? You okay?" Bebe asked.

"Sorry. I didn't mean to disturb you. I'm fine. Just reviewing a potential script for Ryan. I'm just peachy, in fact."

"With sugar on top," she beamed, her adorable dimples willing me to offer the slightest smile back.

"Yeah, a double scoop," I answered forcing my lips to curl upwards. I was once like Bebe -- twenty-two years old and brimming with hope and optimism that each day could be the one where I found my dream job, met the love of my life, or had unprotected sex. I made a mental note that my next assistant should be dumpy and hard-of-hearing. While at it, I made another that stated my next husband should be straight.

"Has Josh had you start on Ryan's campaign?" I asked Bebe.

"Well, we have been discussing things...and we spent the greater part of yesterday talking about..." her voice trailed off.

"Things? Like the media list?"

"Yes! The media list. That's just what we were doing. But we didn't really finish."

If I hadn't known better I'd think Bebe and Josh were, you know, but that was just too icky a thought to entertain fully. Besides, why would a girl like Bebe go for a guy like Josh? Sure, there is the whole moving up the corporate ladder thing, but does that really happen? I mean, don't you have to like the guy a little bit? Then again, Bebe tended to hang on Josh's every word, laughed at his horrendous jokes and on more than one occasion had commented that she thought he had charisma. Gross. I put this passing thought out of my head and breathed a sigh of relief that for once my assistant's inability to meet a deadline was a blessing in disguise.

"That's okay," I said patiently. "Do you think you could start on them again? You might also ask Josh if he has anything to add."

"Will do!" she beamed.

"WHAT HAVE YOU BEEN DOING IN THERE FOR SO LONG?" I motioned to Josh's office.

"Well, we had every intention of starting the lists," she stammered. "And then, it just happened."

"It?" I asked.

"*It,*" she confirmed.

I looked at her carefully. She didn't look that differently, but then I saw it. The look of a woman in love.

"Oh no. You didn't *do it*?"

"He is my boss."

"That's reason not to do it. And for the record, he's *my* boss. I'm your boss," I explained.

"Yes April, I know that. And I'm sorry if I let you down, but I'm in love. Besides, I think you'll find that technically your boss is my boss, so I figured you wouldn't miss me."

I felt sick. Everyone was having sex except for me, not that I wanted to be involved in this type of seedy behavior, but it just reeked with such unfairness.

"Can we just get back to work?"

"Of course, April. Thanks for being so understanding. Josh told me that you wouldn't mind."

"That was nice of him. Since he seems so preoccupied, I'll just fill you in on the new plans for Ryan's campaign."

Signs of her loyalty to Josh emerged immediately. "Josh didn't mention new plans."

I winked at Bebe. "As I said, he's been preoccupied...you naughty little minx."

"Well, you know how it is," she giggled.

Actually, I didn't. If Ryan wanted exposure that was just what he would get. Exposure for being such a meanie. He broke my heart even though I've stood by him when he was blasted for poor performances. I've supported him financially for years. And, I never stopped loving him. For all of those reasons, I was letting myself enter the next phase of the grieving process. After experiencing despair from losing a loved one, comes anger. There didn't appear to be any hope in getting Ryan back, and therefore, I would get back at him.

I turned toward Bebe, "Don't worry about the regular

press. I need the list we usually ban from our events. You know, the gossip rags. Oh, and put a star by the ones who catch celebrities looking badly.

Ryan's act, in which I became an unknowing co-star, lasted two years. Thus far, it was his longest running role. I was ready to swallow my pride and admit that our marriage was over. I was going to tell the entire country.

We worked throughout the morning and by afternoon I felt that we were making real progress. At least, for the first time in weeks I was making progress on my mental recovery.

Josh had stepped away from the office to visit a client. I was elated; Bebe was devastated.

"He'll be back," I assured her. "Now you can work without any distractions." She didn't seem as pleased at the prospect.

"But you have a list of every reporter that has ever rail-roaded a celebrity. Everyone from Us magazine to Star and even the British tabloids are listed. There's more?" she asked bewildered.

"Tons!" I said while leading her to the conference room. I proceeded to outline an elaborate plan to expose Ryan as a two-timing liar without any merit for being attractive to women, thus bringing his approval rating on "Setting Sun" down to the level of toenails.

"Sure, the Calvin Klein ad will probably still run," I admitted, "but there won't be any others!"

"April, are you sure that Josh wants us to do this?"

"Bebe, this is strictly research and development. All the big companies do it. You research the worst possible publicity angles and media outlets known to our society, and then figure out how to avoid those angles. If you're really on top of things, you actually pitch them just so that you can make them issue a retraction later."

"And you're sure this would be good for Ryan's career?"

"Of course. It's like a two-for-one special. They print something horrible one week and then say he's wonderful the next."

I didn't have to tell Bebe that there was the slightest chance that I might be sick on the day that those retraction requests would need to be made.

"This is just the type of publicity that actors hope to receive," I reassured her. "It's meaty. It'll make the public talk. It's like what happened to Tom Cruise after he jumped on Oprah's couch. They said he was insane and now look at him."

Bebe gave me a questioning glance.

"Alright, that's not the best analogy, but what I meant was that Tom is back to his old level of wonderful. Ryan should be so lucky!"

"So this is sort of like a publicity stunt?" she asked hopefully.

"Exactly!"

Cars crawled home on the freeway, but my mind was on the fast-track towards Ryan's downfall. I imagined his last episode of "Setting Sun," a scene that would never allow him to return, no reincarnations for Ryan. Still, I knew that deep down this was little consolation for me. I wasn't over him and I knew that if Ryan claimed a momentary bout of insanity and then wanted me back, I would gladly embrace mental illness over malice.

When I got home Buster and Louie wagged their greetings at me and the answering machine beckoned. It was Mom. "April, we've moved up dinner half an hour. Dad got home early, so more time with my girls. Lucky, huh? See you soon, darling!"

Lucky. That was not the word I would have used. I turned to Buster and Louie. "How could I have forgotten again?" They stared at me with open mouths exposing pink tongues, which bobbed gently up and down. They looked like they were laughing at me. "You two are no help." I quickly dialed Melissa's number at work, hoping she could be persuaded into telling a dating horror story, anything to throw my parents off the subject of Ryan's absence. Only the firm's answering service picked up. Melissa couldn't help either.

I ran the dogs around the block before returning to feed them dinner. Two scoops of kibble for them, and a helping of anxiety for me. We exchanged wet kisses (theirs not mine) and I was back in my car. I set my Pandora to Burt Bacharach radio because let's face it, I was in a melancholy mood and I imagined that Burt and his contemporaries would jostle me out of it. "Wishin' and Hopin'" by Dusty Springfield poured into my consciousness and as I sang along to the sappy lyrics, "You won't get him, just a wishin' and a hopin'...," I contemplated how my parents would react to news of my pending divorce. On the one hand, I would probably get my Visa reinstated. On the other, any new purchases reflecting my suddenly single lifestyle would be up for the scrutiny of my mother. "I Say A Little Prayer" by Aretha Franklin came on next, and I did.

Chapter 4

The songs that poured out of my iPhone became increasingly more depressing until I finally shut the thing off while waiting for Melissa to arrive. I had planned on not entering my parents' home until she also got there. The idea was that perhaps they wouldn't immediately notice Ryan's absence if I arrived as a twosome, even if that pairing was with my sister. The minutes creeped along and so did my annoyance over Melissa's lack of punctuality. Until it occurred to me that this very quality could get me out of what was sure to be an evening of questioning.

Her car finally rolled up the drive and.I bounded toward it. "Hiya!" I shouted while knocking on her rolled up window.

Melissa jumped back at the sight of me. Then, after scrunching up her nose and making sure it was just me outside and not me being held hostage by a crazed lunatic, she opened the door and stepped out. "Ape, you scared me. Why are you waiting outside in the dark?"

"I've got a favor to ask you. But before you answer me,

please try to remember that I would totally do this for you."

She looked at me skeptically. "Where's Ryan?"

"Well, it's funny that you bring that up because he's not here and therein lies my little problem."

"Ryan being late is your problem?" she asked.

I shook my head. "No, not exactly. Ryan being permanently absent is my problem. We're getting a divorce."

"No way!" she shouted and then held me in a warm hug.

Great. I had the sympathy vote. This might actually work. With my face still buried in her hair, I asked the million dollar question. "Could you tell mom and dad you're pregnant so their attention is pulled off me?" I mumbled.

She immediately released me from her embrace. "No way!"

"Oh come on, Melissa. How could it hurt? In a few weeks you get your period and just tell them you were worried for nothing. You can just say that you're irregular from being so thin. I'd actually be jealous of that."

"You know what, April?" she said while heading up the walk, "You're insane."

"Melissa, think about this for a moment. Mom will start baking you batches of homemade goodies and everyone will be sorry they ever doubted your virtue. I bet you could earn sympathy for months to come."

I smiled and nodded my head in the affirmative because I read recently that when one person is trying to convince the other to agree to something, they will involuntarily mimic your actions and if that action is an affirmative head nod they will typically says 'yes' to whatever it is you're asking. Only this time it didn't work.

"April, I'm not going to pretend I'm pregnant. I've got my own problems," Melissa said miserably.

"Alright, I'm sorry. I didn't even ask how you were. I've been so wrapped up in Ryan walking out. How are you?"

"I'm sorry too," she said and we hugged again. "Seriously, he's a fool."

"So what's wrong in your life? Misery loves company," I reminded her.

Melissa started to kick the gravel around on the driveway. "I got laid off...three months ago."

"How have you been paying your rent?"

"Savings, but they're practically gone. I'm trying to get freelance work, but there's not a lot of demand for graphic artists these days."

Suddenly, mom popped her head out the door. "It's about time you two arrived. Why are you standing out there?"

"Just listening to a song; we'll be right in," I hollered out.

"It smells great!" Melissa added for good measure.

"Have you told mom and dad?" I asked when Mom returned inside.

"Are you kidding? You know how they worry and then you know how they meddle."

"That's why I didn't want to break my news."

"April, that's something you can't hide."

"I know, but maybe...you could just..."

Her hands went to her hips, her stance became stiffer. "I'm not going to tell them I'm pregnant." And then, she started to chuckle, "Although I have to say that would certainly take the pressure off you."

"Okay, I've got a new idea. Move in with me. I've been covering my rent by myself for years. You need to save money. And...if you were pregnant, it would totally make sense that you would want to live with me just in case anything were to happen."

To my utter amazement Melissa didn't immediately shout 'no way' again. I could see her mind at work.

"Alright, but only until I get on my feet. I don't want to take charity without repaying it."

I threw my arms around her. "Trust me, you're not taking, you're giving."

"April, what happens if I don't find a job within a few months? I can't just keep on being pregnant," she said making quote marks with her fingers. "They'll expect me to start showing."

"Let's just cross that bridge when we come to it." I motioned to the front door. "So, are you ready to do this?"

Melissa grabbed my hand. "I'm as ready as I'll ever be."

"Mazel Tov!"

MOM HAD GONE ALL OUT ON THE DINNER, MAKING A feast to rival Thanksgiving. It didn't seem right to spoil the ambiance, but with Melissa by my side I gained confidence. Besides, she was the one that was about to take the fall.

"Honey, where's Ryan?" Mom asked me.

"Don't tell us he's hitting the gym at this hour?" my Dad chimed in.

I took a deep breath, gave Melissa the signal and delved in. "Mom, Dad...there's something I need to tell you. Ryan and I have decided to..."

And then Melissa delivered. "I need to say something

first, before I lose the courage. It's been a very difficult time and I know that I can count on my family for their love and support."

I had to hand it to Melissa, when she decides to do something, she puts her whole heart into it. Forget graphic design. Give this girl an Oscar.

My mom spoke first. "What is it, dear?"

"Mom, Dad, I'm pregnant!"

And just like that, all eyes were on Melissa and the whereabouts of Ryan were completely forgotten.

IN WHAT SEEMED LIKE THE FIRST TIME IN WEEKS, I BEGAN to breathe. Melissa moved out of her apartment and into mine. We hadn't lived together since being kids, but the transition was a smooth one and Melissa was finding her new digs quite agreeable. There was no fighting over closet space like when we shared a room years ago because Melissa simply took over Ryan's area. Since he had occupied more space than I did because he had far more clothes, Melissa came out ahead. Fake pregnancy or not, we agreed that she would spend her days job hunting as well as doing the preparations for dinner each evening. Work was getting far more stressful and I was happy to have finally come clean about Ryan, if only to Melissa. I knew that it was just a matter of time before the news found its way out fully.

In the meantime, I focused on the task at hand. Bebe had instructions to tell the tabloid editors to be on the lookout for news about Ryan. As I drove to work in surprisingly light traffic for a Monday, she texted me stating that thus far, five media outlets had called wanting to be the first to break whatever news we were planning on releasing. It was shaping up to be a good Monday. With so much going wrong in my life, I took these minor victories as signs that life was improving. When I arrived at my office and checked mydailyhoroscope.com, it turns out that the stars agreed.

Aries: You remain strong in spite of unusual family tendencies. It was kind of a back-handed compliment so I decided to check out the nearest water sign to my birth since I was thirsty.

Pisces: Hope comes alive when plans become action.

Cool. It probably meant that I wasn't a complete bitch for trying to sabotage Ryan. So for the next three hours I buried myself in research. I had picked up every trashy magazine available at the newsstand and was now carefully jotting down the names of the more widely read reporters. I quickly got a sense of their beats and specialties. One woman seemed to have made a niche for herself by describing celebrity fashion foibles. Another wrote about celebrities and their pets, which is normally a nice subject, but in her case, she described those who looked like their pets. I decided not to include her name on the list since Buster and Louie would not be dragged through any ugliness. One male reporter had developed a series about celebrity females who used to be males. Could definitely come in handy.

My quest continued throughout the day until I was satisfied that my plan would go off without a hitch. I would pretend that some unknown source from his set had leaked a series of stories to the press that painted him in a less than flattering light. It would be karma getting back at him and then I would rectify any damage to his reputation by calling the very same writers who wrote trash about him in the first place. Everything would be right in his world again and he would forever be in my debt.

I came home to the satisfaction of this knowledge as well as an amazing dinner cooked by Melissa. I even found myself wanting seconds since food always tastes better when someone else makes it and it had been weeks since I had eaten properly. Trying to digest so much more than I was used to made me instantly tired so I retreated with Buster and Louie to my way too large California King size bed. I knew it was wrong to let the dogs get in the habit of sleeping on the bed, but it was just so empty these days and frankly, I doubted that I would be needing the extra space anytime soon. I fell asleep to the sounds of Buster and Louie's heavy breathing and snoring, which was oddly comforting.

MY PRESS KIT ON RYAN WAS NEARLY COMPLETE. I HAD reworked his bio to age him up by a decade. When the reporters called to ask about it, I'd mumble something about the wonders of Botox and Restalyne for the appearance and then, when the damage had been done, I'd send out a retraction and claim that a rival publicity company hired by his co-star had done the sabotage.

The rest of my plan included a headline screaming press release. My brain considered the possibilities: "ACTOR OUTED," "PRODUCERS REVOKE ACTOR'S CONTRACT," "BURN OUT FOR SETTING SUN STAR"...

I had a mission. Unfortunately, so did Ryan. After our meeting was over, he had ducked back into Josh's office under the guise of setting up a golf game (I swear, if I had a dime for every time I was excluded from a manly golfing...), but it seems the topic of conversation veered to our relationship status. There was no time to initiate my plan; I was immediately summoned to rejoin them.

Josh nodded toward Ryan, "April, I'm sorry to hear about the two of you."

Oh God, I felt that tight clenching in my throat, the pinching of my forehead, water forming in my eyes. I was going to cry. I was sorry to hear about us too! Thankfully, Ryan's newly developed, asshole-ish mannerism presented itself.

"April, I told Josh that under no circumstances do I want the gay issue to be public knowledge. I know that working with me is extremely important to your firm. I'm perhaps one of your most high-profile accounts. And yet, I believe you're able to handle the pressure."

Arrogant bastard! Sure, I'd hold onto the account, and tear it to the ground.

"April?" Josh asked. "You with us?"

"Of course." I forced a smile at Josh, and tried to send darts into Ryan with my eyes.

"The divorce issue really isn't a big deal," Ryan rambled on.

I must have started hyperventilating or else the grip I had on Josh's desk weight worried him. "April, I think what Ryan means is that divorce is no longer seen as scandalous. It happens." The crass t-shirt slogan kept coming to mind: shit happens. Well, divorce shouldn't. At least not to me.

"Exactly," Ryan said approvingly to Josh. "We're definitely on the same page, Josh. Maybe it would be better if you explained the new campaign direction to April."

Chicken! What else could be said? I already know that you married me for my media contacts, never loved me, would rather be with a man...In the midst of my mental rampage, I finally found my voice, "How could you come up with an entire new direction? You were only in here for ten minutes. Besides Josh, isn't that my job?"

Josh put his hand on my shoulder. "This is a delicate situation for many reasons, April. I just want to ensure that you're able to see things clearly. So," he said with a sudden boom in his voice, "this is how it's going to be handled."

I didn't like the new assertive Josh and I certainly didn't like Ryan's smug smile.

"Your separation and the pending divorce will be kept quiet until...oh, I don't know, how 'bout 'til after Christmas? Nobody likes to be alone at the holidays and walking out of a marriage now won't look good for Ryan."

"We wouldn't want that," I said sarcastically. "Maybe we can announce it just before New Year's so Ryan has an opportunity to kiss someone really special when the ball drops!"

Josh continued, "Our thoughts exactly. After a significant mourning period, say a week or so, we believe it would be helpful for you to set Ryan up with an eligible, young actress. Get something brewing by Valentine's, maybe sooner if we so decide. You know, have him be seen with others who are hot."

Josh must have sensed that either a fainting spell or nervous breakdown on my part would ensue. "Not that you're not," he added quickly.

I was losing energy. "Not what?"

"Hot."

Ryan didn't respond and frankly, I didn't care. I didn't feel hot. I felt bothered. Annoyed that my job was now to play matchmaker to my gay husband. "I thought you were already dating?" I said to Ryan.

"I am, but Matthew is of the wrong sex."

"Since when?"

"P.R. wise. I need Matthew in my private life, but an eligible *female* in my public life."

I stood up, deciding that this meeting had come to an end. "You had one," I replied, making a suitably dramatic exit.

I would have escaped to the bathroom, perhaps to lunch, but Bruce, our firm's president, was waiting outside the door, hovering in fact, which caused me to scream.

Josh and Ryan ran from the office to check on me. "She's gone over the edge," Josh said to nobody in particular.

"Have you?" asked Ryan.

Bruce waved his hand to them. "She's fine," he assured, taking me by the arm and leading me down the hall.

"You'll be okay to start on the new campaign, won't you?" Ryan called out.

———

BRUCE'S OFFICE WAS SITUATED DOWN THE HALL FROM the conference room, on the opposite end of the building from Josh's. The three other rooms along the corridor contained our media screening room (mainly used by Bruce to watch exercise videos and James Bond films), the company library (containing an assortment of public relations journals, reference books, and Bruce's Agatha Christie collection), and his private bathroom (thankfully, of which, I know nothing about.).

With the exception of the slurping, sucking sound Bruce made with his cherry Tootsie Roll Lollipop, we walked down the emerald-green carpeted hallway, which Josh and Bruce use for putting practice, in silence.

"I heard about you and Ryan," he said finally.

"Does everyone know?"

"No, I was the only one standing outside the conference room."

I gave Bruce a look, but decided it wouldn't be in the best interest of my employment to lecture him about eavesdropping.

"I have a solution," he continued.

"Honestly Bruce, it's absolutely humiliating. Could you talk to Josh about resigning this account? He's becoming such a P.R. whore," I said angrily. "The idea of setting Ryan up on dates. He still has a few random items in our house. The bed's practically still warm!"

Now Bruce raised an eyebrow at me. "Forget Ryan. I was talking about you...and me."

"Oh?" I said uneasily.

"What you need is an affair. Hell, I need it too. It would get your mind off of Ryan and make me more productive at work. It would give me a reason to come in each day."

"You would come to work only to leave for an affair?" I asked incredulously.

"Absolutely! It would probably make you more productive, too. Take your mind off your problems. You know that Josh is doing it with Bebe."

"So I heard," I admitted. "Can't you do something about that as well?"

"Listen, the clients love Josh's leadership. I wouldn't want to squelch his creativity. But I need to make sure our employees are happy. I can see how this could be difficult for you. Maybe I am the solution to your problem."

At the moment, I couldn't believe the extent of my problems. He talked about increased productivity clinically, as if he were a workers' compensation adjuster.

"STATE YOUR NAME, PLEASE," BRUCE ASKED PROFESSIONALLY.

"April Monahan."

"April, who is your claim against?"

"My husband, Ryan Monahan."

"The nature of your injuries?"

"Mental, all of them."

"Do you have proof of decreased mental ability?"

"Just frequent and irrational fantasies."

Bruce began writing on his hand. "So noted."

"What do you suggest?"

At that moment, Bruce, a.k.a. my marriage adjuster, began to unbutton his shirt. "I am going to recommend that you enter our firm's treatment program for an unspecified period of time."

I didn't want to ruin my chances of a claim, but nonetheless, I was worried. "You're unbuttoning."

"All part of the program," he said calmly. "Your type of situation is an open and shut case, a no-brainer."

"Meaning?"

"Our firm welcomes your type of claim. It's obvious this husband of yours didn't appreciate you. We feel it will take very little effort on our part to return you to full mental capacity."

"What benefits am I entitled to?"

"Some foreplay, limited post-coital cuddling."

STRANGELY, I FOUND LITTLE DIFFERENCE BETWEEN fantasy Bruce and the real-life form.

"Mind you, April, I realize you're on the rebound. It doesn't bother me. It would be a purely sexual, non-emotional relationship. Nothing complicated," he added.

I wasn't sure if he was referring to the sex or the relationship, and frankly, I didn't want to know. I tried a change in conversation.

"Bruce, what exactly do you do around here," I said gesturing to his office.

"Mainly I act presidential, not much of anything except supply the moola for this little biz," he said with a wink and then picked up a yo-yo from his desk. He thought for a moment and then gave the yo-yo a flick of his wrist. "I always had an eye for business. This one has served me well. Celebrities have an insatiable appetite for publicity and money to burn. But Josh and you do such a good job of leading the direction of the campaigns that there isn't much need for me to be in the office," he paused to look around the place as if seeing it with new eyes. "Yeah, coming in here each day would be good." Bruce continued with his yo-yo practice and then stopped mid-throw, seemingly unsure. "That's what the rest of you do, isn't it?"

I nodded politely, and then realized he might interpret my head's yes movement to my body's yes agreement, and quickly started shaking my head back and forth. "Bruce, this is a flattering and certainly enticing offer, but I need time to think." What I needed was time to figure out how to maintain my sanity.

"Of course, April. My door is always open, except when you want it closed."

There was something to be said about Bruce's candor, especially in the wake of Ryan's deception. Most men pretend to be "the one." Flowers and evenings out. Long conversations on the phone. A massage before sex. Even after.

However, before you even run out of massage oil, the flowers wilt. Conversations replace sex. Dinner is served in front of the television. Here was a man who was honestly offering me nothing, but quickie style sex.

I left the office realizing that up until this point, I had always searched for "something." The allure of nothing had eluded me. A carefree romp may have been what I needed, but certainly not with the president of the company. Had Bruce been a dead ringer for Brad Pitt, maybe I'd make an exception. But for now, I needed to keep my job. I still had a plan to launch, not to mention being responsible for Melissa in her "delicate" state.

Chapter 5

I admit that I may have been thinking about sex more than usual, or perhaps more than the usual woman. I rationalized that my preoccupation was probably normal considering my husband had chosen to end his life with me in favor of one with another man. Still, I found it curious that men suddenly seemed to be paying so much attention to me.

"It's your pheromones," Melissa said after I told her about my incident with Bruce.

"You mean they can sense it?"

"Yeah, you're probably sending off signals," she said knowingly.

I looked at myself in the hall mirror. Same face, same hair, maybe slightly more messy than usual. "Do you think it's this tousled look that's doing it?" I asked flipping my hair around.

"No, it comes from within. It's a good thing -- better than inner beauty."

"What could be better than inner beauty?"

Melissa gave me her best smoldering eyes, lowered her lashes and said, "Inner Sex!"

"What the hell is that?"

"It's the real essence of you. Honestly April, don't you know anything?"

"That sounds kind of icky, like an internal organ, or an innie belly button."

"First of all, innie bellies are far superior; it's a fact. And, it's only an organ if you're a man," she joked.

"Okay, enough. I wouldn't mind having inner sex appeal if the man that I projected it onto was somewhat appealing."

"Maybe he'll do." Melissa pointed out the window and indicated that our mailman was walking up the drive.

"I'll get it," I said heading out the door.

The very idea of a relationship with my mail carrier is ridiculous because he is the consonant professional. He doesn't wish me a good day when delivering bills. He never asks how I am if he's bringing junk mail. Basically, we never speak. But the day the papers arrived was different. Joe or John, something one-syllabled, was indeed walking up the drive and straight up to the door. I opened it a crack and he immediately handed me the envelope.

"Ms. Monahan?"

"Yes."

"For you," he said handing over the envelope.

As I reached for the envelope, my hand grazed his. "Ahh, not so fast. First I need something from you."

"Are you serious?" I couldn't believe the audacity of men! Is each and every one of them a pervy fool?

"Your signature, right here," he said pointing.

"Oh, right. You gotta pen?"

"Yeah, somewhere in here," he said while rummaging through his bag. "Hey, maybe it's your lucky day."

IF IT WERE MY LUCKY DAY, JOE JOHN WOULD BE SOMETHING more along the lines of an older (by about ten years) Zac Efron (Honestly, ladies he's just too young!) whose concern for my well-being causes him to rush over and check a leaky gas line. I have no idea what knowledge of gas lines Zac possesses, or how he knew mine was faulty, but I don't bother to ask. I just invite him inside.

Strangely, my front door now leads directly to my master bedroom suite. Mature Zac takes a good whiff of the air, and smelling only bath oils, believes the problem to now be non-existent. "I must have made a mistake. Sorry to bother you," he mutters sheepishly.

"Don't be silly. It was kind of you to check on me. And I appreciate that you left your throngs of women behind," I answer.

"Oh, them," he says in an off-handed manner. "Nobodies. I only have sex with them so they deliver a good performance."

"And me?"

"I was worried about you. That gas leak could've been dangerous," he says moving closer to me. "I had to check on it, especially since you are now alo..."

I covered his mouth with mine. No need to say the obvious.

Mature Zac was a much better actor than I originally believed. Sure, I was a little disappointed that he didn't break into a song about me a la "High School Musical," but he did suggest we check under the bed for monsters. The ploy allowed us to get on the floor together, rolling easily on smooth, hard wood floors that I don't own. He pulled me onto him and we giggled like, well, high-schoolers. We kissed and petted and play-worried that my parents might come home soon. When sufficiently hot and sweaty, Zac got up to turn on the shower.

"Is that it?" I fretted.

"It's just beginning," he said and extended his hand to me. Oh, what a leading man. I followed him to the bathroom, where the glass walls of my shower were completely steamed up. Zac stepped inside first and tested the temperature. Nice, he assured me.

He washed my back and kissed my neck. I kept my back to him, fearful that at any minute he might lose the ten years I put on him. "Oh Zac!" I screamed.

"Are you okay?" Melissa came running from the house.

"She just started yelling 'Zac'," the mailman insisted.

"I did not," I said vehemently. "I said 'rat.' I thought I saw a rat. I think it ran in there," I said pointing to a bush.

"Anyway Ms. Monahan, here's the pen. Sign here, please," he said and pointed to the dotted line.

One thing was for sure. Joe John was no Zac. The only thing he left me with (thankfully) was the envelope, a thick, ominous mass with a return address belonging to a large law firm. That awful feeling immediately came over me. I could only describe it as a myocardial infarction, although thankfully, I'm not sure what that actually feels like. I envision it's like this, however. Simply holding the papers made each blood vessel constrict. After reading just one paragraph, I imagined my arteries clogging with goo, and it's probably times like this that lead to prematurely grey hair and wrinkles.

"Divorce papers," I said with a sigh.

"I thought you said he wan't going to pursue it?" Melissa asked.

"Not publicly, but privately we're right on track to ending our marriage."

"I'm sorry, Ape."

"Thanks, but I guess it could be worse. I could be like you -- single and pregnant!"

Melissa took the papers out of my hand and led me back to the house. "Shall we go out to dinner? Girls' night? We could call Jessica, too."

"That sounds nice. You mind if I bring these?" I said indicating the papers. "I don't want to read them alone and I don't want to read them in here. I want my home to be my sanctuary. Besides, I might be able to digest them better with a few bottles of wine inside me."

"Maybe you'll get lucky and spill a big bottle of red onto them. Give me half an hour to dry my hair."

***

While I waited for Melissa to do her hair and Jessica to arrive, I stared at the papers. I was right. Just having them in my house was making me feel sad, but I couldn't very well rip them to shreds. Instead, I carefully crafted an airplane out of the cover page and launched it at my formerly favorite wedding picture. Then, I passed the time by rearranging the useless possessions that, during my marriage, all seemed incredibly important.

Some of them were placed in the empty spots left by Ryan's removed belongings. The ones that came from his Aunt Betty, Cousin Arlene, and anyone from his father's side of the family were wrapped in newspaper for Ryan to pick up on his next visit. It's not that I didn't like Betty or Arlene. They just had terrible taste. His father, I didn't like.

"Hey, I just realized the one good thing about Ryan dumping me," I said to Jessica, who had just arrived wearing jeans and a white blouse that draped low in the front revealing a lace camisole underneath. "And why do you look so good? How can you cheer me up if you look hotter than I do?"

"You look amazing. Break-ups agree with you."

"I've lost five pounds."

"See? That's another thing that's good about it. Go on, tell me another."

"I don't ever have to see Ryan's father again? He was miserable company."

Melissa joined us, "Talking about Ryan? Hi Jess."

"No, his father," she answered. "Congratulations on your new house and your new pregnancy. I got you a card," Jessica said handing it over to Melissa.

"Oh, you shouldn't have." But Melissa was already ripping open the envelope and pulling out the card, which she read aloud, "Because you're knocked up, we wanted to give you this...Jessica, that's disgusting."

"What is it?" I asked reaching for the card.

"It's a picture of egg-beaters. Why would I want that for my baby?" Melissa said reaching a protective hand over her stomach.

"Do you know how hard it is to find a pregnancy/house-warming card? They just don't exist," Jessica said. "I had to take the front page of one and tape it to the inside of another."

"But it doesn't make any sense unless you're suggesting I use egg-beaters to....you know, end it," Melissa said, her voice dropping to a hush.

Jessica threw her arm around Melissa's shoulders. "No sweetie, of course not."

Melissa started crying; Jessica started crying.

"It's just that it's starting to seem so real," Melissa sobbed. "I think I really love my pretend baby."

"Honey, if this pregnancy is what you want then we're here for you. Tell her, April."

I stared at both of them with wide-eyed wonder, picked up my coat and said the only thing I could think of given the circumstances. "Maybe we should head out to dinner."

WE DECIDED ON A SMALL CAFE THAT FEATURED
outdoor seating and sat on the same property as a hotel
and dance bar. It was a perfect people watching place as
one got a great view of the bar entrance and we immediately started our hook-up game.

"Black dress will go home with flannel shirted hottie,"
Jessica said.

"Which black dress? The LBD or the one with the
white down the sides?" Melissa asked while reaching for
our bread basket.

"The LBD standing with her friend in the red slutty
dress," Jessica replied.

"Don't be catty. The poor girl is just looking for her Mr.
Right," I sighed miserably.

Jessica shook her head. "That girl is a partier. She's
wanting Mr. Right Now."

Melissa concurred. "You know, we could add to this
game. We have a great vantage point to not only guess the
hook-up, but then watch to see if they go to their own car,
hop into each other's car, or just head straight for the hotel
next door."

"It is nice here," I agreed.

Punctuating my sentiment was the arrival of our
waiter, no doubt an aspiring model given his contagious
smile, high cheek bones and overall perfectness. Jessica
looked up and no sooner spilled her water everywhere.
"Oh my god, I'm so sorry."

The waiter grabbed his towel and started blotting. "I'll
just get you a dry set of cutlery," he said before leaving.

"Why did you do that?" I asked.

"I didn't do it on purpose. He's just so gorgeous that I
got all nervous."

"And your hand decided to bat the glass away," I
teased.

The waiter came back with a dry tablecloth and efficiently whipped off the old one. "You should have spilled it on yourself," Melissa whispered.

"Yeah, that could've been your dress being removed."

Jessica responded by kicking me and then Melissa under the table causing each of us to give a little yelp in surprise.

"Good as new," the waiter reported. "I'm Ian and I'll be serving you tonight. May I tell you ladies about our specials?"

Jessica and Melissa couldn't be more encouraging.

"Oh yes!"

"Please!"

"Do tell," I added.

Ian proceeded to run through the sauces, accompaniments and "cooked to perfection choices" on the specials menu while we sat drooling, not for our impending meal, but for the vision that stood before us.

Ian finished and waited expectantly for our decisions, which were predictable given the circumstances.

"I'll have the salad special, dressing on the side." Ian took down my order and nodded his approval at my low-cal choice.

Jessica followed suit. "Caesar salad with grilled chicken, dressing on the side."

And then Melissa threw us for a loop. "That pasta special sounds amazing. You know, the one with the cream sauce?"

"It's amazing," Ian agreed. "I had it before my shift."

"Well, if you had it, then I want it too," Melissa said giddily.

Ian looked at Melissa and smiled. "I'm sorry that I couldn't have enjoyed mine with you."

Jessica and I watched the scene transfixed. In what

reality does a girl order pasta with heavy cream and the guy just falls over backwards trying to get in with her? In my life, the gay ex-husband actor would tell me that I should be watching what I eat because if I don't, nobody will want to take a second look at me.

Ian left to place our orders and Jessica and I immediately grilled Melissa.

"What was that?" I asked.

"What? He's cute."

"Yes, but you never order fattening food. You're a size four."

Melissa tucked into another piece of bread. "Can you pass the olive oil?"

Jessica dutifully handed it over. "She's one of those types. You can tell by her body. Doesn't have the decency to gain weight and the guys find it refreshing that she eats whatever she wants."

"It's not that," Melissa replied.

"Then what is it?" I asked.

Melissa looked at us with an expression of complete seriousness and answered. "I'm eating for two now."

Okay, I was officially worried.

———

AFTER TUCKING INTO HER MEAL AS IF IT WERE HER LAST, Melissa proceeded to order hot fudge lava cake in spite of the fact that the menu indicated it contained over fifteen-hundred calories.

"I'll get three spoons," she responded when I pointed out the fact.

"I don't want any. I'm on a diet."

"Well isn't that nice for you," Melissa said. "I can't just shut off my cravings."

Jessica had sat by politely until that moment when she gently pointed out, "Melissa, I thought you weren't really pregnant. Has something changed?"

"It feels real and I'm growing. Look!" Melissa said pointing to her tummy.

My voice raised slightly, "Well, you admitted it yourself. You're eating like there's no tomorrow."

"Haven't either of you heard of a hysterical pregnancy?"

Jessica and I shook our heads.

"It's a condition in which the mother being so desperate to have a baby actually takes on the symptoms of pregnancy. I've got it all -- irregular period, swollen breasts, and nausea. Well, except when I just can't seem to get enough food. I must be pregnant."

I had pulled out my iPhone and started to google. "Here it is. Also known as 'pseudocyesis' in humans."

"What do you mean in 'humans'?" Jessica asked.

I continued, "It says that it's most common in dogs and cats."

"Well that explains it," said Melissa. "You know how tuned in I've always been to animals. I'm more evolved than regular humans that way."

"Melissa, the one thing you're not picking up on is that the term 'hysterical pregnancy' is for when these creatures -- human or otherwise -- aren't really pregnant," I said.

Melissa sat and thought for a moment. "I'm not so sure. You see, you needed me to be pregnant and I didn't want any part of it. But the fact that my body is responding in this way is a sign that my mind has accepted it and I think it may be the real deal. My eggs are ready to be harvested. This is a sign that I need to move into the next phase of my life. Stop wasting time with run of the mill men and find a real one to impregnate me and live a happy family life. It's going to weed out the men from the boys."

I put my head down on the table. Jessica stared into her caesar salad before speaking. "Isn't that exactly what April was thinking and we talked her out of it? Remember? We told her that her self-worth was not wrapped up in a man?"

"Yes," I agreed. "Besides, starting a relationship with someone while you're already 'pregnant'," I paused, using quotation fingers, "is not ideal."

Melissa replied simply if not a bit creepily, "Sometimes He moves in mysterious ways."

At that moment, Ian, our gorgeous waiter came back with the check and along with it, a little something for Melissa.

"I'll see you Saturday," he said and presented a plastic container with a slice of chocolate cake inside. All he gave me before leaving for his next table was the check.

"You're going out with him?"

"I am. While you and Jessica went to the ladies room he asked me out. You see? Some men don't mind if you're knocked up. He's going on my 'to-do' list."

THE THREE OF US DROVE HOME SHORTLY AFTER learning about Melissa's new love interest. She went straight to bed citing that pregnant women needed to get two to three hours more sleep than the average adult. Jessica and I, who had not been privy to chocolate cake, sat on the couch with a box of girl scout cookies between us. After polishing off the lot, we turned to a more productive use of our time -- googling Ryan's name to see if my media blitz had yielded any interesting results.

"Who's Samantha Morton?" Jessica asked.

"Publicity stunt last year. Non-threat," I said referring to a model who was photographed on Ryan's arm at a Vanity Fair event held earlier in the year.

"Hey, did you ever notice this picture?"

I turned to look at a shot of Ryan hugging Samantha, but obviously looking over her shoulder at another male actor standing behind her. "Missed that one. It's true what they say about 20/20 hindsight."

"Let's do something else." Jessica took the laptop from me and started typing away. "Here, this is useful...a relationship guru who says that the pain that follows a break up will last at least half the period spent in the relationship."

"That is useful," I said with only minor sarcasm. "By her calculations, my torment is scheduled to last for another year, perhaps a year-and-a-half if I count the period that Ryan and I dated before marriage."

"Hmm, it looks like you're entering a rather lengthy juncture. Maybe we'll figure out how to find a fast-forward switch."

"I can only hope."

Jessica started to yawn. "I have to get to work early tomorrow. One of the partners is arguing a motion and his secretary is on vacation so I'm working for my boss and him. It's going to be a nightmare of a day."

"You go. I'll be fine. There's still some of Ryan's stuff that needs to get packed up."

"April, just dump it in the garbage. Why should you have to pack up his shit?"

"It's kind of comforting. I think it's helping me move on."

Jessica gave me a hug and then retrieved her keys from the dining room table. "Get some sleep," she instructed.

"G'night," I said and hugged her back.

No sooner had Jessica left when Melissa's cell rang. I looked at the caller i.d. -- Ian. I debated about letting it just go to voicemail, but Melissa did seem excited about him so I picked up.

"Hello, Melissa's cell....oh, hi Ian. Yeah, let me go get her..."

It only took a nanosecond for Melissa to wake up and grab the phone. Ahh, young love. Within minutes, Melissa had emerged from her bedroom.

"I need your help," she after hanging up. She had retrieved two dresses, one black the other red. "Which one is better for my first official date with Ian? This one shows more cleavage," she said pointing to the black one.

"I'd go with that one."

"Even though it has major cleavage action?"

"Yeah, why not?" The minute I asked, I regretted it.

"Because I'm with child. Is it appropriate?"

I decided to play along with Melissa's fantasy. "Well, you didn't wind up in your condition by dressing like a nun and if you want a relationship with Ian, you need to show him the goods."

"Good point," she said and skipped back to her room. "I'm going back to bed. Have a good night."

Alone again I started going through my own closet, clearing out the last of Ryan's clothes. In the process I came across a little, black dress of Christmas past. Nearly a year later, the designer piece was still unworn. I acquired the dress while Ryan and his friend, Jack, were absorbed in an almighty football match. Jack's new girlfriend, Kate, entertained me with her latest dress designs and told me that I could see them before the Nordstrom and Ann Taylor buyers. In my book, she was a perfect catch; if Jack didn't want her, I did.

While Ryan and Jack formed an inseparable bond with the couch, the television remote, and the football action, I got to know Kate's designs. I tried on a low-cut red number, a high-collared white dress with Victorian lace, and fell for the little black dress, knowing that a woman can never have too many black cocktail dresses. It was the kind of dress that would incite my father to make a comment about jam or jelly, or some other spreadable concoction and its inability to shake as much as me in the dress. I never was good with adages; in short, the dress accented what Ryan referred to as my best features, a comment that at the time I felt was more of an insult than a compliment, but now would have done anything to hear. Kate offered me a discounted rate. I couldn't refuse, but apparently Ryan could.

Looking at it now, I remember Ryan's reaction to it. "Ryan, what do you think of this?" I twirled in front of him, but remained careful not to block the titillating excitement of men slapping each other's behinds in admiration of a phenomenal catch or some other achievement to surely rival the Nobel award.

"Yeah, honey. Just gimme a second, will ya?" He turned to Jack, "Sweet Mary, did you see that run? God, what were they thinking trading him? He could've been running for us."

"Ryan, will you just look at me? What do you think?"

"Honey, that's beautiful, really nice." He looked up at me for long enough to spit out the sentiment and then returned to the business at hand. "So Jack, how about spotting me ten points, huh, buddy?"

Despite such incidents, prior to Ryan's announcement, I believed my life to be virtually free of strife. I now wondered if I also had the power to ignore catastrophic disasters, such as flood and famine. Yet, I was still in

danger of believing that an inept husband was better than
no husband. In nearly two months it would be Valentine's
Day, the most depressing of holidays for a single woman.
The day when if you didn't receive candies and flowers
you felt like a complete loser was fast approaching and I
didn't have anyone in my life to send me those niceties. I
considered sending a token gift to myself. Too pathetic.
Angrily, I banished the little black dress to the back of the
closet where it would be safe from violating hands trying
to unzip its back, lift up its bottom, or merely caress
its front.

I went into Melissa's room to see if by any chance she
was still awake, but she was sound asleep, lightly snoring.
The dogs followed me into her room and I quickly led
them out before they decided to jump onto her bed. They
followed me obediently and jumped onto my bed instead. I
smiled and climbed inside, mildly content in the knowledge
that I had not one, but two warm bodies on my bed.

"Good morning," Melissa greeted me when I
finally emerged from my bedroom. "Man, you slept late."

"I didn't go to bed until late. Couldn't sleep."

"Thinking about everything?"

I nodded and poured myself a coffee.

"Then I might as well hand this over now. I thought
about waiting, but you might actually have a good day and
then I would ruin it." She handed me an envelope, and
one glance at the return address told me that she was right.
It couldn't be good news as it was from a large law firm
downtown.

"How come I didn't see this when we came home
last night?"

"It was stuck to my magazine. I nearly threw it in the trash by accident."

I opened it up and immediately regretted that it hadn't ended up in the garbage. The embarrassment of being cast aside by Ryan did not compare to my outrage over what the contents of this envelope brought.

"Oh my god. He wants to take the boys."

As if on cue, Buster and Louie ran up to me, tongues at the ready. I hugged both of them to me, their furry faces nuzzling me, their tongues lapping up my tears.

"He's launching a custody battle," I cried.

"Can he do that?" Melissa asked. "I mean, does it count with dogs?"

"They're like people."

Melissa nodded her head sympathetically.

"You know, he doesn't know the meaning of quality time," I said, my sadness turning to anger.

"The whole thing is ludicrous," Melissa agreed. "You shouldn't give it a second thought.

"He says he'll keep me from even visiting the boys if I damage his image. You think he knows what I've been wanting to do?" I couldn't bear to think about the answer. "That is actually the one thing keeping me going. Take that away and he's taken away my last hope for happiness."

"Bastard!" Melissa responded dutifully.

"I just can't believe the nerve he has to drag Buster and Louie into this. Who adjusted their work schedule to spend extra time at home when the boys were young?" I implored.

"You did."

"Who goes to the park everyday? Who prepares their meals?"

"You do," she said on cue.

I was working my way from frenzied anger to hysteria. "Who has always been there to teach the boys not to run into the street when we play ball?"

"April, relax. Any judge will see that you're the one who takes on all the responsibilities."

"There's more," I sniffed hard while continuing to read. "He's also threatening to take his account elsewhere if I sabotage his publicity campaign."

"Good. Let him."

"I can't. If I lose his account it could be disastrous for the firm. His agent and manager subsidize the fees. Ryan is a cash cow."

"Well, he's something, alright."

"Melissa, if he walks, I could lose my job."

"You'll get through this, and the divorce."

"You think?"

"I know."

I FELT CONFIDENT THAT NO JUDGE WOULD CHOOSE RYAN over me, but I worried nonetheless. A preliminary hearing and deposition would be set up. I needed a lawyer, and a Valium. I wanted to book a massage and facial, but decided that I needed a more pro-active approach to improving my situation and called Jessica at her office.

Her cheery voice answered, "Law Offices of Abrams, Schuster, and Schwartz." It was such a mouthful, I wondered if she ever had the urge to abbreviate the three partners under the heading A.S.S. Even with my limited experience in hiring attorneys, the moniker was appropriate.

Last year, an angry client, Hillcrest Preparatory, sued our firm, claiming the campaign we launched was a disaster. I pitched the concept that Hillcrest not only gives children lessons based in academics, but also in social skills, preparing graduates to enter the business world and succeed. I suggested a survival of the fittest theme, explaining that Hillcrest children learn the skills necessary to be top in their fields. The client thought it was fabulous; Josh and Bruce took me to lunch.

It wasn't until a few parents became squeamish at the site of tanks with sharks, tarantulas, and rattle snakes and a banner above that read, "We prepare your child for the real world," that the misunderstanding began and my chances of landing more vacation time were shattered. I lost the extra summer holiday, but inherited Bebe. Bruce said that I would be thankful for the extra help considering I was expected to take part in no less than seventeen meetings with opposing attorneys who argued the merits of my campaign. The nerve.

My only other experience with an attorney involved a one-night stand. His choice, not mine. It's no wonder the idea of Jessica being the rescue line for my furry family and the one who would attach me to another attorney, made me nervous.

It's not that I didn't trust Jessica's judgement, it's just that she's never really been in a tight spot so I worried that she wouldn't be able to relate to my quandary. In fact, ever since I met Jessica in elementary school it seems that good things simply land at her feet, or at least she makes living life look a lot easier than the rest of us.

I remember when she performed Tina Turner's "What's Love Got to Do With It" at our sixth grade talent show. She didn't strut around stage like Tina. She didn't belt out the number. She looked almost reserved or melancholy as she sang the lyrics sweetly and ever so softly. When she was finished, she got a standing ovation with my own parents being among the first to jump out of their seats. It didn't bother me, though, partly because I knew that she was singing about Jeff Mussman, also known as the most gorgeous boy in our grade. Jessica had believed that she and Jeff were going steady until a week before the talent show when she told him she loved him and he replied that he only loved his parents and turtle. Jessica immediately came to my house for one of my peanut butter, Fritos and chocolate syrup sandwiches. It was between mouthfuls when she decided to change her talent show song. She said it didn't matter if she couldn't sing and dance like Tina as long as she could relate to the lyrics. And she was right. Jessica not only found her own groove, she learned the important lesson that one should not let their own self-worth be affected by another's opinion of yourself. Jessica learned this at age eight. I was still grappling with the concept.

Jessica also became a serial dater. She lasted longer at the Law Offices of A.S.S. than the young associate who introduced her to the job. After he gave her an introduction to the head of human resources, Jessica convinced him that he would be happier with a girl who shared his ambition. She explained that she had no interest in pursuing the law and therefore she imagined their future together would be full of strife since he would be working late and she would be toiling away at home, waiting expectantly for him. "The last thing you want is a needy girl," she said emphatically and he naturally agreed. The thing is Jessica had wanted to end things with him for a few weeks so she could pursue another guy, but she never wanted to hurt anyone's feelings the way Jeff Mussman had hurt her. She had the rare quality of being able to date every man at the party, remain friends well after the inevitable break up, and ensure that the men also stayed buddies with each other. Jessica was the United Nations of dating.

As for her career at A.S.S., she had systematically worked her way through the roster of other potential suitors. Her boss, a man of fifty, was convinced that Jessica, with her short skirts and filmy blouses, was the cause for his wife's renewed interest in him. Fearful that Jessica would leave the firm if one of her love affairs turned sour, he persuaded her to stop dating within the firm by offering her a substantial raise and an annual bonus as incentive. It sounded like a good deal, but it wasn't without its own ramifications.

"This means you'll probably never marry an attorney," I said.

"It's okay. My boss probably did me a favor. They can be pretty stuffy, you know. It's always the missionary position."

"Wow, I never knew that."

"Yeah, you should probably avoid them as well," she warned. "Hey, I hear that accountants are givers."

So with Jessica's job safe and her theories about attorneys duly noted, I dialed the number. After enduring an extremely long three minutes on hold, Jessica answered the line: "Hello. William Barrows' office."

"Can't your firm hire someone to pick an appropriate radio station?"

"Having a bad day, April?"

"Worse than awful. And the love songs didn't help."

"I would think the opposite. What's up? I'm busy."

I could hear her typing. "Jess, can you recommend a lawyer? Custody case."

"Sure, who's it for?"

"Me. Ryan wants Buster and Louie."

The keys stopped. "You're kidding."

"Terrible, isn't it?"

"I meant, you're kidding."

I was becoming irritable. "Don't you care? I appointed you their guardian last year."

"April, I actually have the respect of my boss around here. Why would I want to jeopardize that?"

"Because you're my friend and I'm falling apart."

"Well, I can't argue with either of those facts. So okay, I'll see what I can do."

I hung up with Jessica after telling her that I wanted a fighter, someone who believed children should not be separated from their mother. I needed a lawyer who understood how hard I worked and still made time for Buster and Louie's walks, visits to the park, and rides in the car. Surely one of the lawyers at A.S.S. would appreciate the time I took out of my busy schedule to make homemade dog biscuits. Jessica merely hoped to find someone willing to take on a canine custody suit.

"PANIC IN THE CONFERENCE ROOM, APRIL," BEBE squealed as I approached the building. She was waiting for me by the back door like a well-trained pooch, but far more chic wearing black leggings and furry Ugg boots from their new designer collection.

"Those are amazing," I said leaning down to pet them.

"Thanks! They're vegan," she said.

"Vegan?"

"Yeah, like not real fur. No animals harmed."

"Oh right. Anyway, shall we go see what the *dilemma* is all about?"

I stressed the word because in truth, I wasn't allowed to use words like 'dilemma' or 'problem' in Josh's presence.

His idea of running a successful company meant never saying "no," "I can't," or "I've got a problem." In theory it was a great plan. In reality, it's a futile idea. Clients are big fat headaches with large egos and unrealistic goals. I should know and how anyone can stomach the thought of never saying so, is unrealistic. The customer is always right phrase is a perfect example of lunacy. The truth is that the customers are never right. But, because they pay our bills, we pretend that we know they dreamed up the great idea, but were just too busy with more important issues to actually execute their brilliance. In their infinite wisdom, they hire a P.R. firm to behave like lemmings with M.B.A.s, able to convert even the silliest concepts into award-winning campaigns. So if today was one of those days that I was expected to soothe bruised egos, I would need reinforcements.

I stopped by the company kitchen and grabbed a tray. A peek in the cupboards revealed Josh's favorites so I piled them onto the tray. Salt and pepper popcorn, Vitamin Water (the pink variety) and Keen-Wah, a protein bar made from quinoa that is actually much better then it sounds. Josh wouldn't be able to resist.

When I got to the conference room, Bebe was sitting by Josh's side, taking notes. However, it didn't take long to realize that the notes involved his grocery shopping list. "Here, maybe this will help," I said offering the tray. "Start with the bar, wash it down with the Vitamin Water and then polish off the popcorn. It's the preferred consumption order for alleviating stress," I said with authority. I had learned that Josh responds amazingly well to bullshit.

"Is that true?" he asked.

"Absolutely. The process of chewing popcorn releases endorphins and you should feel better in about two-and-a-half minutes."

Bebe and I watched as Josh munched, drank and seemed to relax. "That is better," he agreed. "You know, April, you're surprisingly good at this sort of thing."

"What sort of thing?"

"Making people feel better. It's a shame it doesn't work on Ryan. Well, never mind about that. Anyway, I might have just the thing for you," he said leaning forward. "Nothing like a new campaign to get your mind off your troubles. Yesiree, I think you'll be pulling an all-nighter over this one."

"That sounds great, Josh. After all, there's nobody waiting at home for me."

Josh turned to Bebe. "You see, I told you."

Great. Now it was official. Even my assistant knew about my personal problems.

Chapter 6

Josh invited the rest of the staff to "pop in" on the meeting. He made it sound like he was inviting everyone over for tea. Once everyone took their seats he reached for his pad of paper and started doodling while Bebe read his notes aloud. I looked over at Josh's artwork and noticed that he had a fondness for kittens, devils, and square boxes. I haven't yet made the connection, and am frankly afraid of the day it comes to me. What I do know is listening to my co-workers battle like divas for stage time is far more painful than even leg waxing.

The ideas flurry back and forth through the air. I've taken to experiencing the meetings like a spectator sport, watching the holes in each person's face open wide with enthusiasm, angst, or anger, depending upon the topic. New clients bring enthusiasm for the belief that they will stay forever. I had similar thoughts about my husband. Now, at least I know better. My idealistic co-workers, many of them single, have yet to learn. The client who has not received recent media attention brings the most angst for they're the ones threatening to leave. Anger comes when they are late paying an invoice, marking the end of the courtship. If we're successful, the media salivate over our pitches, valiantly rewrite our press releases, and turn out slightly changed versions of our stories. The result is an article as processed as bologna with nearly as much merit. On this particular Monday, our meeting focused on our newest cause celeb, The Arthritis Foundation.

"We need someone who evokes virility; that's what they want," Josh declared. "Any ideas?"

The associates jumped, eager to please and be noticed.

"Taylor Lautner?"

"Too young."

"Ashton Kutcher?"

"Too divorced."

I sat motionless, aware that if my eyes opened much wider they would dilate. The reaction was not caused out of intimidation or being awe-struck at the prospect of working with these great actors; rather, I was dumb-founded at the stupidity of it all.

"Which actor, excuse me, which *virile* actor," I corrected, "is going to want to be associated with this cause?"

"There's nothing shameful about the Arthritis Foundation. It's a high-paying account," Josh challenged.

I stood my ground. "Sure, nothing shameful for our books, but to a hot actor, it's bankruptcy. You get Pierce Brosnan going on television to say he's got arthritis, along with millions of others, and he's no longer James Bond. Suddenly, he's one of us. Getting grey, instead of distinguished. Slowing down, instead of becoming more deliberate. I guarantee that if he's associated with arthritis, he'll have to start doing his own stunts."

"April, did you sign on Brosnan without informing me?" Josh asked, trying to avoid civil unrest in the office.

I wore the smile especially designed for occasions such as this. The upper lip, tilt on the left side with a slight crinkling of the eyes. The meeting was adjourned and my team was off. By lunchtime at least two dozen of Los Angeles' top agents would know that a hot gig was available for any top actor able to convey sophistication, sexiness, and an arthritic condition. Now that's acting. I walked to my office wondering if Tom Cruise was ready to change his image.

It didn't take long for my staff, who an hour earlier wore the optimism only available to the young, to age substantially after enduring phone calls with some of the meanest theatrical agents in Los Angeles.

It's a known fact that with every million dollars earned by their clients, the agents become incrementally more obnoxious. It's getting to the point where the agents receive nearly as much press as their clients. The ones who represent the hottest performers are themselves dubbed "celebrity" agents. To keep up with the image, they shop at Neiman Marcus, lunch at The Ivy, drive BMWs, or perhaps, the Range Rover if their nanny called in sick and they are forced to actually drive to the supermarket after work. Tough life.

Bebe suggested the hideous idea of holding another meeting. "To flush out the campaign," she said. Before anyone could say anything to the contrary, Josh bellowed his approval, winking at Bebe as if they shared some sort of indecent secret. Bebe literally swooned and looked as if she might take flight. Please God, tell me my boss is not boinking my assistant. I shuddered as my mind contemplated the possibility.

"*BEBE, CAN YOU TAKE DOWN SOME OF MY THOUGHTS?*" *Josh asked.*

"Right away," she cooed.

"Alright, let's start here. Take this down," Josh ordered, pointing to his pants.

Suddenly, Bebe appeared only in a bra, sitting across from Josh and holding a writing pad and pen. They placed a new, demented twist on the act of dictation.

"Jo-Jo," she cooed, "don't be such a silly-willy."

"I'll have you know there is nothing silly about my willy," he returned with an under-the-desk lob. I didn't want to listen to any more sick, double entendres, let alone witness Bebe topless and God forbid, Josh bottomless, but I was stuck. I had come into Josh's office to find the Book, the one that holds photos of the sexiest and hottest actors on our roster. All I wanted was to sneak in one after lunch looksie at Ryan. Instead, I got caught because of the location of the damned thing...the tippy-top shelf of Josh's mammoth bookcase.

Why must all adults have a shelf, where the good stuff is hidden beyond reach of children? I nearly broke my neck trying to get it. I climbed on top of his leather chair, jumped atop his desk and proceeded to use each shelf as a ladder until I reached the very top when suddenly, out walks Josh and Bebe from the private bathroom adjoining to the office. I couldn't do anything, but sit paralyzed on top of Josh's bookshelf holding the Book, my own version of "The Joy of Sex."

I stared down from twelve feet above to see the top of Bebe's head poised above Josh's lap. "Joshee," she said, over-emphasizing the "ee" sound to make at least his name an unbearable length. "We must finish your letter."

"Of course, my dear. That will be sufficient," he said moving her back to her seat. The only time I had heard that phrase was in the context of my nanny asking if I had eaten enough of my chicken pot pie. "Have you had sufficient, April?" My reply was always, "Yes,

thank you, I've had quite enough" since the pie was never very good. It was the one thing Bebe and I had in common. She didn't protest when seconds of Josh's pie weren't offered.

"Are you ready?" he asked seductively.

"And able," she replied in her sugary voice.

Josh's dictation began, "When they first met, they were strangers, mere associates in a stale, office environment, but that would change," he said, pausing for dramatic effect.

Bebe's pen moved furiously across the page and her breasts bounced lightly as the speed of her dictation increased. Josh was momentarily memorized by their movement, something akin to watching a metronome gently swish back and forth. He shook himself from his reverie and continued, pausing only to adjust himself.

"They began arriving early and staying late, but even those fleeting hours together were not enough. He started following her into the ladies restroom where they would stay for hours, touching and groping..."

"Oooh Jo-Jo," Bebe interrupted. Are you getting to the good part?"

The story continued at nauseam, bringing Josh and Bebe to a frenetic wanting. They clawed off what was left of each other's clothes and climbed atop Josh's desk. As Josh pounded into Bebe, I was struck by two fears. The first: Bebe would get pregnant and I would have to find another assistant. The second: Bebe would open her eyes and see me sitting above them.

THE HORROR OF BOTH THOUGHTS JOSTLED ME FROM MY daydream -- err daymare, and within minutes I had intercepted Bebe from Josh's grip, at least figuratively speaking. Along with three account executives and one junior executive, they marched obediently into my office to brain storm ideas for the Arthritis Foundation. We scoured the agency lists looking for a well-known actor to be our spokesperson, an unknown actor to play the part of our arthritic-inflicted man and finally, a gorgeous actress/model to be the hot, young girlfriend. The campaign had just the right amount of absurdity to be believable, at least in Los Angeles.

The rule of thumb was that men of a certain age like to believe that their ideal match should be half their age plus seven. That means a 50-year-old man believes his ideal match is a 32-year-old woman. But since we're in the publicity business, it doesn't hurt to push the envelope a bit and therefore, we looked for a virile looking old guy and a "half his age" girl, a model of about 25-years-old.

I assured the execs standing in front of me that our actor was out there; they just needed to find him.

"Okay everyone, remember that we're not just looking for a pretty face. Make sure you scan the resumes for special skills. Our guy needs to be able to do something like rock-climbing or something else that involves agility."

"What about fencing?" one of the execs asked while scanning a headshot.

"Sounds good. Put that one in the consider pile."

"So let's go over the campaign. We'll see our guy in the midst of his busy work day in which he must climb to the top of a telephone poll or something equally physical. When it's quitting time arthritis doesn't stop him. He's still got the strength and energy to play some sort of sports match. Afterwards his woman is waiting for him -- this is where we need the young, hot model type -- and they'll walk off holding hands presumably for a quickie."

"One question," Bebe asked.

"Shoot."

"Do they need to speak English or will it be a voice-over?"

"Good question. Accents don't matter in this campaign

since that's where our known actor comes in. Our Tom Cruise or Pierce Brosnan will provide the voice-over for the whole campaign. Something like, 'Arthritis never slows me down, blah blah blah,' and we'll cut to their face at the very end."

My team excitedly returned to their offices; I looked at my watch and calculated the minutes until lunch.

By afternoon, they returned with the news that Tom Cruise's people gave a polite, but formal "no." The remainder of their report was not nearly as positive. Dennis Quaid and Bruce Willis were favorites after Tom, but each one failed in one major area. Their "people" neglected to call us back. I wondered at what point in one's career do you become surrounded by people rather than co-workers. I have assistants, yet surely I couldn't be so egotistical to consider them my people.

"How's the arthritis front?" I inquired.

"The staff seems to think we're making progress. I'm not so sure, though," Bebe whispered conspiratorially.

"How come?"

"We've only got two to choose from." Bebe placed two photos on my desk. "Here's the head shots."

The first was of a man that looked to be about fifty, with salt and pepper hair, and a strong jaw line. He had a James Brolinish look about him. Definitely not bad; certainly the right age. His name was David Benedict and the cover letter from his agent divulged that he actually suffered from arthritis. I suppose they believed it would lend credibility to his performance.

The second head shot belonged to Richard Wyatt. Shoe-polish hair and eyes with exclamation mark extensions made Matthew look as if he had the aging process under control. At least it was nothing a few trips to the tanning salon and the dermatologist couldn't handle.

I scanned the photos. "Who does the client want?"

"They left it up to us."

In my experience, this was a set-up. "And?" I asked, waiting for impending bad news.

"They said as long as one of them looks like a real celebrity, they'd be happy."

I stared at the faces again. "This Richard guy--who's he supposed to be?"

"Burt Reynolds. Before the beard."

"Am I the only one who doesn't see it? And who's David?"

"We're thinking James Brolin."

I studied the photo carefully. "That actually works for me. Done."

Well," Bebe responded slowly. "There's just the teeniest problem."

I nodded for her to continue.

"David doesn't want his public to know he has arthritis," Bebe explained.

"The public doesn't even know David!" I exclaimed. "The only benefit to David is that he does have arthritis and he looks like Barbara Streisand's second husband, James Brolin. If he's good enough for Barbara, even with arthritis, he'll be good enough for everyone else." I started pacing the room, becoming more irate. "I swear. Actors and their egos. Any 'problems' with Richard?"

Bebe kept her sugary composure. "Richard doesn't mind if everyone thinks he has arthritis, even though he doesn't have it, but he wants his stunts to be over-the-top and apparently it's hard to get insurance on him due to a drug incident a few years ago. By the way, he mentioned skydiving as an option."

"If we can't get insurance on him then no. Skydiving is

not an option. Neither is bear wrestling, bungee cording, or a menage a trois in a pit of warm chocolate!"

"I'm sure he never thought of that," responded Bebe dutifully. "Should we go with David?"

"Who does Josh want?"

"He told me that if you asked I should say that he trusted you implicitly, especially with a half million dollar account."

"Great."

I asked Bebe to schedule a staff meeting in half an hour. I would go over the basics of our P.R. strategy: how to fool the public, win over the client, and manipulate the actor.

"OKAY, WHO ARE THESE MEN?" I ASKED MY STAFF WITH mock enthusiasm, hoping their youthful exuberance would rub off on me.

"Our newest Associates?" one of the account executives cried out.

"The answer to our client's problems?" another yelled.

I smiled the part of the patient teacher. "Au contraire, mes amies." They looked totally confused. French was lost on them. "Come on, you said it yourself. They're James and Burt!" I whispered under my breath, "Just not as sexy."

"Personally," I continued, looking back at the photos, "I think that David is much closer to James Brolin than Richard is to Burt Reynolds. What do you think?"

They didn't dare argue. Kiss up time.

"So David it is. And he has arthritis to boot!" I said like a cheerleader.

"April, I told you, we can't say that," snipped Bebe.

I stared at her perfectly turned up nose, eyes with lashes that reached toward the ceiling, and bouncy breasts. She was so beautiful. If Josh were doing her I bet he wouldn't change his mind and decide to switch over to David or Richard. Bebe simply defied gravity and it just wasn't fair.

ONE OF MY UNDERLINGS DISTRACTED BEBE WHILE I LEAPT across the table in one fell swoop to her seat. Then, while her mouth opened out of sheer shock, I began to force feed her an entire package of Hostess Ding-Dongs. At first she resists, but then when the entire staff begins cheering -- it's not clear whether they're rooting for me to fatten her up or for Bebe who has suddenly become more human --but either way, Bebe begins to enjoy the process, polishing off the package and then turning her attention to a platter of bagels that are left-over from the morning.

"And to think that I once said bagels were the most evil of carbs," Bebe laughed while piling on the cream cheese.

I handed her another. "That's crazy. They're soft and yummy and nicely round. How could all that be bad?"

And then the best part...a giant scale appears, the kind that reads the weight out loud. One of the associates folds out a red carpet and Bebe walks toward it, tentatively taking baby steps until she reaches her destination.

"Bebe! Bebe!" we chant.

She takes a bold step and the robotic male voice, of course it's male, drones, "105...108...172!"

Bebe smiles, as if preparing to give an acceptance speech. "Good thing I've never been sensitive about my appearance."

A NAGGING FEELING THAT THE ENTIRE ROOM WAS

waiting for my response crept into my brain. Bebe stared at me expectantly and then sighed with slight annoyance.

"I said," Bebe repeated patiently, "Josh specifically told me that David is highly sensitive about his condition. He has his image to consider. And now, David feels it's up to him to consider the image of James Brolin." She paused momentarily and then threw up her arms as if in explanation. "Josh told him that we were considering him as a James substitute."

Naturally, it would be David to be sensitive and not Bebe. She wouldn't be sensitive about anything in the looks department. And that's when I realized that my very satisfying daydream about Bebe not being so perfect actually collapsed into reaffirmation about her confidence.

"What image? Nobody knows who he is. He's not the real James Brolin. He's living vicariously in James Brolin's body, sort of. He's probably never even been in the same room as Barbara Streisand," I answered. "Forget his condition. We'll work around it."

"How?" Bebe asked hopelessly.

"Call David's agent and tell him he has the job. Whatever you do, do not promise that we won't mention he has arthritis. I mean, gosh, that's actually a reason to hire him in this case. If we can't promote it then what's the point?"

"But Josh said..."

I scanned the room. Eager eyes waited for my response. "Guys, let's not forget that this is a commercial for the disease. Don't you all think it's our duty to promote it to the best of our ability? Doesn't the Arthritis Foundation deserve that? I'm thinking they do."

Across the board, the staff nodded their heads.

"Alright. It's decided then. Bebe, if David threatens to walk because we will reveal he has arthritis then tell him to go. If he's on board, let him know that we see him as a more virile version of James Brolin, the type of man that is ready to pounce every time he hears that song from "Cats" that Barbara used to sing.

"Memories?" asked Bebe.

"Exactly," I answered. "He'll go for it, so will the Arthritis Foundation and every woman over fifty who sees him on television. Tell him that as long as his penis works, the Arthritis is incidental."

"Uh April, do I really have to say that?"

"Alright, just tell him that we can see this leading to a gig for one of the E.D. drugs."

"Wouldn't that mean he's not virile?"

THE SUDDEN BUZZING OF MY TELEPHONE'S INTERCOM made me jump out of my seat. Two years and still I wasn't used to its rude interruptions. "April, someone from Artists United on line two."

"Who do they represent?" I asked our receptionist.

"Didn't say."

The woman on the phone indicated she represented Leandra Lawson, a "new talent" she described as having wowed critics during her performance in "The Glass Menagerie."

"And where did she perform it?" I asked politely.

"Oh, a highly prestigious theater group in Ms. Lawson's home town of Shaker Heights, Ohio."

Small town apples. Another actress who was willing to do anything to be discovered, even act in an Arthritis commercial. The agent assured me that although Leandra was only twenty-two, she had tremendous depth and could play roles within a twenty-year span. Also, she was willing to act the part of a young trollop after an aged actor with arthritis. I took down her name, agreed to review her resume and then proceeded to field eighteen similar calls before the afternoon was over. It was amazing how many young women were desperate for the chance to act in a thirty-second commercial just so they could skip to the local Screen Actor's Guild office with their new contract in hand in order to get a S.A.G. card.

"Is my name written on the back of a bus?" I shouted through the office.

"April, line three."

"Take a message."

Within minutes our receptionist let me know the details of the call. In a nutshell, David had decided his virility could not be compromised and walked away from our offer. When I inquired whether they had called back Richard, our second choice, I was told that his agent passed citing that Richard doesn't like to be anyone's second choice, but would make an exception if the offer was increased by $25,000. I felt a migraine coming on. We were expected to shoot in less than a week and thus far, we were cast free.

"Bebe, we've got a problem. You need to call all the casting agents and get me a 25-year-old female and a 50-year-old male stat."

"Cool."

"Cool? How do you figure?"

"I didn't know you could speak hospital."

I took a deep breath to steady my nerves. "I'm just full of surprises. So, about those calls?" I urged.

"No worries, mate!" She beamed back at me. "I'm crummy at hospital, but amazing at English. I just did Australian English, which is totally different from American English and English English."

"That is so amazing." I smiled knowing that I had totally made her day.

THE PHONE JUST WOULDN'T STOP AND IT DIDN'T MAKE any sense. The gig wasn't bad paying, but it certainly didn't warrant this type of attention, especially from top casting agents. "How did these actors find me?"

Bebe brought me a magazine in the form of an answer. "Well, you indicated that it would be hard to find an actor and that the casting agents may not respond fast enough, so I improvised and placed an ad in Dramalogue."

"What exactly did you write?"

I looked at the ad copy in Bebe's extended hand with horror.

IDEAL JOB FOR ENTERPRISING ACTOR

Must be a versatile, experienced performer who can portray pain and suffering with conviction. Call (310) 805-0785.

She may as well have written my name on the bus because every actor coming to L.A. with hopes of making it big goes straight to the newsstand to buy that publication. The worst part was the average age of the callers was eighteen. They weren't decrepit enough to appear arthritic, nor were they old enough to be considered for the girlfriend.

"Bebe," I said evenly, "with the way this ad is worded every actor from here to New York City will believe they fit this part. Shopping for jeans is more specific."

"We got a discounted rate for being under 20 words," she offered hopelessly.

NOT ONLY WAS EVERYTHING A TOTAL MESS WITH MY half-million dollar account, my concern over Bebe getting too close to Josh remained. The two of them together was bad news for so many reasons. First and foremost, it was just plain icky to think of them in *that* way. Secondly, I knew that if I ever needed Bebe to do anything that remotely resembled busy work, Josh might interfere and then before you know it, Bebe is no longer my assistant because Josh has decided to promote her. And, even worse than these two valid concerns is the horrific combining of both of them. Bebe and Josh become too intimate and then during their pillow talk she convinces him to give her my job!

I had enough to worry about between my marriage, the custody suit, and now my job security. I passed by Josh's office to see if I could have a word, but sure enough, Bebe was already camped inside. When I saw that she was sorting through an array of nail polish colors and comparing each to Josh's skin tone I tried to sneak by unnoticed. Unfortunately, my heels betrayed me.

"April, is that you?"

"Yeah, it's me."

"Come on in. Bebe is here and I'd like her to see us do one of our campaign briefings. You don't mind, do you?"

"Of course not!"

"Well, take a seat. Over there," Josh indicated the opposite side of his desk. Bebe, on the other hand, seemed to hold the coveted spot next to Josh.

"Bebe's helping me with my ulcer," he explained.

Upon hearing this, Bebe no sooner got up and kneeled in front of Josh's feet. It was then that I noticed his pant legs had been rolled to the knees and his loafers were waiting patiently under the table for their inhabitants to return.

"She's amazing. Works on my stomach through my feet!" he exclaimed gleefully.

"It's a pedicure combined with reflexology," Bebe informed before launching into 'this little piggy went to market'.

"Bebe," Josh interrupted. "Which piggy represents my stomach?"

"This one," she said pointing a red-polished finger toward the second appendage, a hideous specimen that extended beyond the big toe's domain.

Josh massaged his stomach. Bebe massaged his toes. I massaged my temples. Now was as good a time as any to launch my attack.

"Josh, I think I have the answer to our arthritis problem," I said.

"It's ulcers," he corrected.

"And corns," Bebe noted, while busy pumicing.

I looked at both of them, who were oblivious to the crisis at hand. "No, the arthritis account. We lost all of our cast. I think we should send Ryan up for the part."

"He'll never do it," Josh said with a wave of his hand. "Not good for his image."

I couldn't argue that point. It wasn't particularly good for anyone's image, which is why we were in this position to begin with. But, it occurred to me that this small slice of the negative pie could become Ryan's just desserts.

"Nonsense," I said. "Ryan needs exposure. He told us that himself. This is a national-running commercial."

Josh didn't respond, but he seemed to be mulling it over. At least that's what I think he was doing since he had retrieved his foot from Bebe's grasp. Time to tighten the bolt.

"It's not like we're asking him to be a spokesperson for

Viagra," I reasoned. "Besides, it would be great residuals for him and a hefty commission for us."

Josh nodded, "True, but how are you going to get him to go for it?"

I held up the script. "If you read this, you'd think you were selling aspirin. All it talks about is the pain of living with pain and how there's something that can help. We'll tell Ryan that the phone number he gives at the end of the commercial refers to a test project for a new aspirin-like drug."

"April, if you can pull it off, I'll stand behind you," Josh replied and then turned to Bebe. "Love that shade. What do you call it?"

"Peachy keen," she said breathlessly.

It figured.

***

WHEN RYAN CAME TO OUR OFFICES I HAD PROMISED myself not to notice his strong arms, flowing blond hair, deep-set green eyes. After all, I had to focus on my job. That was, until I told myself that in truth, my job was to focus on Ryan. Win-win. I got to admire his gorgeousness and save the account. And, as I predicted, his excitement over a new commercial caused him to ask little other than when he was due to audition. Josh was right and given the script, Ryan never suspected anything was amiss and happily skipped to the audition the next day. He wasn't even half bad.

"Barely a day went by that I didn't suffer from pain," Ryan said with feeling. "Thankfully, help was nearby."

"Good, Ryan. Now give us the 'B' script," the director instructed, his face hidden from Ryan by the bright lights that shone onto the stage.

Ryan cleared his throat and began: "Just because I'm an actor doesn't mean I'm immune to pain. But if pain does strike, I get the help I need."

Presumably, after that cut is when the FDA warnings about Mobilax potentially leading to a wide array of problems far worse than everyday arthritis would be announced. But Ryan would simply smile blissfully at the camera and then walk off with our actress of choice, making every man watching it believe that the risk of dying was incidental if he could pull such a young hottie in his arthritic condition.

"Great!" the director yelled from his post.

"Yeah, that one felt right," Ryan concurred. "My 'Setting Sun' fans will probably relate."

"Good point. You got your share of the senior set watching that show," the director said to a confused Ryan. "Congratulations. You've got it."

"Terrific," Ryan said. "When do we roll cameras?"

"We've just got to get the release from corporate for the logo to be superimposed over your image and we're set."

"Fine," Ryan said nodding. "By the way, do you want me to hold up a bottle of aspirin?"

"No, not necessary. The Foundation doesn't want to endorse any specific brand. Too political. Might effect their corporate supporters."

"Foundation?" Ryan asked as a young girl began to powder his nose.

"I don't know how you guys do it," the director remarked. "You're probably on so many calls, you've actually forgotten the client."

"Right," Ryan said in a worried tone. "Just who is the client?"

"The Arthritis Foundation."

"That's impossible. I can't be right for this," Ryan said, fighting back hysteria.

"Modesty. Nice touch. You don't see that in actors much," the director laughed.

Ryan stood suddenly. "I'm serious!" he shouted, causing the powder girl to drop her brushes, powder to scatter to the floor, and Ryan enough time to make a dramatic exit.

———

"THIS IS THE TYPE OF P.R. THAT YOUR FIRM SEES AS positive?"

Ryan was indeed throwing a temper tantrum. Apparently, I wasn't "senior" enough to be privy to his rantings, although it was easily heard down the hall. "Bruce, I assume you'll get to the bottom of this."

"Ryan, I assure you that no damage has been done. Your agent probably just got your casting call mixed up with someone else's."

"The tip came from your office! Probably from April! Where is she?"

"Right here," I said on cue. "I thought you wanted privacy to talk about me behind my back."

"Ahh, April," Bruce said in a dreamy voice.

"Jesus, Bruce. This could have been disastrous. I never would have known until it was too late. They were going to turn me into the poster boy for the decrepit," he said in a tone that sounded close to tears.

"Nonsense. You're not decrepit, ol' boy," Bruce said through a sincere smile.

"What are you going to do about this?" Ryan asked in a threatening tone.

Bruce scanned the hallway once more. "We're going to

make sure you're seen with a young, sexual, hot woman!" Bruce said closing his eyes, visualizing the possibilities. "The type of girl who wouldn't accept a worn out carpet, let alone man."

"Excellent," Ryan said smugly looking at me.

"You know how to get to him," Bruce said.

"I don't know what or who you're talking about."

"Come on, April, that casting call was a low blow."

"Nonsense. I was just doing my job. Think of the positive press we could get for Ryan if he would just start doing a little charity work."

Bruce put his hand to his chin and rubbed an imaginary beard. "Yeah, I admit, charity work gets the media going."

"You see, no harm done," I answered sweetly. "I always have our clients' best interests at heart."

"Hmm. There's only one thing that gets the press moving faster than a sad, charity case."

"What's that?"

"Sex."

"I tried that. We were married."

"Young, fresh, undiscovered sex," Bruce replied in a knowing manner. "April, we need to start the set-up phase of Ryan's publicity campaign. It's time the press started talking about the new whoever in his life."

"Bruce, I'm really busy. And frankly, I don't see that this would..."

"April, you'll have to make the time," Bruce interrupted. "I know it won't be easy, after all there's still probably some hurt feelings, but try, dear," he said while putting his hand on my shoulder.

The heat of it burned through my sweater. I was reminded of elementary school plays when all the kids had to file onto the stage, hand-in-hand, to take a final bow. We all fought over who had to stand next to Alex Wrencrest, the fat kid with the sweaty hands. Inevitably, I was placed next to Alex because we were the same height and the teacher wanted a uniformed, precision type of look -- kind of like a Nazi troop.

"April, placing your feelings aside is what you need for your own recovery and what better way to do that then find a suitable replacement for yourself? I figure we need someone about this tall," he said placing his hand in level with my head. "Someone with your coloring, skin so white and creamy. Maybe even someone with your eyes," he said placing his face obscenely close to mine.

Thankfully, Josh walked in at that same moment. I think it was his first well-timed entrance of the year.

"Good, you're here too. Aren't we forgetting something?"

Bruce and Josh shook their heads in unison.

"Bruce, you're describing Ryan's ideal woman as someone who looks just like me, but he obviously doesn't want me." In spite of myself, I felt my shoulders slump causing Bruce to grab me in a bear hug. Not wanting to ever be outdone by Bruce's efforts, Josh embraced me from behind, making a sandwich out of me.

I coughed from the squeezing. "Guys? Also, if I set up Ryan then we'll have to address the divorce issue."

"Not necessarily," Josh said. "Celebrities are always cheating on their spouses."

"Right you are," Bruce concurred. "You know, April, you're onto something. We probably should've set up Ryan years ago. Being seen with another woman is never bad for a man's image."

"Absolutely," Josh agreed. "Makes him seem desirable."

"Try your best, April. Get him a date by next week. The holidays will be here before we know it and that's always a good time for celebs to step out with a new love," Bruce said while finally releasing me.

Josh let go as well and I breathed a sigh of relief that they mistook for acceptance.

Chapter 7

"Ian, which one do you like?"

"You look good in everything."

"Ohh. April, Isn't he sweet?"

I looked up from my laptop and nodded politely. Melissa was trying on various sizes and shapes of prosthetic baby bumps.

Ian grabbed Melissa by the arm and pulled her in for a hug. "Come here."

"With pleasure."

It was all too much in my fragile state. "Hey guys, do you realize what I'm doing?"

They looked up from their lip lock. I indicated my laptop for Melissa to look at the screen. Images of smiling faces stared back at her.

"Wow, that's great April. You're taking the plunge." Melissa turned to Ian, "She's going on match.com."

He gave me the thumbs up.

"I'm not on match.com for me. I'm looking for girls for Ryan."

"That is so messed up," Melissa noted, before whispering to Ian, "total denial."

"Who's Ryan?"

"Her ex."

"Soon to be ex," I corrected.

"That's big of you," Ian noted, albeit a bit leerily. "So you guys are pretty amicable about your separation?"

"Not even," Melissa piped up.

"Then...why are you setting him up?" Ian asked.

"In a nutshell," I started to explain, "he's an important account of my firm's, the bosses want to keep him happy and the public interested in him, so I get to act like his pimp. Call it a job perk."

"That's more like workplace harassment," Ian duly noted.

It was my turn to hug Ian. "He is sweet."

Melissa concurred, "Told you."

Who was I to question their relationship or pending fake pregnancy especially when Ian came up with the obvious solution that was staring me in the face, but I was too blind to see.

"Why don't you just pick a loser?"

"He wouldn't date a loser. He's used to someone like me."

There was a moment of awkward silence before Ian explained his thought process. "Of course not, if she's a dog, but if she's beautiful...," he let the idea percolate. "Listen, you pick a gorgeous girl. He'll go for it, so will your bosses and your problem is solved, especially when she turns out to have the personality of a sloth."

I smiled for the first time all afternoon. "Wanna help?"

"We'd love to," they said in unison and took a seat on either side of me.

AFTER AN HOUR OF SIFTING THROUGH SMILING FACES and their corresponding online profiles, we made notes of the most viable women, those who were attractive enough to be deemed worthy by Ryan, but had a predilection for puppies, rainbows and other giveaways of their vacuous mindset. Ian and Melissa decided to check out free pre-natal classes at the local hospital, leaving me to search my horoscope for an indication that lightening might soon strike Ryan.

Aries: Attention revolves around sex drive, marital status. Must I be reminded? Pisces seemed more appealing: *Life only seems to be against you. It's merely an illusion.* Well, I could only hope. I kept searching for something more to my liking.

Taurus: Family member urges, "Live a little. Don't be afraid to experiment." Thankfully, I haven't had time to speak to my mother today. If I had, no doubt her idea of "living a little" would be to march Ryan straight into marriage counseling so that the two of us would live a little more in the bedroom and give her grandchildren. Melissa's advice would be the converse: dye my hair red and go on the prowl. Fortunately, Dad kept his opinions to himself.

I glanced at Gemini's horoscope, a virtual catastrophe in my current state: *"New discovery alters your destiny."* Sounds ominous.

Aquarius was no better. *"Falsified vow is restored."* As if I could kidnap Ryan to Las Vegas, force him to renew our wedding vows in a cheap, heart-laden, "weddings-are-us" type of place and then immediately surrender to the nearest hotel to consummate our new and improved marriage which includes sex, the kind with insertion! Yeah, right.

There's roughly only one month of shopping days left

until Christmas. In soon-to-be-divorced-woman-speak this meant only four weeks to accept the fate of holiday depression brought on by my mother's worries that I would never give her grandchildren (mine too), Josh's concern that I wouldn't locate a suitable actor for the Arthritis Foundation (ditto), and the reoccurring fear that one day I would be referred to as the "crazy lady who chatters to her two dogs" (not such a bad thought).

I wondered which was worse: attend Aunt Joan's brunch alone and explain that Ryan has a date (courtesy of my new matchmaking skills), or show up as the "happy couple" knowing that news of our divorce would soon hit like a firestorm. Attending the party with Ryan wouldn't be so terrible if he hadn't developed the nasty habit of constantly reminding me that he is a "transitory" gay man. He explained that this means his choice is to be gay, but because of current obligations that depend on him to flirt with women other than his wife, it's important that he still appears to be the straightest guy around.

And then as if my mother had spy gear inserted into the recesses of my subconscious, the phone rang. The caller I.D. indicated it was my mother and I know that I should know better, but I just couldn't bring myself to answer in my current state. Answering machine to the rescue.

"Hi honey, just thought I'd swing by to bring you some soup."

Oh no. I lunged for the phone, hoping to head her off at the pass, but she had already hung up. God was punishing me for not answering when I knew it was my mother.

The truth was that the more I avoided family dinners, the more intent mom became to be in the same room with Ryan and me. It was a menage à trois that was surely more neurotic than erotic. My marriage was a trophy on my mom's mantlepiece of accomplishments. Apparently, she had entered the lifelong, offspring competition with Aunt Joan. It started when Mom found out she was pregnant and claimed she knew she was having a girl because she was on top. Joan argued that the missionary position produced females. First point, Mom.

She had only just left the message when the phone rang again. Caller I.D. showed my mom's number. There is a god. I answered feeling redeemed, but then was surprised to discover that it was Dad, calling to warn me about my mother's latest plan to keep me married.

"April, your mother will call you within the hour."

"Transfer your psychic abilities to commodities trading and you'll make a fortune."

"Make jokes if you want, but it's true and she's on a mission."

"You're too late. She already called. I'm supposed to come over and pick up soup. Can't you do something?"

"She's your mother."

"She's your wife."

Passing blame is a long-standing tradition in my parent's home. Whenever either Melissa or I did anything hair-brained when we were young, Mom and Dad would debate whose daughter we belonged to with both parties pointing to the other.

I thanked Dad for the notice and immediately texted Melissa: *Mom will b here soon. Pls come home. Need u.*

The lovely ping arrived almost instantaneously: *In pre-natal class.*

This was too much. What was the point of Melissa's fake pregnancy if she wasn't here to make good use of it? *Repeat. I NEED U!*

And then finally, a reply that I could get behind --

Melissa's request about her protruding front. *Can I wear my tummy?*

Yes, just get here.

On the upside, Melissa and Ian arrived before Mom, but her appearance was a matter open for debate. She wasn't just sporting your everyday, run of the mill, had a heavy lunch type of tummy. This was a full-blown preggers stomach.

"You remember why we're doing this?" I asked shaking my head at her.

"Of course I remember. Your relationship is kapluie and as usual I'm having to make you look good."

"That's not totally true," I argued.

"Please."

"First of all, there may be a chance in salvaging my marriage and second, you can't say that you're making me look good *as usual*."

"Look at me!" she said pointing to her stomach. "You're going to owe me for a long time."

"Yeah, about that," I said indicating her stomach. "Mom's going to die."

"I know, pretty cool, huh?"

Melissa was starting to enjoy this waaay to much.

"Melissa, we haven't even broken the news to her yet and you're wearing the six month pillow."

Melissa turned toward the hallway mirror. "This one makes my legs look thiner. Don't you think?"

I had to admit, a larger stomach does make legs look thiner, if only in comparison.

"It's even better than wearing black," I admitted. "But, don't you think we should ease her into the whole idea?"

"Fine," Melissa said and pulled off her pillow. "I'll go and change into the pillow that makes me look like I've just eaten a large burrito."

"Honey, I think that one's at my house," Ian chimed in.

"How can it be at Ian's house!" I shrieked. "Mom is going to be here any minute. How could you leave your child alone?"

"Relax, April," Melissa walked calmly to the hall closet. "See? I'm totally prepared for motherhood," she said retrieving another prosthetic tummy.

"Not that I'm complaining, but why do you have two?"

"In case I found out that we were going to have twins," Melissa replied sweetly, giving Ian a peck on the cheek before going into the bedroom to put on her tummy.

Ian looked after her wistfully. "She thinks of everything. She's going to be a terrific mother."

I had to admit. He was right.

MOM WOULD BE HERE ANY MINUTE AND THE HOUSE looked like a hoarders dream place. I hurried around picking up stray articles of clothing, magazines, mail, dishes, you name it, hiding everything in the hall closet that was now our depository for everything unwanted (after Melissa pulled out a second tummy there was no telling what else was lurking inside) before focusing on myself.

It's amazing what a fresh application of mascara can do for the appearance. I started applying with one hand while using the dust buster with the other. The place looked decent, but I had managed to stab myself in the eye when the doorbell sounded.

"Ehhlow," I answered while attempting to stop my eye from watering by opening it widely and simultaneously stretching my mouth into a big "O" to stretch the cheek away from my lower lashes. Clumps and smears would only make the matter worse.

"Oh April, it's worse than I thought. You've been drinking!" Mom shrieked.

"I aven't een inking."

"Cocaine?"

I couldn't even respond. My eye was burning. The reality of having to face my mother was giving me heartburn. I merely shook my head.

"Alright good. That's good," she said more to herself than to me. "Unless...unless it's one of those designer drugs. You were always a trend-setter."

"Mom! I'm utting on makeup."

"You're what?"

Resolved that my makeup would be finished faster if I simply stopped the process, I answered. "I'm fixing my face. I was in the middle of my left eye."

"Oh, that's a relief. Here," she said shoving a drippy pot toward me. "Soup."

Mom believed homemade soup to be a colossal achievement. Whenever she made it Melissa and I were summoned to the house, ordered to report for soup claiming duty armed with two large Tupperware containers. (Brownie points for me ever since I got a set for a wedding present; Melissa still resorted to regular bowls.)

"Well, if everything is okay than where's Ryan?" she asked suspiciously.

It was my cue to bring out the savior sister. "Melissa! Mom's here and she can't wait to hear our big news."

Melissa came out with Ian in tow. The two held hands, looking every bit the united front, ready to ambush mom with news of their illicit sex, irresponsible birth control practices and total lack of respect for mom and dad's repeated lectures about the importance of settling down after one is firmly established in a job and then after say five years of marriage, and only then, would it be wise to consider having children. Ooh, this was going to be good. I gave Melissa a surreptitious thumb's up sign, nodded my head and waited for her to spring the news of how she got knocked up.

"Hi Mom."

"Hi Darling. Give me a kiss," mom said leaning her cheek in Melissa's direction. "You look nice. Is that a new dress?"

For the first time, I took in Melissa's outfit. It was a very flowy dress -- completely inappropriate for it didn't hug one ounce of her body. It was the sort of dress that Jennifer Aniston would wear in front of the tabloids before she spilled the beans of her pregnancy. In other words, it was a maternity moo-moo, which is a definite no-no in my book.

"You can't even see the baby," I whispered in a panic to Ian. "What's she doing?"

"We decided to wait," he said simply.

"Wait?!"

Mom, Melissa and Ian all turned to me, mouths open and looking as if I was losing my mind. Perhaps I was.

"Wait, right here and I'll get us some tea. Melissa, would you like to help me?"

I dragged Melissa into the kitchen, leaving Ian alone with mom where he could win her over with his charming smile and easy personality. It was a nightmare.

"What are you doing?" I screeched when Melissa and I were a safe distance away.

"Listen Ape, I know you're probably wondering why I'm not doubled over in back pain and feigning nausea, and maybe it's because I'm having a fairly easy pregnancy, but it just doesn't seem like the right time for Ian and I to you know, spring the news. They barely know Ian and shouldn't dad be here?"

I pulled Melissa closely toward me because it was the

only way I could keep myself from shouting at the top of my lungs. "First of all, I seriously think you've gone insane."

"Why thank you, April. Coming from you, an esteemed expert on the subject, I'll take that statement as a simple reflection of your concern for my well-being."

"It's meant as a threat. You made me a promise. You're living here rent free. You owe me!"

Mom suddenly yelled to us from the other room. "Are you two coming back in here soon? And where's Ryan?"

"He's out with the boys," I yelled back.

Mom's voice carried into the kitchen loud and clear. "And you're not with him? On a Sunday? Oh God, that's terrible."

I grabbed Melissa by the arm. "This is not supposed to be happening. The attention is supposed to be on you and Ian, not Ryan and I."

"Just make something up for now. Ian and I, well...I think we have a real future. April, just give me some more time. I don't want to mess things up."

I looked at Melissa, who really did seem happy. I rolled my eyes, knowing that I couldn't deny her happiness or that feeling you get with a new relationship. What was that feeling called again? Oh yeah, hope. It was something that was quickly draining out of me. I ladled a cup of soup into a bowl and led the way back into the family room. "Come on."

"So?" mom prompted, accepting the bowl from me.

"He and the boys are probably having such a great time that they lost track of time. You know, we're not tied at the hip."

"It just seems that lately, you're not spending any time together. Is it because Melissa moved in because I could have a word with her," she whispered.

Melissa took that as a cue to leave and grabbed Ian to head toward her bedroom. "Bye Mom. Ian's going to help me with my computer."

I rolled my eyes. "Oh, is that what the kids are calling it today?"

For the life of me, my mom never gave me the breaks that Melissa gets. "How come she's allowed to have a boy in her room and I never was?"

"Because she's the baby and would never do anything wrong," mom said simply.

It wasn't fair when we were young and it's still not fair now.

"Besides, we're not talking about Melissa right now," mom chided.

"Ryan is just....busy," I finally came up with. Apparently that was the totally wrong answer.

"Oh my god. Did he say that? April, you know what 'busy' means, don't you?"

"Umm, he's occupied, industrious, unavailable?"

"April, you need to learn how to seduce your husband immediately. I obviously failed as a mother," she moaned.

"You haven't failed as a mother."

"Well then you must have failed as a wife. Tell me, April, do you perform your duties?"

"Melissa!"

Melissa came out of her room with hair mussed, cheeks flushed and staring daggers into me. "Yes?"

"Mom wants to know all of your news."

Melissa looked at me, eyebrows raised. "What? You mean *all* of it?"

"Yes, tell her about your work, *or lack of*," I whispered. "Then, give her the real kicker," I winked and motioned my chin at her stomach.

Melissa took a deep breath, looked at mom and with

resolve spoke those magic words that will make any mother quake in her sensible shoes. "Mom, there's something I need to tell you."

Five minutes earlier, Ryan's arrival would have been a godsend. But he chose this moment to arrive. Of all moments, why now? Now, was certainly not fortuitous. Now was just irritating. He opened the door, calling for Buster and Louie to follow, which they immediately did by bounding into the room and jumping at Melissa, who stumbled into my mom causing her to spill a healthy amount of soup onto the front of my mother's dress.

"Oh, I'm so sorry," Melissa said. Ironically, the apology was directed more toward me than mom. "Here, I'll get you a washcloth."

"There's no need. I'll just go home and put it in the wash," mom said simply, as Ryan followed the boys in. "Well, this is 'hi' and 'goodbye' for me. We'll have to catch up tomorrow night."

Ryan gave me a questioning look, but was thankfully too caught off guard to verbalize his confusion.

"Tomorrow?" I asked with the sinking feeling that I had forgotten to get out of something I definitely didn't want to be a part of.

"You couldn't possibly forget," she stated staring between all of us. "The annual holiday do at Aunt Brenda's! Melissa is bringing Ian, and I'm making a roast."

Melissa gave me the look. Tomorrow was the night.

In my mother's mind everything was so simple. I was destined to spend an evening hearing how sex could rectify a marriage and a weekly dinner could reinstall the value of family. "Should I bring anything?" I asked miserably.

"Just yourself, dear."

I FINISHED MY MAKEUP WITH NEGATIVE FIFTEEN ON THE clock. No sign of Ryan. I leaned in close to Buster, then Louie. A slight smell of D.O.--doggie odor--reached my nostrils. "Okay Buster, are you the Channel or Paloma Picasso type?" I asked while surveying the perfume bottles on my dresser. Not enjoying Buster's new signature bouquet, Louie retreated from the bedroom.

"Not so fast," I yelled after him. I had him cornered under the kitchen table, perfume bottle in hand, when Buster came to his rescue. I got a fresh whiff, "Uhgg, I now realize that even a classic like Channel No. 5 can be overdone."

I looked back at Louie, still cowering, obviously repelled by Buster's feminine side. "I get it. You're not one for Channel. How 'bout something more masculine?" I asked.

I considered forgoing this part of my newly invented grooming regime, but knew that Ryan would detect "eau de unwashed dog". I couldn't risk it. "Listen Louie, I know you're troubled by this, but we can't give daddy ammunition," I said in a sing-song voice as I grabbed him by the rear leg. "You wanna live with mommy, don't you?" I pleaded.

Louie seemed to understand as he nuzzled my neck. I softened as well. "Oh the hell with it." I left Buster smelling like a runway model and searched Ryan's departed bathroom cabinet for any forgotten supplies.

Some razors, vitamins, Mennen deodorant, and Band-aids. He probably left these believing them to fall into the "household supplies" category. I grabbed the Mennen roll-on and proceeded to smear up and down Louie's back, periodically stopping to extricate fur from the gliding dome. We were all pleased with the outcome, dressed and ready, when the doorbell rang.

"Hi, you got here fast," I noted.

Ryan checked his watch. "I'm late. So, you got their stuff packed?"

"Yes, but honestly I don't know why they can't just spend the night here. Aren't you bringing me back home after the party?"

"Yes, but I'm certainly not staying. We agreed that we would get them used to spending time at my place. So, like we said, I'll bring them over to my place and then come back and pick you up for the party."

As if on cue, the dogs ran to him. "Hey boys," he called, and then, turning to look at me, "What's that smell?"

"Nice, huh? New groomer."

"Louie feels...," he struggled for the word, "sticky."

"Oh, it's his hair gel," I said with a nonchalant wave of my hand. "The newest thing in dog grooming," I said while fluffing and teasing Louie's fur.

"Well, why doesn't Buster have any," Ryan asked.

"Oh, uh...well he doesn't have fly-away fur," I whispered, so as not to upset Louie. "Do you want to have a snack when you get back. Something light before we go?" I asked hopefully.

"April, we're going to spend an entire evening together at Aunt Brenda's."

"Being in a house full of people is not the same."

He ignored my comment and moved to follow the boys outside. "I'll be back in half an hour."

I FOUND BUSTER'S FAVORITE STUFFED ANIMAL TUCKED under the coffee table and Louie's bedtime pillow. Ryan had left in such a hurry that I didn't search the house properly. Or maybe I was just too preoccupied with his taking them to his place to remember. I had watched them climb into Ryan's car from the living room window. Ryan was laughing; Buster and Louie were panting, giving the illusion that they, too, were in on a joke. A tear weaved a snail trail down my cheek.

I was tempted to drive over to Ryan's new place. I wasn't exactly in a party mood and if there was one thing that Ryan and I did agree on it's that Aunt Brenda's events could never be in the "can't miss" category. I thought about what would happen if I turned up unannounced, wearing my best...towel.

"April, you look different." It was working. I knew it would. He was a man, after all, and the Target ad said that this was the plushest towel they carried. It was practically a designer item. Ryan, on the other hand, was wearing his swim trunks. He and the boys were frolicking in their wading pool. "Wanna join us?"

"Well, I don't want to get all wet," I said indicating my carefully selected ensemble. (Did I mention that somehow a new pair of Jimmy Choos, which I don't currently own, were magically on my feet and complimented the pale blue of the terry cloth perfectly.)

Ryan obviously couldn't resist. "Come on, the water's great."

"Actually, I just thought you might need this while the boys were over." I handed him the latest copy of <u>Dog Fancy</u> magazine. The cover article was about how to calm your pet in a new surrounding.

"That was thoughtful, but as you can see, unnecessary. So, what do you say you ditch that sexy little towel and jump in?"

"I'd love to," I beamed, no sooner dropping my towel and stepping into the ankle deep water of the wading pool. It was like the parting of the sea. Buster and Louie must have sensed our need for privacy and jumped out. Ryan took the opportunity to pull me in closer to him and kiss me like we haven't done in far too long.

STUPID FANTASY SEGMENT. IT WOULD NEVER HAPPEN. I'M not sure why my subconscious wanted to pair stilettos with a bath towel, but I was certain that Ryan never liked the color blue on me. And that was only the half of it. In reality, he would argue that the dogs should not be left unsupervised and he would be right. Not only was I facing divorce before Christmas, regardless of Josh's promise that Ryan would "wait until after the holidays," but I was also showing increasing signs that I possessed inept parenting skills.

Ryan had started taking Buster and Louie on "meaningful" outings to locales such as the dog park in the Hollywood hills where they could socialize with other four-legged children. He had a point. A judge would certainly consider the hours both of us spent at work compared to the time we spent at home with the boys. Quality time would have to be gained if I were to win the battle.

As if mirroring my thoughts, Ryan returned with tousled hair looking slightly more lived in than he did when he left.

"Why did it take you so long?"

"We decided to stop off at the park and then we were having so much fun I couldn't just break it up."

"We decided? Don't do this, Ryan."

"Do what?"

"Try to make it out that they have more fun with you. I'm plenty of fun!" I insisted.

"Good. We have a party to go to. Got your coat?"

It was a long ride to Aunt Brenda's with the only sound coming from the car radio and my stomach.

"Can you stop that?"

"What?"

"That noise," he said and pointed to my abdomen.

"Excuse me," I replied sarcastically. "Had you been on time, we would already be there and my stomach would be content."

"At least one of us would be happy."

"What's that supposed to mean? You're the one who wanted to continue this charade until New Year's."

"Forgive me if I'm not looking forward to your mother springing one of her acting hopefuls on me."

"That's not fair. You flaunt yourself like a peacock. 'Look at me; I'm on the number one soap.'"

Ryan took his eyes off the road long enough to roll them at me. "That's ripe coming from Miss Power Publicity."

"I don't know what you're talking about."

"I guarantee within minutes of arriving you will have given unsolicited advice to the nearest ear willing to listen."

"Don't be ridiculous, Ryan. If I have ever doled out advice it's from a true desire to help someone save time and money. Surely, you remember how much my firm makes off your account."

"Whatever. Can you stop arguing now?"

"Me?!"

"April, we're here. If you want to keep my account, try to act happy. Give me a little peck on the cheek from time to time."

"I'll make a note of it."

Apparently, Brenda was still busy in the kitchen with her Christmas matzo ball soup, a specialty that was served for all of December, so Mom answered the door and immediately commandeered Ryan and I to our posts. "Oh good, you're here! Everyone has been asking about the happy couple. Ryan, I want you to talk with Elaine Gold-farb, a big fan."

Ryan gave me an "I told you so" look, but not before I could lob one right back at him.

"April, Jack Binger has a publicity question for you," Mom continued.

Ryan left my side in search of his latest fan, but before I could do the same, Mom placed my arm in a clamp-like grip and steered me to a quiet corner. "Melissa told me that you two were fighting."

This wasn't happening.

"I didn't want you to know. What exactly did she say?" I said in a desperate attempt to find out how much exactly Melissa had spilled.

"That's all. I asked her why I never saw the two of you in the same room. At first she said nothing. Actually, she never did say anything. I just made that up to see what you would say. So, spill it.

In spite of my best intentions to protect my mother from worry, to keep Ryan happy and to ensure that my job was secure, I let the tears flow.

"Come here, sweetie," Mom said, leading me into the hall bathroom.

When we got inside, she hugged me and I melted into her arms. It was the first time in ages that I've done that -- just allowing someone to hold me -- and it felt better. It allowed me to at least tell her a little bit.

"We've just been having troubles," I admitted.

"Every married couple has troubles."

"I'm not sure we can work through ours, but I'm trying. The problem is that he doesn't want to try any more."

"April, you need to take action. Look at that blouse you're wearing," she pointed accusingly. "Undo another button," she ordered.

"You hate it when I dressed suggestively."

"That was when you were sixteen. At your age, with a husband about to leave, I want to see some cleavage. Now unbutton!" she ordered.

Instantly, I remembered being eleven-years-old and shopping for my first bra with Mom. It was September and Los Angeles' Summer was still in full force. The stores' new Fall line of sweaters, long-sleeved tops, and wool pants had arrived, so to combat the heat wave and inspire shoppers to try on Winter wear, the air-conditioned blasted. Frigid air was not an ideal environment for a bashful girl to try on bras. I was so exposed. To make matters worse, Mom, who earlier declared herself an expert bra shopper, decided a second opinion was needed and called in an elderly sales woman to also examine my blossoming breasts encased in their new, nylon home.

"Mom, it's not like Ryan hasn't seen my cleavage before."

"April, your father still gets a thrill when I..."

"Stop, I'll do it," I said so as not to get an x-rated earful of my parents' exploits. I undid my button. "Happy? Now if you'll excuse me I going to find Melissa."

Maybe Melissa had shown up wearing real fur or some other Los Angeles social faux pas that would drive attention away from me.

Chapter 8

I wish I could say that the party wasn't as bad as I had thought it would be. In actuality, it was worse. Driving to work, I gave Jessica the lowdown.

"It couldn't be that bad," she insisted. "This is a prime example of the typical April mentality."

"What does that mean?" I said suddenly swerving out of the way of another car whose driver decided that my lane was preferable. "Watch it! You inept…"

"You see? You even suffer from road rage," Jessica said in an annoyingly calm voice. "You need to start looking at the positive side of things. It'll change your life. Go on, try it."

"You're right. There was an abundance of food, plenty to drink, roomfuls of cheerful people."

"Oh April, it sounds ghastly. When did you get home?"

"Around ten. Ryan praised me for my performance."

"Always a kind word from him, eh?"

"Yeah, soon it will be his turn to start acting. I'm supposed to find him a date for some big industry charity gala. Oh, and the date has to be female."

"I thought he was gay?"

"He is, but the firm wants him to maintain his *image*," I said stressing the word.

"Then you should do the same. Every Hollywood publicist has a gorgeous guy on their arm. You need a young pup. Cute and stupid. You must know tons of actors like that who want to be seen around town."

"Too depressing. I want someone who actually wants me," I said sadly.

"You know what? You're going to be okay."

"I am? How do you know?" I asked uncertainly.

"Because with what you just said, you actually made the first step toward dating."

"I'm not sure that's a good thing. I'm not even divorced."

"April, it's not as if you're going to get back together. You and Ryan have irreconcilable differences. And, for all intents and purposes, the two of you have been separated for ages. You might as well get back in practice. God, how long has it been?"

"For what?" I asked suspiciously.

Jessica was all too knowing. "You know what. Do you still have the lipstick that's not really a lipstick?"

I smiled remembering the pocket vibrator that Jessica had bought me on my last birthday. "It's here somewhere," I said searching my purse. "God, I wonder if it still has battery power."

"You know that I recently saw one that can be charged in a USB port?"

"No way!"

And that's when I plowed into the car in front of me.

"April? April, you okay?" Jessica repeated.

I bent over to retrieve the phone. "Yeah. But I sort of

hit the guy in front of me. I really shouldn't go looking for vibrators during rush hour traffic, Jess. I gotta run."

"That's when we need them most. Bye."

I tentatively got out of the car. The guy I hit was already inspecting his bumper and I couldn't help, but take notice of his. He was gorgeous. Maybe there is a god.

"Do you have your insurance?" he said briskly and in the most beautifully sexy English accent. Double goodie!

"Oh, do we have to do that? It's just a little fender bender, as we say here."

"Well, as I say, I don't want to leave it like this. So, will you be paying for this or will your insurance company?"

He was becoming less cute by the minute. "I'll pay. Here's my card. Call me!"

He gave me a peculiar look before getting back into his car and drove away. I grabbed my cell once again. Jessica answered on the first ring. "Are you okay?"

"Yeah, I'm fine. My car has good taste."

"What does that mean?"

"It means that maybe the cute guy whose bumper I crumpled will forgive me and ask me on a date instead of asking me to pay for damages."

"Or, I could just set you up with someone."

"I have pretty high standards," I admitted. "He needs to be..." I kept thinking back to Ryan, to my parents happy relationship, to the sexy English stranger who just drove out of my life. "He needs to be as well-suited for me as Buster and Louie are for each other."

"I'm not sure that's what you need," she replied tactfully before we hung up.

I HADN'T EVEN MADE IT DOWN THE HALL TO MY OFFICE

before Bebe informed me that a call was holding. Ooh, sexy traffic accident guy, here I come!

"Hello?"

"April, tell me what I'm reading is your firm's idea of a publicity stunt."

I exhaled loudly; my hopes dashed. It was my mom and I had no idea what she was talking about, but it sounded bad. I covered the mouthpiece of the phone and whispered to Bebe, "Today's paper. What happened?"

She looked like a scared rabbit "You didn't know? I thought it was your doing."

Mom continued her rant, "Did you have to announce this on the front page of the entertainment section?"

"You know me, Mom. I've always been good at my job." Finally, Bebe brought up the Times' website and I stared at a photo of Ryan with the caption, "SOAP STUD READY TO GET DIRTY."

"Oh my god. How did this happen?" I said aloud, not actually meaning for my mother to hear.

"Oh April, please!" she shouted. "This is no time for jokes. You should be trying to get a retraction printed, or whatever it is you do in situations like this one."

"I'm sorry you found out this way, Mom. But, in situations like this, I'm supposed to learn to accept it."

"You have to do something," she whined desperately. "What about grandchildren? Think about your future, dear."

"I am Mom," I said and hung up the phone.

Bebe stared at me expectantly.

"What?" I asked miserably.

"I'm just waiting. Are you going to yell or cry?"

"Which would be more advantageous given my situation?"

"Oh April, I'm sorry. Josh felt you needed a little push to start Ryan's new campaign."

"You knew?"

"For the record, I was against it all along."

I nodded. It's not like Bebe would've had a choice. "It's okay. It's the worst surprise ever, but he was right for doing it. Now I have to move forward. You mind giving me a minute?"

"Of course not. Do you need anything? Coffee? Latte? Green Monster juice blend?"

"Just a good cry. Don't tell anyone, will you?"

Bebe just gave me a hug in response. Strangely, it was just what I needed.

I took a few minutes to consider my life and realized that the advice everyone had given was right. If I didn't consider the future, I may never escape the misery of the present.

There was a lot to be done. After all, I was expected to find Ryan a date and keep my sanity. The quickest route to my rescue was the list of actors who applied for the Arthritis Foundation commercial. By the time Bebe checked in on me again, I had recovered Leandra Lawson's resume from our reject files.

"Bebe, remember Leandra Lawson? The actress who applied for the Arthritis gig? Could you get a hold of her and set up a meeting as soon as possible?"

"I thought you were looking for a man."

I longed to blurt out "never again," but thought better of the idea. "It's for a different job," I explained.

THE INDUSTRY COMPOSITE CARD LISTING LEANDRA'S physical attributes read like a description of a beauty pageant contestant: 5' 10", 125 lbs., brown hair, blue eyes, measurements 38-24-34 (Nobody naturally has a 38 bust and 34" hips — so L.A.), enjoys sports and reading in her free time (she can read!).

The card also listed her latest acting roles. She had performed in "A Chorus Line" in a small home town theater. Not surprisingly, she sang "Dance Ten, Looks Three" about a girl who didn't get the job until she renovated her assets. Yet, Leandra's most watched performance was a small bit role on "Saturday Night Live" in which she was hired to do a parody of the national commercial where girls croon, "Don't hate me because I'm beautiful," as they hock some sort of shampoo. Leandra again focused on her voluptuous figure with the memorable line, "Don't hate my breasts because they're big."

I scanned the resume one last time when Bebe buzzed me that Leandra had arrived.

"Show her in," I said cheerfully.

Any actress will tell you that their entrance is as important, if not more so, than the lasting impression they give. The entering patterns usually feature hold your head high, but don't make eye contact, let the hips lead the oh so sexy body, or a combo wiggle walk and direct gaze that is meant to say I'm too sexy for the likes of you, but please go home and dream about me. Leandra's entrance into my office was one I had never seen from a would-be starlet.

She wore a simple dress covered by a modest sweater, low heels, hair pulled back in a ponytail, and walked with a distinct limp, which prompted her to carry a cane with one hand and clutch her lower back with the other.

"Leandra?"

"Yes, nice to meet you," she said while positioning her

bottom over the spare chair and letting her body crash to its waiting surface. "Oh, down we go," she said with a grunt followed by a martyr smile.

"Uh, are you okay?"

"Pretty good, huh?" she said sitting straight up while simultaneously loosening her hair, removing the sweater, and crossing a long leg. "Told you I could do it."

"Do what?"

"Be an arthritic. You know, the commercial."

"Oh, you were acting," I said with more conviction than I felt. "I asked you here to fulfill a different role. Something very important."

"Something better than a commercial?" she asked hopefully.

"Much."

"I've never heard of her," Ryan said into the phone, his voice sounding arrogant.

"Well, she's very pretty," I answered.

"Leandra who? What has she been in?" he pushed.

"It's Leandra Lawson. Has a nice ring to it. Don't you think?"

"April, what has she done?"

"What difference does it make? It's bad enough I have to find you dates. Listen, she's pretty and willing. What more do you want?"

"Clout. I have my image to consider."

I rolled my eyes, which was a useless gesture considering we were on the phone. "I'll see you later. Leandra will meet you at the event," I said and hung up.

THE VALET WAS JUST DRIVING OFF WITH MY EXPLORER when Ryan pulled up in a red Jaguar, rented for the occasion and no doubt billed to my firm as one of his new, but necessary expense items. However, it wasn't the car as much as what Ryan had with him in the passenger seat that shocked me most.

"What do you think you're doing?" I yelled as he got out.

"April, you look nice," he smiled. "Let me introduce you to Matthew."

A good-looking man crossed to the driver's side of the car. He was about six-feet tall with blond hair and green eyes. He was stunning and younger than me by about five years. It didn't take me a moment to notice that he was also appearing in the role of Ryan's date for the night.

"Nice to meet you," I said in Matthew's direction and then grabbed Ryan by the elbow to pull him closer.

"I thought you were concerned about your image," I hissed in his ear. "How could you bring a man to this event? What about Leandra?" I asked protectively.

"Relax. Matthew has his own ticket at a separate table. As for Leandra, I checked up on her, and honestly, she sounds like a nimwit. Besides, Matthew is not just any man, he's my..." Ryan hesitated. It was the first time since our separation that he showed some compassion for my feelings.

"He's the one, isn't he?" I asked. I didn't need Ryan to answer. "Just keep him out of sight. You asked me to arrange for a date and I did. Don't you dare ruin things for my firm, especially after putting me in such an uncomfortable position. Besides, she's really quite sweet and better than you deserve."

Ryan waved his hand at me like he was swatting away

an annoying insect. "I know, I know. I'm here and I'm virile, completely at your call and heterosexual."

"You better get inside," I instructed. "It's time for the happy couple, you and Leandra," I said for emphasis, "to be seen."

I WALKED IN AHEAD OF RYAN FOR TWO REASONS. THE first, we didn't want the press to mistakenly assume we were still together. The second, it gave Ryan the chance to make sure Matthew was safely tucked away from the fanfare.

"Ooh April, he's absolutely dreamy," Leandra cooed having spotted Ryan across the room.

I quickly turned her around to ensure she didn't notice Matthew, who was still trailing behind. I looked beyond Leandra's shoulder at Ryan's mystery man, the one who uprooted my happy home and miserably took note of his muscular physique. I suppose if Leandra questioned it, I could argue that he was security detail. God I was good at my job. If faced with the choice of grabbing a bread knife to attempt the decapitation of Ryan's over-inflated head or protecting Leandra's feelings, it was obvious that I would choose the latter. I smiled at her. She really had no idea what was going on. "Why don't we take our seats," I said leading Leandra. "Ryan will join us in a moment."

Josh and Bebe were already seated, and Bruce had marked out a spot next to himself for me. Great, I was seated next to Bruce the Lecherous with Ryan's date, Matthew the Muscular, right behind me. I was sure that the worst of the evening had presented itself. Unfortunately, I was wrong.

An hour later, Leandra stood up after allowing one

strawberry of her fruit tart to enter her digestive system, and asked, "April, could you come to the little girl's room with me?" I hated the Noah's Ark bathroom culture. I had never felt the need to relieve myself in pairs, but then again, I was old enough to call it a bathroom, lavatory, ladies' room, even a loo, but never "the little girl's room. I also really wanted my dessert and in this case, felt that I more than deserved to consume large amounts of fat and sugar.

"Sure," I smiled sweetly, and in my head repeated my new mantra -- corner office with a view, corner office with a view.

Leandra moved surprisingly fast for a woman teetering on six-and-a-half inch heels even if they did feature a two-and-a-half inch platform. Louboutins, of course. Price tag: $6,395. I knew because Leandra had crossed her leg in front of me and the small sticker remained under her shoe. I wasn't entirely sure that this was a mistake. One thing that was for certain, this girl was a chameleon. She strode with purpose to the restroom, smiling at cameras as she made her way through the ballroom, but once inside the bathroom, Leandra crumbled. "He has eyes for someone else," she wailed.

"Who?" I asked, strangely hoping that she was talking about anyone other than Ryan.

"Your husband!" she cried.

"Well, it's not me," I assured her.

"I know it's not you. That's obvious," she paused and then said, "I'm sorry; you know what I mean."

"You're probably imagining the whole thing."

"He keeps getting up between courses — I think to meet someone."

I wanted to strangle Ryan. I imagined how nice it would feel -- for me, that is.

My hands reached for his perfectly knotted Bvlgari silk tie. I tightened it ever so slightly.

"Thanks, April. You always tied them better than I did."

"My pleasure," I said sliding the knot a bit closer to his Adam's apple.

"That's enough," he eeked out.

"Oh, I'm just beginning." I tightened it a bit more, causing his eyes to bulge. "This is for wearing such an obscenely priced tie in the first place and claiming it as an expense. Did you know that the IRS is auditing me?"

"That's because you cheat on your taxes."

"I cheat because you spend money like there's no tomorrow!"

"Can we discuss this without your hands around my neck?"

I squeezed harder in response. "And this," I said with emphasis as I pulled upward on the silk, is for making Leandra cry. How dare you put me in the position of having to comfort your dates."

"She's not really my date. Not my type."

"AAAAAAHHH."

"April?" Leandra looked scared.

I realized that I had released a rather blood-curdling scream. "I feel better now. Don't you?"

"Err, not really," Leandra admitted.

"Don't worry, Leandra. After tonight, with all the photos that were taken of you and Ryan, every entertainment publication from Daily Variety to Entertainment Weekly, and even Premiere, will know that YOU and not someone else who may or may not be seated at the table behind us, is Ryan's official girlfriend. I'll make sure of it.

Leandra dried her tears and smiled. At least one of us was happy.

Chapter 9

Melissa wanted me to get out of the house more, although I suspected it was so she could spend more time alone with Ian. Jessica insisted I should start a new life, which to her meant a new man. The two of them planned a not so secretive intervention over brunch, but making matters worse, Jessica insisted that we go for a run first "in order to work up an appetite."

"Keep up," she hollered over her shoulder.

"You're going uphill," I complained.

"You're stamina is shot," Jessica yelled back without even the decency to be out of breath.

"It's because she never has sex," Melissa replied in a similarly fit and non-breathing impaired manner.

"In my defense, I don't really work out much. My trainer has developed this nutty idea that if you push people too much, it only sets them up for failure," I lamented. "He's always talking about his new boyfriend and the amazing dinners they cook together. It's depressing because I get hungry and I start thinking about Ryan and Matthew doing the same thing."

"You have a trainer?"

I nodded sheepishly. "Everyone in Hollywood has a trainer. It's how I network."

"Hmm, and to think my boss still sends me to Chamber of Commerce meetings," Jessica sighed and took a quick swallow of a pre-packaged wheat grass shot.

"How do you do that? It looks disgusting."

"Well, you workout. I don't eat. I like my way better."

"You must eat sometime."

Jessica took the last drag of her drink. "Sure I do. Saturday and Sunday, but only until 5 p.m. And, today because you're in crisis."

Even Melissa was in agreement on this one. "What? Don't you feel the need to chew, once in awhile? I'm so glad I have the excuse of eating for two."

Jessica exchanged a look with me before answering. "Chewing is what happens on weekends. I'm following The New L.A. Diet."

"How does it differ from just the plain ol' 'The L.A. Diet'?" I asked having heard of this supposed miracle practice.

"It's totally different," Jessica explained. "In the old The L.A. Diet you had to eat healthy everyday, but you could indulge on anything during the weekend. In The New L.A. Diet, you can only drink your food until 1 p.m. Then, you're allowed a piece of fish and as much of any vegetable that you want. I had an entire bowl of brussel sprouts last night and I swear, I couldn't eat another thing. But what really sets the new and old apart is what you do on the weekend."

"Tell me," I begged.

"You can eat anything you want, just like the old diet, with the exception of anything that contains salt, sugar, butter, white flour or anything carbonated because, you'll bloat."

"How is that indulging?"

"Well, you just have to get imaginative. Last weekend, I had a brownie made with wheat flour, Splenda and olive oil."

"Eww, who makes that? I mean where would you even find such a thing?" Melissa asked.

"The health food market on the corner of La Cienega and Third. It's not bad."

"I'm pretty sure that wouldn't do it for me. But this place," I said pointing ahead to the House of Blue's, "is going to be amazing."

We walked inside and the sound of a choir, rich and full voices reaching to the heavens and singing as if there was no tomorrow greeted us. One couldn't help, but feel more rhythmically inclined even if you were like me and born with two left feet.

"This is inspired," Jessica agreed.

"And, they have normal desserts," Melissa pointed out.

I inhaled deeply and eyed the table at the far end of the room. "Chocolate is my serenity."

We passed the omelette station, ignored the pile of bagels, lox and cream cheese, and went straight to scope out the dessert table first.

"Ohh, this is enough to make me rethink the diet," Jessica admitted.

"It's my heaven," I agreed.

Melissa closed her eyes before uttering, "I'm so glad you said that because fruit is totally for dessert under-achievers." She turned to me, "Are you feeling better?"

I nodded. "Chocolate mousse, hazelnut torte, every type of coffee cake you can imagine. Yeah, I'm feeling better." I reached for a plate. "Let's do it in reverse order;

desserts first, omelette later, or we might not have room for the good stuff."

Jessica suddenly grabbed my arm. "You know, April, now that I think about it, I can't risk the sugar rush. How 'bout we try the place that just opened down the street?"

The singers were filing in and the brunch line was beginning to resemble the Post Office on the eve of April 15. "We're already here. Honestly, Jess, what's with you? You can splurge just this one time."

But the answer came without Jessica having to reply.

Something caught my eye at a table located just beyond the desserts -- Ryan. I stared wide-eyed at the woman who sat across from him. She leaned forward with intense interest in Ryan, her eyes staring boldly at him without blinking. She must have felt cold, or at least pretended to because she slid her hands over her arms as if applying lotion. Occasionally, her hands would drop under the table, presumably to adjust a snap or pull at a strap and then resurfaced to her cool glass of orange juice, smoothing beads of condensation away from its surface. She toyed with the brightly-colored plastic straw, running her fingers up and down it, while casually allowing her pinky to dip into the liquid and offer it to perfectly-lined, lipstick red lips. She was a sitting seduction.

"What the heck? He's supposed to be gay and if he's going to be with a woman, it better be Leandra."

"Wanna go?" Melissa asked.

"No. I want to stay and make him miserable."

Melissa and Jessica casually tried to hide. I promised to behave like an adult, and then walked directly toward Ryan and Blondie's table. I stuck my hand out toward Blondie, nearly causing a collision with a forkful of eggs benedict, and introduced myself as Ryan's soon to be ex-wife, the one who believed that divorce happens even to couples who love each other and didn't she believe that a certain unspoken amount of time should pass before couples began dating, kind of like a respect for the dead period?

I could see Melissa and Jessica out of the corner of my eye. They alternated between waving frantically and beckoning me to return, their hands clasped together as if in prayer, in keeping with the restaurant's gospel singers. The woman stared blankly at me. Ryan seemed worried that I might be carrying a concealed weapon.

In a nerve racking, annoying calm voice that always drove me mad, he spoke, "Hello, April."

"That's all you have to say? Hello?"

"Uh, no. April, this is Trudy."

"Pleased to meet you," she answered nervously. "We're just having a late breakfast," she said dabbing her napkin to her lower lip to retrieve some run-away hollandaise sauce that preferred her to the poached egg.

I glared daggers. "Got a late start on the day?"

Ryan was getting nervous as well. He looked around the room and then smiled with relief at the sight of Melissa and waved her over, much in the same fashion as she had tried to do to me.

"Ryan, why are you having breakfast with a woman?" I continued. "You had one and didn't know what to do with her. I even brought you Leandra, who by the way is another example of someone who is too good for you. So what is it today? You're bored? Decided to try out a new model, literally?"

Melissa turned up at that moment. "Mel, good to see you," he said grabbing her hand and pumping her arm. The introductions continued. "Trudy, you've met April, my err-wife, and this is Melissa, my sister-in-law, at least for the time-being. Ladies, Trudy is my psychiatrist."

"Are you crazy?" I asked hopefully.

"I'm just getting some advice about my change of life-style," Ryan responded. "I'm not crazy, just a little confused. Trudy came very highly recommended."

"So you're still Gay?"

"Yes. Still Gay."

The gospel chorus began on cue: "Hallaluyah!"

I was actually relieved. "I don't know what I was thinking. Sorry to interrupt your breakfast. Ryan, there's a cocktail party this week. I'll call with the details." I started to back away from the table, but turned to add, "Make sure you're faithful to Leandra; she'll be your date again." I grabbed Melissa's arm, "Nice meeting you," I said to Trudy and retreated with my hand automatically moving to my temples, the reflex reaction to an oncoming migraine.

"God April, do I have to say it?" Melissa asked when out of ear shot.

"Yes."

"Why did you do it?"

"Which part? Verbally accost my husband's physician or make a fool of myself?"

"That was intense, even for you," Jessica added.

"It's like fattening stuff. It's easy to pass up dessert until someone reaches for the last cookie." Melissa looked at me in confusion. I continued, "It's only then that you know how much you want it. I thought she was after my last cookie," I explained.

The three of us walked in silence for a couple blocks. Melissa had apparently forgotten the exact location of the other brunch place. I didn't mind.

"It's up ahead," she said victoriously. "You'll love this place--not as crowded."

Alert the Media

Chapter 10

One more week until Christmas. I could do it. I could get through the holidays wearing a smile, content in the knowledge that the New Year would bring all sorts of new challenges to my life. I will have gained the experience of going through a divorce, a custody battle, having married a Gay man, resorted to accepting favors from my sister, and financial rewards from my parents. It wasn't such a new concept. Tons of people do it everyday. I told myself that I could come through it without scar damage.

Yet as I continued through my day, it seemed perfectly reasonable to be filled with annoyance when the corner Santa Claus, the one that smelled of Ben-Gay ointment, wished me a merry day and shoved his tin cup in my face. I fantasized screaming, "Don't tell me what to do!" as I elbowed him in the eye, kneed him in the groin and then stepped on his tubby tummy as I passed over him, but not before I leaned down to collect his tin cup and made a run with it. However, since I was a generally nice person, I resorted to avoiding his eyes, holding a newspaper in front of me, and increasing my walking speed.

Last year, I gave him a dollar every Monday, Wednesday, and Friday, the days I passed by him on my way to the gym, but then I became resentful of all the people who could keep going without even a glimmer of guilt for not donating.

Then, as Valentine's approached, the man in the Santa suit morphed into a new character. He was dressed in red tights, a pink neon top, and had three-foot wings taped to his back. He was supposed to be Cupid, he informed me, but looked more like a skinny preying mantis. Like Santa, he was soliciting funds for charity.

"Have a heart; spare a gift for the children of Saint Lukes," he said in a put on ethereal voice that sounded more stoned than soothing.

I eyed him closely, "Weren't you Santa Claus two months ago?"

"What about it?" he said and pressed his cup into my line of vision.

"I dunno," I pondered more to myself than to him. "It just seems like false advertising. I mean, one minute your fat, jolly Saint Nick collecting for Vietnam Vets, and now you're Cupid Man, soliciting for someone else."

"So what's your point? Are you gonna give or what?" he said, now in a decidedly Brooklyn accent.

"No, not if you put it that way." I was proud. I had stood up to Cupid Man and my adrenaline was pumping.

"Oh, like you can't afford it," he said giving my Jones of New York suit, and matching pumps and handbag the once over.

"That's not the point," I argued.

"Oh? What is the point? You decided to play dress-up like an executive and treat everyone else like ants on a sidewalk?"

"You have no right to say that. Besides, do you really

think people who dress like this do it just for fun? Perhaps you think I'm getting ready to go prune my fruit trees? Or, maybe now would be a good time for me to rush home and bathe the hounds? On the contrary," I said with emphasis, "I am on my way to a real job, one that contributes and offers something to society." He didn't have to know that I promoted actors and other entertainment entities that merely managed to provide meaningless brain candy to the masses.

His demeanor changed rapidly. He was no longer a bullying insect-looking Cupid, but a sniveling, skinny man in a ridiculous suit. "I've never contributed anything. My mother says I'll never amount to anything and she's tired of giving me handouts. I came to L.A. two years ago to be an actor," he said defeated.

This was not what I needed. I was too good at guilt, other people's, my own, you name it. My mother had taught me the skill at an early age, and I've had over three decades to perfect it. "I'm sorry. I've just been having a really crummy day, no, a crummy life. I, uh, shouldn't have taken it out on you. Here, take this dollar for your cause. I'm only a publicist," I offered.

"You know, this is the steadiest gig I've gotten. Holiday work is pretty consistent," he sniffed. "I hear some major industry execs go shopping here at lunchtime. I'm hoping to catch their eye."

"I'm sure you will," I lied and started to walk away. I turned back to see him return to his Cupid act. Nothing had changed. He was still a struggling actor; the people on the street still tried desperately to ignore him; and I was determined to lighten up.

SO HERE I WAS, ANOTHER YEAR HAD PASSED AND I WAS still hoping to avoid Santa/Cupid. I worried that he would recognize me, remember our conversation, and then find out that I was the loser. I took to avoiding lunch time shopping trips only to make the mistake of eating at my desk while reading a romance novel before checking Bebe's whereabouts. Honestly, I might as well paint a scarlet "L" on my forehead and trade in Buster and Louie for twenty or so cats as I was already projecting that type of loner image.

"Hi, good book?"

I displayed the cover without looking up from the riveting prose.

Bebe nodded, "Looks steamy."

"I'm living vicariously."

"April, maybe you should get out more? At least at lunchtime."

"There's nothing to see, nothing to do."

"Well, have I got news for you. This is just going to brighten up your day like fresh-squeezed orange juice on Sunday morning," she said in her syrupy Southern accent.

Bebe's concept of good news is irritatingly naive. I wasn't able to close my door fast enough before her news that we had been chosen to promote the Seventh Annual Rutabaga Festival erupted. Root vegetables? I had heard of the Strawberry Festival, even the Pumpkin Festival, but the Rutabagas? They didn't tie into a season or holiday. They had no purpose other than to give people indigestion and stink up a kitchen.

"That's your idea of good news?"

"It'll give you something other than Ryan's account to focus on. Josh just landed it last night. I just happened to be working late."

"Of course you were. You have a sex life, even if it is inappropriately tied to your work life."

"Anyway," she smiled sweetly, "you know Ari, the new guy with the hairs popping out the top of his shirt?"

"Yes?"

"He totally wanted this account, but I nabbed it for you. Come on, Sugar, put that away and I'll brief you."

"Fine, I'll just put my book in my drawer, where it will wait faithfully for me until tomorrow."

"That's better. I'll tell you what the client wants and then you can work your magic to deliver it. Come on," she coaxed, pulling me out of my chair.

After half an hour of Bebe's briefing I had the full picture. I would get to lead my anxious group of banshees in the pursuit of Better Homes and Gardens, Martha Stewart Living, and other lesser known publications, which would no doubt be taken in by our crafty tales of "down-home fun," "family entertainment," and other catch phrases that were sure to weave an image of what our friends at the Rutabaga Council would want to promote. The arthritis campaign was suddenly becoming more appealing.

"Alright, last night Bebe sent out the standard event release on the wire," I told the room of junior account executives. "I need everyone to pick five editors and call them immediately. Ask them to send you a reprint of the article they ran yesterday."

Ari started to bristle. "What do you mean? How would they have run it yesterday if we just sent it on the wire last night?"

"They'll think it was an oversight on their part. Speak with authority and I guarantee, you'll hear them apologize for the mistake and promise the release will run in the next edition. Come on, everyone, let's get going. This only works once and we're on a time crunch so it's now or never. If all of you take five editors, we'll have the top thirty publications covered within 15 minutes."

Within an hour, Bebe came through my door. "April, the response is overwhelming," she squealed. "The article is running all over, but there's a call on line two that insisted on fact checking with you. She said she heard you were on to something nouveau."

"Nouveau?"

"Her words," said Bebe pointedly.

"Thanks, Bebe. I'll take it," I said and hinted toward the door. When Bebe was safely outside I picked up the receiver. "It must be you."

"How'd you guess?" asked Jessica. "You're no fun anymore."

"Sure I am. I go to my parents for dinner once a week, and come home each night to not one, but two mammals who love me."

"Things must be getting bad. You called them 'mammals'."

"Divorce isn't necessarily bad, is it? It just means I'll have to change my checks to remove Ryan's name, change my driver's license if I decide to change my name, and hide from the embarrassment of seeing my mail man."

"Don't you like your mail carrier?"

"He'll know, Jessica. It's a suburban scandal. I won't be able to attend my 15-year high school reunion because I will look like a failure. I won't be able to learn to play bridge, because only couples do that."

"Did you really want to do that?"

"Not the point," I said and continued. "I'm actually getting a divorce," my voice starting to raise in panic. "I know now."

"How about a nice lunch with someone who thinks you're wonderful?"

"Male or female?" I asked, "because if it's a male, I'm not interested or ready."

"That issue is up for debate, but I was referring to me. I'll meet you in half an hour at The Ivy. You need cheering up."

"I can't afford to be that cheery."

"Live a little," she countered and hung up before I could argue.

I KNEW JESSICA HAD A PLAN. I ONLY HOPED IT DIDN'T involve changing my hairstyle. The expensive lunch would only bother me for a day, but that could last months.

"Why are we doing this? Neither one of us can really afford it." I said while taking my seat. Jessica had arrived early in order to scope out an ideal people-watching table.

"Because you need this," she said matter-of-factly. "It's good for you."

"The Caesar salad here is bad for my health since it is made with real egg yolks, the menu reports; the cost of probably everything, including the mineral water, is bad for finances; and, the atmosphere is definitely unsuitable to my mental state due to the over-population of beautiful women with bodies better than mine despite the fact that they are older than myself."

"April, they get that way by reducing their worries." She leaned in close and whispered, "Wealthy husbands, work that they enjoy, and limited, neurotic experiences."

"I can claim one of those," I reasoned, referring to the latter.

"That's debatable. Anyway, remember what happened the first time we came here?"

"A total disaster that I refuse to relive and if that's why you brought me here, you're the one experiencing neurotic fits."

Before I met Ryan, Jessica decided that we needed to put ourselves in the position to meet "quality men." Her definition was slightly less discriminating than mine. I wanted someone with the same religion, similar educational background, someone good with children, the usual. She would settle for someone rich. I got what I wanted, plus the divorce. Jessica got a two-month affair with Ritesh, a Persian oil tycoon, and learned how the other half lived.

They would make love atop a Duxiana bed with down pillows and Egyptian cotton sheets inside his 8,500-square-foot French, chateau-styled manor, behind the gates of Sherwood Country Club Estates. They drank wine from his own private reserve, fed on delicacies prepared by his private chef, and when Tiger Wood's participated in a golf tournament at the country club, they would watch it without the necessity of a television by just stepping outside to Ritesh's backyard, which backed up onto the green.

It was a great two months for me as well. Ritesh gave her his membership cards to all of his clubs and Jessica brought me whenever he was away. We started to breakfast at the Polo Lounge, lunch at The Ivy, and play tennis at North Ranch Racquet Club, an exclusive, members-only club where women and men sweat in style, enjoy power breakfasts, and then drive off to work in their Suburbans, Land Cruisers, BMWs, or Mercedes. The only downside was having to park my Jeep Explorer at the far end of the lot because "it didn't fit the image conveyed by the membership."

It was a great two-month run, which may have continued if Ritesh hadn't suggested that Jessica would get along *very well* with his other girlfriend.

"It's been a long time since we ate here," Jessica began, "it's time we returned to our snooty roots."

"I don't think we did this often enough even back them to lay down 'roots'."

"We're probably better off that way," she agreed. "Hey, two eligible lawyer types at three o'clock," she said pointing her chin in the general direction. "Maybe they're stock brokers, but don't look now," she ordered.

"I wouldn't think of it," I said sarcastically. "Jess, I'm not interested. Really."

Rationally, I concluded that getting out is what led to marriage and then divorce, so I reasoned I could be happy staying put for the time being. Not surprisingly, Jessica was not happy with this idea. I was beginning to suspect she might have stock in one of those matchmaker services and was working the system on the sly. The only other explanation was that she was trying to live vicariously through me. She always said the early dating stage, before the relationship grew predictable, was her favorite time. When Ryan and I first started dating she wanted to know every detail; and, myself, being so excited about the whole thing, willingly let her pump me for information.

She said it was only to appease her addiction for gossip. "I just missed my weekly talk show fix and need something to get me through 'til Monday," she explained. Jessica had a policy of only allowing herself to watch one drippy, staged television talk show a week. She loved them, and after seeing an episode of *The Dr. Oz Show* where addictive personalities were discussed, she feared she had one and believed it was necessary to start limiting her viewing of talk shows. If only Dr. Oz' program director knew. By the way, this philosophy is also what prompted her to only eat sweets on the weekend, but then she started to believe that in itself could lead to a habitual, addiction so she decided to venture into her crazy diet realm "just to switch things up."

To help her break the talk show habit, I played along, and provided benign details of my dating pre-Ryan. Not much had changed because even today, Jessica was relentless in her pursuit of the daily dish of gossip at my expense.

"Dating would be good for you," she insisted.

I stabbed a leaf from my salad and waited to respond until the waiter, who was obviously too good-looking to be just a waiter and was more likely a model or actor waiting to be discovered, finished refilling our water glasses. "You're wearing me down."

"Good!"

"But tell me, Jess, does dating mean spending what little time I have laughing at some guy's jokes over a meal that is actually comprised of liquidized vegetables because all of the men in this city expect women to be the waif-like creatures who are never seen eating solid food, have a sound-bite at the ready in case they're 'discovered', has done at least one Maxim magazine pictorial and has a secret sex tape of their involvement in a threesome that is ready to be leaked in order to boost their acting career? If that's the case, that just wouldn't be good for me."

I couldn't help myself. The tears started to roll down my cheeks. Naturally, the Ivy has white linen napkins, which were now splotched with black.

Jessica came round to my side of the table to give me a good hug. It was just what I needed; I cried even harder.

At that moment, my cell rang with an unfamiliar number posted. I picked up and spoke my name in case it was work related. Within a second my tears flowed even harder.

"No, I'm not faking tears to get out of it. Wow, you have nerve. And for the record, I'm upset over something else. No, I didn't hit someone else."

"What was that?" Jessica asked when I had hung up.

"Guy from the traffic accident. He wanted to give me his address where I could send a check. I'm obviously not getting a date out of that encounter."

"You're going to be fine," she assured me.

"You're sure?" I sniffed, composing myself quickly as I was starting to attract inquisitive looks from the paparazzi that always camped outside the restaurant's front patio on Robertson Blvd.

"Yes, I'm sure, but I don't think you know what's good for you if it bit you on the bottom. Ryan proved that fact. Well, actually he never came close, but you get the point. It's time to start the power meal program again."

"I can't afford to," I explained.

"If you keep it up regularly, you're sure to see the results and then you won't have to worry about any debt you've incurred," she reasoned. Jessica made it sound like a retirement plan rather than a man hunt. "Besides, I had a dream that I think was meant for you."

"This should be good. I've infiltrated your subconscious. What did I do?"

"Well," she started, "you didn't really do anything. I mean, you weren't exactly in this dream, but I know it was meant for you since I was talking about your predicament to the girls at my office."

"I'm not in a predicament," I countered. "And so glad that I now serve as water cooler fodder."

"April, you're pushing forty, have had no children, and have an affinity for Gay men. That's a predicament."

"I'm still mid-thirty," I replied glumly.

"I want to introduce you to Peter," she said cheerfully.

"Office mate? How convenient. So, what about the dream?"

"I dreamt that I gave birth to nine possums, all connected to one another. Amazing, huh?"

"I failed to make the connection, and was sure it could only be evidence that Jessica was the one with neuroses. "How does that sick dream apply to me?"

"You're an animal lover; I'm not. You're obviously in need of having real children..."

"Don't imply that Buster and Louie aren't real," I interrupted.

"As I was saying," she continued, "I want to set you up with Peter," she said emphasizing the "P." Get it? Peter. Possum. I'm sure there's a connection."

I wasn't convinced, but nonetheless, agreed to my first blind date since the demise of my marriage.

Chapter 11

M elissa's fake pregnancy may not have taken my mother's attention from my marriage as planned, but somehow it did land her in what was strangely the healthiest relationship I had ever seen her in. She and Ian were growing closer by the weeks. They had yet to consummate their relationship, although they couldn't admit that to my mother for fear of being labeled the Virgin Melissa, and instead spent quality time watching movies and talking. As I simultaneously prepared for work and my set-up with Peter, they offered their advice for what not to wear while watching reruns of the television show that bears the same name.

"What about this?" I said twirling before them.

"If you wear a dress, he'll think you want him to feel you up underneath it," Melissa said.

"No way! That is so not true. Besides, didn't I just hear the hosts of that dopey show you're addicted to tell their newest fashion refugee that she should show some leg?

"First off, Stacy and Clinton are the hosts and they are anything, but dopey," Melissa answered. "They totally help millions of women. The difference is that this woman," she said indicating the T.V., "...is wanting to attract a man. You've already got one lined up. Trust me, if this girl were going on a date, Stacy would dress her in black skinny jeans and a blousy blouse."

"I don't have time for this. I have to get to work."

"How can you go to work and have a date?" Melissa asked.

"Because I'm a multi-tasker, one of us has to pay the bills, and I agreed to a *lunch* date."

"Hmm, I suppose that'll work. Definitely wear the jeans in that case."

"My thighs are too big for skinny jeans. Ian, what do you think? This is good isn't it?" I said holding up the dress.

Melissa leaned forward, "No Ian, it's totally asking for it, isn't it?"

Melissa and I stared him down. "Well, I'm not Clinton. I just don't know."

"Would you want to feel me up?"

"April! That's my baby daddy you're talking to."

"First off, you're not really pregnant and second, I didn't mean it literally. I just meant that I think you're totally off base and I want Ian to remark on that fact."

"Sorry April, I can't do that," he answered.

"You see? That's why I love him," Melissa leaned over to kiss Ian.

"Not so fast," I countered. "You can't comment because you don't want Melissa to know that you are among the group of men who would want to feel me up, because if that's the case, then you're actually agreeing with her."

"Oh, in that case, she's right."

In a split second, Melissa smacked Ian over the head with a throw pillow.

"What?" Ian complained. "I was just trying to agree with you. I wouldn't do your sister."

"I'll leave you two alone to sort this out. I'm going to change. Thanks for the fashion lesson, Mel."

"That's what sisters are for," she said leaning into Ian, the drama already forgotten. "Now go put on something less slutty. Try a skirt."

I went back to my room and smiled at the irony that I was getting advice from Melissa. My life was certainly taking a new direction.

Six months into my marriage, when the bickering first began, I tried desperately to locate our Katuba, the decorative, Jewish marriage contract the rabbi had presented to us on our wedding day. I thought framing it and including a nice note would make a good half-yearly anniversary gift. It seemed as good a reason as any to celebrate, but the thing had mysteriously disappeared, along with the top layer of my wedding cake.

Eventually I found the cake, or more specifically, the culprit who had taken it. Melissa.

"That tradition is ridiculous," she said referring to eating the top layer on the one-year wedding anniversary date.

I was incredulous. "You stole our wedding cake."

"Don't be so melodramatic. I ate your cake; I'm not a thief. Anyway, like it matters. You're getting divorced. I saved you from eating stale, pink champagne cake," she responded.

"With raspberry filling," I said glumly.

As a sister, Melissa was the best. As maid of honor, she was a disaster. Three days before the wedding, Melissa tried on her bridesmaid gown. It was a lucky twist of fate, because she discovered that her new exercise regime had added a full inch to her bust size and she was no longer able to zip the back of the dress. She decided it was best not to upset me, and her method for not doing so involved a seamstress with an eye for plunging designs. The demure bridesmaid dress was redesigned to reveal Melissa's now toned back muscles. Admittedly, she carried the look off well, easing into the dress and the reception hall. It was like watching maple syrup pour over pancakes; no space was safe. Melissa didn't just stand in the room, she occupied it. Forget the bride getting the attention, all eyes were on the Maid of Honor. I had my own Pippa Middleton in my midst. The men drooled, the women glared, and throughout the evening, "It's only one dance," was meekly uttered to unforgiving wives.

As soon as the Rabbi signed the Katuba, I handed it to Melissa for safekeeping. It wasn't my best decision, as reliability was not one of Melissa's strong points. She was the natural choice for maid of honor, yet when it came to showing up on time the morning of the wedding, bringing the guest book she had promised to buy, and holding onto the damn Katuba, she became the Inspector Clouseau of weddings. She had insisted she had given "the tuba" to Jessica who, in turn, thought she had given it to my mother, who was sure she had it waiting for Ryan and I when we returned from Hawaii. I should have known then that the relationship was doomed.

Having successfully poured myself into a pair of black leggings, matched it with a sweater and slipped on a pair of boots, I thought I looked pretty good. Melissa begged to differ.

"What is that?" she said pointing to my legs.

"Uhh, appendages meant for walking?"

"You have muffin top on your thighs," Melissa said

disapprovingly. "How are you going to get Peter into your pants looking like that?"

"Hey, first off, you just told me to change out of a dress because I didn't want him making a move and second, I don't even know this guy. Who says *I* want *him*?"

"You misunderstood a very important point," Melissa said with strained patience. "You don't want him thinking you want him to make a move, but trust me, you want every guy to think they want to make it."

Ian flipped off the television. "Is anyone else confused?"

"Ian...April, we have a few hours. Just enough time to get *that*," she said indicating my body, "sorted out. It's half-yearly sales season and the mall opened at 6 a.m. You're going to be a little late for work today. Jump in the car."

OUR SHOPPING CONCLUDED AT VICTORIA'S SECRET. Melissa firmly reminded me that lingerie should be considered a bit like children in Victorian times where parents told them they were "to be seen, but not heard." She said that if the mood hit me I should remember that my new bra and matching panties were "to be seen, but not touched." Melissa said the only reason to wear them was to feel sexy and therefore, exude an availability, which I was obviously not used to portraying.

"What do you think of this one?" I asked holding up a pink polka-dotted set.

"Nice if you're trying to attract a pedophile," she retorted. "Here, try this one," she said

shoving an ivory lace thong in my direction. "It's more sophisticated."

I looked at Ian for his thoughts, but he was doing his best to become invisible.

Another man walked by, trying on the same I'm-not-looking-at-anything-I-shouldn't-be expression as Ian.

"You should talk to him. He's gorgeous."

"He's in Victoria's Secret alone. Chances are he's not available. Or, he's a perv."

"For practice sake," Melissa argued. "You're certainly not in the swing of things yet," she said taking a pair of underwear away from me that she said bordered on being old lady.

"These are not old lady style. They don't even get near my belly-button. To be old ladyish they have to cover any trace of umbilical cord entry points," I said clinically.

"Why don't we agree to settle on the classics? Here." Melissa handed me the ivory ensemble and with Ian in tow, who looked relieved to be out the embarrassment zone and was sporting a little less color in his cheeks, we went to pay.

THE SHOPPING MISSION WAS A SUCCESS AND I ARRIVED AT the office only an hour late. In less than half an hour I had located a new skirt and a powder blue, silk camisole to dress up and sex up my sweater. The sweater was buttoned only at the top, so my camisole, along with its accompanying cleavage, were revealed. Melissa suggested that I view my backside in different light to test for VPL. As I stood in the bathroom at work, I realized she was right (annoyingly) so I tried removing my panties and had to admit that the outfit looked much better without. Note for later! I was just about to slip my panties back on when Bebe walked into the bathroom announcing an impromptu meeting with our newest client. I was frozen with panties in hand, desperately trying to shove them up my sleeve rather than slip them over my legs and explain how they came off in the first place. Like a naughty child, I followed my secretary down the hallway.

I can't imagine what could be worse: a meeting with three men sans panties, or learning that Bebe does it all the time. Today she was wearing black. Nothing unusual with that because Bebe, being the slave to fashion that she was, often wore black. What was different about today's ensemble was the obvious transparent glow that showed through the lace bodice. Her skin. A creamy white that looked translucent. Fortunately, for all of us who did not desire to see more of Bebe than we already encountered at the office, the nipples of her top were thankfully covered by the pattern of roses. She bounced down the hall, and disappeared into Josh's office before coming back to the conference room.

"Josh thinks we may be behind implementing the Rutabaga Festival," she said.

"It's a root vegetable festival. Just tell him it needs more time before it's harvested."

Humor was lost on Bebe. "April, the client expects ideas today. Do we have any?"

"The stupid roots don't even come out until Fall," I said rummaging through a stack of files. Bebe sensed what I was up to and produced the client's file immediately. I scowled at her.

"Okay, get the staff together. Put together a media list on all gardening publications, local and national. Research any public radio and cable access stations that might want a tip show on how to grow rutabagas like the pros. Maybe something along the lines of our client going on-air like Martha Stewart. While you're at it, go to the bookstore and start looking at cookbooks. We need to find rutabaga recipes. Pitch the food section of the papers, and start developing festival cuisine worthy of being swallowed."

Having barked out orders with the confidence and experience of an Army captain, Bebe had yet to jump to action. "I sometimes cook in the nude," was her only response.

"Good to know."

"APRIL, I'D LIKE YOU TO MEET JOE BREWER, FARMER Joe, as we're going to call him," Josh said while sidling up to beefy man with a steak-like complexion to match.

"Farmer Joe," I said in disbelief, extending my hand.

"Ah she's a perty one, Josh. Know we'll be in good 'ands with this one," he said in his Southern accent, the kind I imagined could be heard in backyards over the spit of barbecue pits and the yells of children swinging from tires, even the occasional grunt from the family's pet pig.

"Well, Joe, why don't you set yourself down here," Josh said pointing to a chair, "and we'll listen to April's ideas. They both smiled encouraging at me. Joe held his head between his hands and placed his elbows on his knees. The man had the largest head I had ever seen. Perhaps it was the redness of his face, but the thing looked like it might explode right between his hands. I cleared away the idea of brain deposit soiling Josh's business suit, and began my presentation.

"Well, Mr. Brewer..."

"Farmer Joe," he corrected.

"Yes, uh Farmer Joe, the rutabagas have virtually disappeared from the everyday dinner table, not to mention the finer restaurants of Los Angeles." For good reason, I wanted to scream, but restrained myself. "Our idea," I continued, "is to kick-off our campaign for your festival by inviting top L.A. eateries to submit their finest recipes incorporating this tasty and healthy root vegetable. As you know, our city is blessed with a number of celebrity chefs. Mary Sue Milliken, Wolfgang Puck, Evan Kleimann, to name a few. We might even extend the competition nation-wide to those chefs such as Emeril Lagasse who might want to throw their spatula into the ring," I said at an attempt at kitchen humor.

Joe loved the idea. "Bam! Bam!" he shouted. I was petrified. Josh looked equally concerned. "Bam!" Joe screamed again, and started laughing crazily. "Farmer Joe?" Josh asked hesitantly, "you okay?"

Bebe came to the rescue. "Bam is an Emeril term," she said with more drawl in her voice than usual. "Farmer Joe, I just love his sweet potato pie. Have you tried it?"

"I can't say I have little lady, but I just love that show. The way he's always shouting 'bam' when he wants to 'kick it up a notch' and make the food hotter. Can you imagine the attendance at the Rutabaga Festival with Emeril promoting a week of Cajun root recipes?"

Neither Josh, nor I could. Instead, we smiled nervously at each other. It was perhaps the first time in this ridiculous campaign when Josh was thinking with his head, rather than wallet. Farmer Joe waited for us to return to our presentation by singing quietly to himself. He repeated, what he later told us was an "Emeril tune," one that was quite easy to learn for it only included the word, "Bam!"

Confident that Joe and I were onto something big in the way of rutabaga publicity stunts, Josh excused himself, grabbed Bebe in tow, and led her down the hallway to what was no doubt a chance to catch a cheap thrill before lunch.

"So back to yer ideas little darlin'," Joe remarked. "I thinks we best hop the next flight to New Orleans to meet with Emeril live. Ha. Get it? That's the name of his T.V. show."

I had never seen the show, but suddenly prayed for its early cancellation. "Farmer Joe, we've got this wonderful new thing called Skype. No need to fly anywhere! We'll just turn on our little 'ol computers and invite Emeril to a chat."

"Well, I'll be."

With the crisis of spending a weekend with Farmer Joe averted, I continued to tell him our other ideas. "We plan to host a community rutabaga cook-off, and develop some fun, family-style games involving rutabagas. Maybe something like a rutabaga toss, or a competition for the fastest rutabaga peeler."

"How 'bout a rutabaga rub?" he said lecherously.

I was afraid to ask, but then again, was pleased that he had forgotten about Emeril. I took the bait, "Rutabaga rub?"

"You peel the vegies, like you suggested," he said, trying to involve me, "and then dunk them into water so they're all slippery-like. Wearing nothing, but a bikini, the girls hold the rutabaga between their legs and have to get to the finish line without dropping it. It's a lot of fun to watch."

"I'm sure," I said horrified. Joe pronounced the word, bikini, like it was "bee keeny," convincing me that it was anything but a keen idea.

"Bet you'd be good at the Rutabaga Rub," he said and elbowed me in the ribs. "Got you some child-bearing thighs on you," he said eyes dropping to my lap. "I always love seeing the well-endowed women do the Rub. In Kern County, where I come from, Becky Anne Thornton was the top Rutabaga Rubber for three years running. Her thighs never lost their grip, not even when we poured melted buttah on the vegies. My buddies and I used to spend hours imagining what it must feel like to be that lucky rutabaga."

"That sounds like lots of fun," I said nodding my head furiously, like an apple bobbing in water. I had read that if you wanted to convince yourself of an idea, you simply nod "yes" and soon, you will buy into the concept. Fat chance.

"So what you say, you gonna take part?"

"Oh I'm sure that I'm no Becky Anne."

"Nonsense. Those thighs are womanly. They would hold the rutabagas in place nicely. Lots of rubbing going on with those thighs," he said and pointed to my lap once again. "How 'bout a date, Darlin'?" he asked suddenly.

I stood up, declaring the meeting over, and escorted Farmer Joe to the door. I promised to put more thought into getting Emeril to do a segment on rutabagas, and left Farmer Joe's lovely offer for a date on hold while I left the office for the one I already had scheduled.

Chapter 12

J essica insisted dating was a statistical equation. One should expect to experience the bad dates and actually be pleased when they occur. This rationale escaped me. Yet, she insisted that with every bad date experienced, one is that much closer to finding a dream date. As I drove to the restaurant where I had planned on meeting Peter, I recalled her virtuous description of him. He was an accountant. Boring, but excellent news as that meant he was steadily employed. Passed the C.P.A. exam on the first try. Good looking. Jewish. He sounded frightfully as "perfect for me" as my first husband.

I was in need of a horoscope fix. Aries listing: *"Take care of business, travel plans. Financial success fulfilled. Pisces figures prominently."* Well, that's not applicable to my life even if it is my sign. I decided to snag Pisces' reading for today: *"Get prepared for romantic interlude with left-brain type. Be thankful for good friends."* It couldn't have been more clear if it had shouted, "Jessica has found your ideal love match whom you will marry and have babies with!"

I envisioned my fated lunch... We're not in a restaurant, but a grand mansion where a team of six tuxedo clad butlers, walk into an ornate dining room. Three men stand on each side of a large, rounded table that is covered by a silver dome. They wheel it into the dining room where guests, stylishly dressed, are enjoying a party. It's all terribly boring and proper with the women sipping on Dubonets or Mint Julips. The men, however, wear mischievous grins. Something is up. They elbow each other as the table is left in the middle of the room.

And then, a gong sounds and seven belly dancers appear from behind a sunken bar like zeniths rising from the floor. They push their way past the bartender standing guard at the top of the steps leading to his domain. He stumbles backwards and lands at the base of the bar where the girls first appeared. One last dancer, a small one, not more than five feet tall, steps across his chest in spiked heels as her serape flows across his face. He is angry and humiliated and grabs at this fleeting opportunity for revenge by attacking the silk with his mouth. Oblivious to his action, the petite girl continues, trying desperately to catch up with her buxom counterparts, completely unaware that as she walks, the bartender's toothy clench is stripping her of all modesty. But the show must go on.

As the belly dancers surround the table, the butlers signal for the guests to gather round. In a tremendous show, they raise the domed lid off the table, and out pops me. Thankfully, I'm wearing more than a sarape. In fact, I'm totally elegant, dressed in an Yves Saint Laurent black evening gown, one that is the epitome of simplicity with long sleeves, a mock-turtle neck, and flowing folds of fabric that drape smoothly over my body. It even makes my thighs look thin and I imagine that Farmer Joe would be dismayed. In contrast with the belly dancers, particularly the one who lost her sarape, the only bit of my skin that shows is a tear drop cut-out between my breasts. In a word, it's perfect.

One of the butlers helps me off the table and as I disembark it's as if my mere presence parts the sea of guests; and, there in the clear-

*ing, appears The Accountant. I wait expectantly, wondering if this is
the man of my dreams, only to see him reach into his pocket and
retrieve a water pistol. He immediately takes aim and begins shooting
directly at that teardrop opening of my dress lying between my
breasts.*

"JESSICA, YOU HAVE TO BE AT THE RESTAURANT WITH
me," I said into my cell.

"No way. I would ruin it."

"I don't think I can do this. I had a vision, maybe it
was a panic attack. Anyway, I'm not ready. Besides, I have
so much work to do I shouldn't even be taking lunch. Have
you eaten yet?"

"No," she said miserably.

"It's just an hour out of your day. Please."

"Only because Peter is a sweetheart and I don't want
you to stand him up."

JESSICA ARRIVED AT THE SAME TIME THAT I DID; PETER
was already waiting inside.

"Typical," I muttered to Jessica, "wouldn't be an
accountant if he wasn't punctual."

"Be nice," Jessica warned and floated toward the door
in a white dress that made her look like an angel.

"Peter, I'm so glad you could make it," Jessica said,
while approaching a dorky-looking man of about thirty-
eight. "This is April!"

Jessica's announcement made me feel like the
unveiling of a Botticelli painting gone awry. In spite of my
earlier shopping trip, I didn't feel like the elegantly dressed

woman of my dreams. Instead, I felt conspicuous, like I was meant to be something I wasn't...a potential girlfriend.

I had to admit that Peter's appearance seemed more put together than my own. His shirt sleeves were immaculately pressed and poked out from a yuppie looking plaid sweater vest. He was so careful to appear presentable he even wore a matching tie and suspender belt. I was so nervous that I felt a sudden urge to snap him from behind, but thought better of it.

"Nice to meet you," I said, hoping that it would indeed be so.

"It's a pleasure," he replied.

"Well, isn't this fun? Should we grab a table?" Jessica asked merrily.

Like obedient children, we followed behind her. It seems our tongues were left behind, however, and my vow to be a good listener was soon cast away as Jessica shot me imploring looks and mouthed "say something," punctuated by exclamation marks that could have come from eyes that shot darts.

"So…Peter, what type of accounting do you practice?" It was lame, but the best I could manage.

"Actually, I've dabbled in all areas - taxation, audit, management services. Presently, I'm a manager in the taxation department at Coopers and Lybrand."

"That's one of the big ones," Jessica interjected.

"Well, if I ever need help with my taxes…" I let my voice trail off. Oh my god, this was torture. I couldn't think of anything to say. And Jessica kept staring at me as if to say that I better grow an interesting gene.

"You must be getting ready for your busy season," I said while looking at Jessica. If my thoughts could be heard she would know that I was thrilled to have found use of my vocal cords. However, she only gave me a pained look and a roll of her eyes as a response.

"Truthfully, every season is busy for me," Peter replied. "I don't like to wait to the last minute for anything. Take hunting for instance."

"Hunting?" I asked.

"Yeah, they say the sport is in the showdown, man against beast, face to face. But, I don't want to be faced by a bear, do you? If I see one when I'm out there, I'll just bag it. I'm not going to wait for an invitation from Mr. Grizzly himself."

"Charming," I said to Jessica and shot her a how-could-you-do-this-to-me look.

But Jessica was not going down without a fight. "Let's get back to accounting, shall we? How did you get started with it Peter?"

"Well, believe it or not, unlike the jokes about the profession, I actually found accounting quite fascinating. It must stem from my belief in numerology, what with the universe being connected by numbers."

The floorshow followed.

"Could you explain that, Peter?" I coaxed him. Unlike him, I was beginning to enjoy the hunt. With a little prompting, Peter would be reeled in and I would be safe to throw him back like an underdeveloped guppy, without any repercussions from Jessica.

"Numerology is the study of how the numbers in one's life add up, so to speak, to the meaning of life. Some people say it's a system of the occult, but that's hogwash."

"It is?" Jessica asked timidly.

"Sure it is," Peter said emphatically. "It's a system of life, or so it should be."

"Oh, do go on. This is fascinating," I said enjoying the fact that he was going down for the count.

"Numbers told me to go into accounting. It was the only left brain profession that made sense. I contemplated investment banking, but that involved too much travel and that would have been complicated, what with having to ensure that the flight numbers, times of departure, and arrival were all in sync with my numbers of the day. You'd have to be crazy to go through all that," he chuckled.

"Crazy," I mumbled under my breath.

"So accounting it was," Peter continued unfazed. "One day I was checking Sun Angel's Number quest report and it indicated..."

"Sun Angel?" Jessica interrupted.

"You haven't heard of it?" He sounded shocked. "Oh, if you haven't experienced it, you must. It's a website that gives daily numerology readings."

"And you run your life by this?" I asked.

"Of course."

"Of course," I responded back and excused myself from the table.

I felt ill. Ill at ease, ill in my stomach, just plain ill. There was also something decidedly uncomfortable about feeling sick outside of your own comfort zone. Right now, I longed to be in my own bathroom, with the sound of Buster and Louie begging to get in. Home. Away from well-intentioned friends who grant me an afternoon of terrible company with a man who could never be part of my life, mixed with conversation so ludicrous it breeds heartburn resulting from wolfing down my food in an attempt to end the meal sooner. I must've actually begun to look ill, because Jessica actually took my hand.

"You okay?" she asked. "You look kinda off."

"I'm not feeling too well," I admitted. "Peter, I'm sorry. It was a pleasure meeting you, but I have to go."

"I can walk you to your car, if you like," he said standing up.

"I wouldn't want to interrupt your meal. I'll be okay." I turned toward Jessica, "Thanks for suggesting the lunch. I'll call you later in the week."

"And the great company?" Jessica asked sheepishly. "Don't forget that!"

I gave her a hug around her neck, "Don't push your luck."

"He's only mildly peculiar," she whispered back.

I GOT BACK TO THE OFFICE TO FIND THAT I HAD FIVE voicemail messages. I punched the code numbers with trepidation.

"April, just reminding you that I'll pick up the dogs at ten on Saturday. Make sure they're ready." Click. Damn Ryan, ordering me around and calling the boys "dogs."

Beep. "Honey, would you like to spend the weekend in your old room for old time's sake? We could make pancakes and waffles on Sunday morning, just like when you were little. Call me." Mom was having a psychic vision about my impending state of depression, or she simply knew me well.

Beep. "Hi April, it's Bruce. I suppose I could walk down the hall to your office, but I though you might want a voice recording of my voice to replay whenever Ryan was being an asshole. Oh, and I need you to make yourself available on Wednesday for lunch." Available. I didn't like the sound of that coming from Bruce.

Beep. "Hey Ape, it's Melissa. Good news. I think I found an attorney dumb enough to take on your custody case." Surely she means lucky enough.

Beep. "Honey, it's mom again. Just wanted to remind you that if you start dating make sure you, you know, use protection." Oh god.

Five calls and still I feel depressingly unpopular.

"I love my job. I love my job."

"April? You okay?"

Bebe had heard my mantra and as one would, gave me a look like I was sitting on the edge of a cliff with nothing, but my sanity keeping me from veering into the rocky canyon below. It was unclear to both of us whether I'd win that battle. "I'm just prepping for an event."

"Oh, it'll be fine," Bebe said with her typical positive and sunny attitude.

If only I could bottle her up and just take a good long swig. "Yeah, what could go wrong?"

Chapter 13

"I don't have to remind you that the cameras will be everywhere," I said to Ryan sternly. I drummed my fingers on the table, and switched my cell to the other ear. The thing was starting to heat up as much as I was. I had already been having this conversation for fifteen minutes. It was bad enough that I had to have this conversation; I wasn't going to make matters worse by developing a minor brain tumor.

"Your point?" Ryan responded.

"Matthew and Leandra don't mix. In fact, Matthew doesn't fit into the mix at all."

"April, the evening will be unbearably long if I don't have Matthew by my side."

"Grow up, Ryan. Since when did you two get joined at the hip?" I reconsidered the question. "Forget that. The point is that Leandra is supposed to be your new love interest. God, do you know how hard it is for me to say that?"

"Exactly. You only chose Leandra because you're hurt and she's a bubble head."

"You know, Ryan, I should let you have your way.

Tomorrow night, show up with Matthew and let the watchful eye of the media see you together."

"That wouldn't happen. We're discreet."

"Obviously," I said wryly. "Should I also leak the fact that you're a cheater?"

"I don't know why you can't just accept him. The boys love him."

"What do you mean the boys love him? They've met?"

"Naturally."

"I can't believe you. One is never supposed to introduce children of divorce to new dates. They can get attached. You don't know if this is going to be long-term with Matthew."

"First, that study applies to human children; and second, we're very serious."

"You know what? I don't think they can go to your place this weekend."

"The preliminary court hearing said I was entitled. Do you want to go on record that you went against the court?"

"Fine. I'll see you in the morning with the boys. Be on time."

———————

"Mmm, it smells so good." Melissa wandered into the kitchen just as I was pulling out a welcome home meatloaf out of the oven for the boys.

"It's for Buster and Louie, but there's enough for you too."

"Excellent. I love eating dog food, if it's prepared by you. How come you're not having any?"

"I'll be at the Regent Beverly Wilshire," I said with all the enthusiasm of a slug making its way across the sidewalk.

178

"La tee dah. Why so glum?"

"It may sound fancy, but it's still work. And for me that means spending another boring cocktail hour and dinner with my boss, about ten reporters and a potential sponsor for Ryan's new campaign. Basically, it's a group of people who think Ryan is *perfect*," I said with emphasis and rolling my eyes."

"Well, you used to think the same. Hey, what's this doing in here?" Melissa had pulled a squeaky toy out of the freezer.

"Oh my god. It's Mr. Noisy, Louie's favorite squeaky. He sleeps with it every night."

"Why is it in the freezer?"

"I wanted it to be extra refreshing so I put it in the freezer, but when Ryan arrived to pick-up the boys, he was rushing me and making me angry and Jessica was on the phone wanting me to have a repeat date with this boring accountant..."

"And you forgot the toy. It happens," Melissa replied nonchalantly and popped an ice cube in her mouth.

"You don't understand. Normally, Louie would be devastated without this toy, but Ryan hasn't even called, which means that Louie doesn't need his security toy when he's with Ryan because Ryan is security enough."

"You don't know that. Ryan's a man. He's not going to call and admit that things aren't perfect."

"You think Louie really was upset?" I said with the slightest trace of hope in my voice.

"Absolutely."

I felt horrible for feeling relieved, but the alternative was far worse.

WHEN RYAN BROUGHT BUSTER AND LOUIE HOME THEY immediately circled me like prey, licking my legs and jumping up to my waist. I hugged them both, gave them their meatloaf in new ergonomically correct feeding bowls, treasures I discovered in one of the endless mail order catalogues that comes to married people. It sits six inches above the ground so your happy hound doesn't have to bend over too far to inhale the food. I sat back and watched contentedly as they went to their favorite spots for an after-dinner nap.

"Why are they so tired?" I asked suspiciously. "Didn't they sleep well?" I hoped it was the Mr. Noisy fiasco and Ryan wasn't enough for them.

"Seemed to. They probably just had more exercise than usual," was his somewhat smug reply. "We went to the park...and the beach."

"Oh. Well I made meat loaf...and chocolate chip cookies," I countered.

"For the dogs?"

"Chocolate is bad for dogs. Who do you think I am?"

He eyed me with a questioning look and the conversation soon turned into a "discussion" outside so as not to wake the boys. We sat under the expansive umbrella that covered our faux suede patio furniture, the way we used to do when we had other couples over for dinner parties.

"April, you don't have to prove anything," he started.

"Who's trying to prove something? I just don't understand why you felt the need to take them on two outings and risk heat stroke and obvious over-exhaustion?"

"They're fine. As you can see, they're sleeping happily."

We looked inside the window and were speechless.

Louie noticed the cookies that were still cooling on the sink, and decided I wouldn't mind if he helped himself to some. Knowing Louie, he carefully sampled just one, and then since it met with his approval, went back for more. Buster, of course, would watch in dismay, knowing that eating off the counter was not in the doggie etiquette guide, but once those cookies were on the floor, he was ready for them. I returned inside knowing something was wrong and found Buster lying on the kitchen floor, unmoving, Louie by his side, staring down at him with a worried expression. "My God, Louie, you ate them all!" It was a brilliant observation on my part, and Louie confirmed his annoyance by burping at me.

I stepped over the mixture of leftover cookie crumbs and dog bile, dodged the chocolate paw prints, and reached for the telephone to call the veterinarian. "Don't just stand there," I screamed at Ryan. "We have to do something."

"What about the dinner?"

"Forget the dinner. They're more important."

"April, I want you to know that this wouldn't have happened if you hadn't been so irritating."

THE VET'S OFFICE SAID TO COME "RIGHT AWAY," WHICH naturally put me into a panic. "How do I get him to you? He's 98 pounds."

"Is he on the floor?" the voice asked.

"Yes," I said in my panic, wondering what kind of idiot I was dealing with. After all, could a 98-pound Golden Retriever be swinging from the chandelier?

"Then you can slide him as far as possible before getting to the carpeted area of your house. Find his favorite toy, or perhaps a treat to entice him to get up."

"I hardly think he's interested in any more 'treats'," I said snippily.

"You'd be surprised. Dogs like yours don't know their limit."

"Dogs like mine?" I was getting defensive.

"Dogs with eating behavior problems," the voice said matter-of-factly.

"Buster is not anorexic, bulimic, or overweight. He just succumbed to peer pressure."

The voice ignored my explanation. "We'll be waiting for you. Call us back if you have any trouble getting him in your car."

I looked at Buster and questioned which end was safest. "You go down there," I told Ryan, pointing to the hind quarters. On hands and knees we pushed Buster along the floor until we reached the carpeting before the door to the garage. Then, I don't know what made me more angry, the fact that the voice was so sure he would accept a doggie treat, or that when the cheesy-bacon dog biscuit was offered to him, Buster struggled to his feet, the first time standing since he had been discovered. With lumbering apprehension, he made it to the car and then whimpered in the back seat until I gave him his doggie cookie. Naturally, I had to bring two: one for Buster's decoy and one for Louie who had to come along.

Ryan drove since I was too upset. Buster was lying on his side again with Louie licking his head. They loved each other, which made me recall a parody book called, "Everything I Need to Know I Learned from my Cat." Ryan and I could both learn a lot about love and devotion from our pets.

Louie was petrified, despite the fact that he wasn't going to be treated. Buster was still feeling the effects of the cookies, and was also less than enthused to enter the office. Louie, at 40 pounds, was wiry and strong, fighting all the way, stretching his front legs out like arms to prevent himself from being thrust into the waiting room. Buster simply sat down and refused to stand up again. When I finally got them both inside, Buster apparently was not sick enough to warrant seeing the doctor immediately. We waited patiently for three-fourths of an hour, watching a woman bring in her cat that had been hit by a car, and a man with a dog that looked like it had mange, but in actuality was going bald due to cancer treatments. When it was our turn, I realized that I had misjudged the danger factor associated with the front end. Buster once again vomited on the way into the examining room.

"I'm sorry," I said feebly.

The nurse replied, "We're used to it," but seemed less than thrilled at the prospect of cleaning up the mess anyway. "Why don't you just take him in," she pointed to the empty room ahead. "The doctor will be right in."

Boredom and nervousness, mine, not Buster's, caused me to start searching the place. I opened cupboards and drawers, afraid that I would get caught, but too nervous to stand and do nothing.

"Will you sit still?" Ryan implored. "You're as bad as the dogs."

"I can't. I'm too worried," I said and picked up my cell phone.

"Bebe," I said into the receiver. "We've had a little emergency and are going to be late...or maybe no-shows. Call Jane Ramsey at the Los Angeles Times and tell her we'll give her an exclusive if she agrees to meet tomorrow morning. She's the most important of those coming tonight. We may be passing up potential coverage with the others, but this way, we can explain away our absence tonight."

"Good thinking," Ryan said when I hung up.

"So glad you approve," I said sarcastically.

"Can I call Matthew?"

"No."

"Please."

"Oh, alright," I said.

"I left my cell at home. Can I borrow yours?"

I rolled my eyes and handed over my phone so my husband could call his boyfriend.

As Ryan dialed, Buster burped, Louie whimpered, and I continued to search the cupboards. Most everything I found was in fact in my own bathroom cabinet. Q-tips, cotton balls, gauze, some gooey stuff that looked like Neosporin or Vaseline were neatly tucked away. I snatched a tube of the goo since I was out. Apparently thievery agreed with the dogs because Buster stopped vomiting and Louie was wagging his tail, urging me on.

The doctor came in, and my breath went out.

He was beautiful, around forty-years-old with a look that would be appealing to women across the generations. There aren't many men who can as effectively pull a twenty-something year old as well as women from the next two decades, but Dr. Emerson no doubt could do it. Thankfully, he didn't catch me at anything more criminal than being on his side of the examining table. He merely showed off his smile of perfectly even, square teeth, offered a strong handshake, and didn't seem to possess any doctorish sort of ego that would preclude him from bedding a divorcee. I politely moved and pointed to Buster.

"It's this one."

In that tone that all doctors use whether they are

internists, dentists, veterinarians, or chiropractors, although I have trouble considering the latter real doctors, he said, "Mmm, what seems to be the trouble?"

"Too many chocolate chip cookies."

"He shouldn't have any."

"I realize that. It was their idea," I nodded toward the dogs.

"Well, they're like children. You need to use a strong hand."

"You like that don't you?" Dr. Emerson asked as he softly stroked my hair.

"Nice," I agreed. "But stronger would be nicer."

Suddenly, he tugged my ponytail backwards, pulling my head back and exposing my throat, which he explored with his mouth.

"That's even better."

And then, without warning, he smacked me on my bottom and delivered a devilishly handsome smile.

"Pardon me?" I asked, feeling slightly out of breath.

Ryan repeated the phrase that had sent me into such a delightful reverie. "The doctor said you need to have a strong hand with pets."

"Absolutely," I smiled taking note of Dr. Emerson's waves of black hair, clear blue eyes, tan, healthy skin. Oh my. "He just helped himself," I said in an annoyed tone.

"So you left inappropriate food at his reach?"

I felt like a criminal and contemplated screaming, "Yes. I'm a bad doggie parent. I left sugary snacks at nose level. And I stole gooey stuff from your drawer!" I decided against it, however, and simply said, "It was a terrible accident. It won't happen again," I replied humbly. He could tell me off any day.

"Dr., I totally agree with you," Ryan said to Dr. Emerson. "This type of incident seems to occur most often at April's house. You see, we're separated. Actually, separated is a bit of an understatement."

I couldn't believe him! He had Matthew and yet he was hitting on our vet as well. This was not fair especially since this gorgeous man, being a doctor, was totally the type of man my mother would approve of.

"He's mine," I said.

"Not yet, he's not," Ryan countered.

"Do you want to step into the ring?" I challenged.

"It would be my pleasure," he said while removing his shirt. I did the same, miraculously discovering that I was wearing a bikini top.

"After you," Ryan said in a tone that was hardly gentleman like.

I dipped my big toe into the vat of hot oil. Warm. Nice. Comforting. But then, Ryan's hands gave one forceful shove and my demurely planned entrance into the slimy pool was replaced by a terrible splash. Ryan followed with a graceful swan dive.

We splashed each other like children until Dr. Emerson called to us: "Don't you two think you've been in long enough? Should I pass you a towel?"

We didn't know who he was speaking to, so both of us called out in eager unison: "Yes! Oh, yes!"

THE DOCTOR SEEMED SATISFIED. "WELL, HE APPEARS okay. I'm just going to take some blood to check his serum levels. We'll be back in a moment. You can wait in the lobby area."

I glared at Ryan as we went to the waiting room with Louie. "I hope you're happy. You know, that little stunt made you look bad."

"What do you mean?"

"Trying to make me take all the blame. That is shameful. We were both there."

"You made the cookies," he reasoned.

"You brought the conversation outside!"

"Let's not talk about this here," Ryan said stiffly. "Anyway, he seemed a little stuffy. Like he was passing judgement on us."

"I don't know. He seemed quite capable. Probably just takes his job seriously. Quite an admirable quality, if you ask me."

"I thought you always said we were supposed to be a united front, especially when around the boys. If I don't like the vet, you don't like the vet."

"So, you don't like the vet?" I asked.

Chapter 14

Bebe held up the morning edition of <u>The Hollywood Reporter</u>. "I don't believe it," I said in response.

"Josh says the publicity will be as good for the firm as it is for Ryan. He's in a fantastic mood,"she said with more elation than necessary.

Nothing could improve my mood. According to the trade magazine, Ryan's recurring role as a blind jockey got him nominated for a Flamingo, the top award for the daytime dramas. His absence at the dinner only increased the industry buzz. Overnight, Ryan was propelled from "B" actor status to stardom, and just as quickly an entourage emerged, ready for kiss up duty.

Messenger services deposited baskets of homemade cakes and cookies with cards from wanna-be friends congratulating Ryan on his "sweet" success. Florists brought bouquets from producers of competitive daytime series, commercials, and product placement bureaus. All were hopeful to lure Ryan away from "Setting Sun" and into their deliberate and profitable care. Hair stylists from the celebrity-laden Beverly Hills salons of Jose Eber and

Umbertos fought in our waiting room. Each had shown up to entice us to give them the chance to create Ryan's new look for the Flamingo Awards night. An astrologer emerged through our back door with the generous offer to foresee into Ryan's future. Designers from the biggest Rodeo Drive boutiques left fabric swatches and photos of suits, which they believed would make a statement shouting that Ryan was a winner. Even competing public relations agencies had the nerve to send well wishes, promising top PR exposure suitable for an actor of his stature. The implication was that we could lose Ryan as a client if we didn't follow suit with our own accolades.

In addition to the fury of uninvited visitors, entertainment reporters from a myriad of print and electronic media were requesting interviews. After months of snubbing our requests, even Honoria Vitale, a virtual media celebrity herself, wanted an interview.

I dodged reporters and fans, slowly making my way down the long hallway leading to my office, but there was no escaping the Ryan commotion.

I closed and locked the door, shut my eyes to gain a moment of quiet, until my chair pivoted and squeaked causing me to nearly jump out of my skin.

"Wonderful news, isn't it, April?" Leandra spun around in my chair.

"What are you doing here? Did Bebe let you in?"

"Naturally. I'm Ryan's girlfriend."

"Naturally," I wearily admitted.

"That's why I'm here. I want your blessing, April."

"My blessing?"

"Yes. When I first met you, I wasn't sure what to make of the fact that you were allowing me to date your ex-husband."

"Soon-to-be ex," I corrected.

"Yeah, whatever," she continued. "Anyway, I now know that you were just a messenger of fate. Ryan and I are meant to be together."

Inadvertently my eyes rolled upward. "How did you come to this conclusion?"

"The Flamingo Award," she said simply. "It's my favorite bird. A definite sign."

"Sign of what?"

"That I'm supposed to have Ryan's love child! The media will be all over it."

"Oh God," I said feeling ill.

"If you research the Flamingo you'll find that it's very similar in nature and physical attributes to the stork, the baby delivering bird!"

"Leandra, I really have a lot of work to do now that Ryan is up for this honor," I said trying to usher her out of my life, or at least my office for the time being.

"But, April, I need your blessing."

I was quickly becoming hysterical and more nauseous. "Fine, just leave," I said opening the door.

"You don't sound sincere," she said warily. "Are you going to try to get back with Ryan? Should I talk to Bruce about this because it was your firm, after all, that suggested I hook up with him in the first place."

Bebe was lurking in the hallway and for once I was pleased. "Leandra, I give you my blessing. Ryan deserves you. In fact, I think you should waste no time in finding something exquisite to wear to the awards dinner, which you will naturally be attending, courtesy of our firm." I motioned for Bebe, who didn't miss an opportunity to come closer to the action. "Bebe, will you take Leandra shopping for something nice?" I pulled her in close and whispered, "Make sure it's expensive and that it's charged to Ryan's account."

LEANDRA WAS GONE. BEBE WAS THANKFULLY WITH HER. Just when I thought it was safe, Bruce came calling. "April, let's face it, the entire office is dillying each other, why not us?"

I could only stall for time. "Dillying?" I asked.

He spurted an obscene chain of explanation. "You know dating, screwing, fucking, love making, making time, dilly dallying. Dillying!"

"The whole office?"

"Might as well be. Your ex and that actress. Your secretary and Josh. You're practically involved in every affair without any of the fun that goes along with it." He leaned in close, his breath hot on my neck. "April, you get the feeling that you're missing out?"

"Never," I said quickly and took a step backwards. "Bruce, you realize that you are head of this company and this could be misconstrued as sexual harassment."

"Nonsense. With the entire firm going at it, it's obviously condoned. Besides, I have graphs to prove it."

I was outraged. "Graphs!"

"Have a seat." In spite of Bruce pulling out a chair for me, his behavior was certainly not very gentleman-like. I imagined that it could only get worse.

"No, NOT LIKE THAT. LIKE THIS," BRUCE INSTRUCTED.

It had been a while since I was in bed with a man. I guess I was rusty.

"According to my calculations, you should be experiencing a rise in temperature, just about now," Bruce said, putting a hand on my forehead.

"Hmm," I said, feigning interest.

"Don't be surprised if this increased body heat makes you feel slightly dizzy. I have that affect on women."

"Oh. I'm not surprised," I responded.

"Now April try to concentrate on your orgasm. This whole process need not take more than ten or fifteen minutes if we're efficient."

"Do we really want to strive toward efficiency?" I asked naively.

"April, you're so young," he chided. "Now pay attention to your breathing."

"APRIL, ARE YOU WITH ME?" BRUCE ASKED.

"Huh?" I said, coming back to his obscure reality.

Bruce had made a fairly strong argument for why we should become a couple. He outlined the benefits of a healthy sex life, citing improved physical as well as mental health.

"It's not that you're unattractive, Bruce." I still had my job to think of. "It's just that the whole thing sounds so clinical."

"Ah, a romantic, are we?" Bruce said with obvious relief, his masculinity still intact.

"That's it. I'm just a dreamer."

"Well, you'll be happy to know that you'll be my date for the Flamingos. Our first date," he said with a knowing nod.

Whenever my mom left dad in charge of Melissa and I, she would return home and he would ask if she wanted the good news or the bad. Good news was usually something like the girls ate a hearty lunch. Bad news was that it consisted of dirt from the garden. I had a date for the Flamingos. In light of the fact that Josh would be there with Bebe, and Ryan would be there with Leandra, this was good news. But, my livelihood depended upon my boss having a good time with my assistant, my ex-husband having a good time with the wanna-be actress that I set him up with, and my boss' boss, Bruce, seemed determined to have a good time with me. That could only be bad news no matter how you spun it.

———

Chapter 15

"You're going to come with us, aren't you?"

"No April, I can't see the point," Jessica replied matter-of-factly.

"I can't believe you. I go on so many of your set-ups, none of which have improved my psyche or my life, and you won't do this one thing for me?"

"It sounds weird."

"Melissa does it," I countered.

Jessica just raised her eyebrows. "Enough said. I'm staying home."

"Don't be ridiculous. It'll be good for you. And, potential business for your firm. Two birds," I said knowingly.

"Not so fast. I don't see this leading to a new client. You convinced me to give another one of your weirdos some free advice." Jessica lowered her gaze, "In fact, your exact words were, 'I think I'm going insane so you must come with Melissa and I to a weird freak's retreat so that I can see that other people are worse off than myself' or something to that extent. And also, "He's being sued and I thought you could play lawyer and help him."

"I didn't say it like that. Anyway, I know you have nothing better to do. Besides, it's sure to be good for a couple laughs."

My attempt at humor won her over and Jessica finally agreed to go with Melissa and I to an Indian Laughter Club. Melissa had discovered the idea of a laughter club during a discussion that erupted during her pre-natal class a week earlier. Ian had gone outside when the instructor passed out photos of the baby's head crowning and he felt like he might pass out. Once outside, he met Sanjay, another man who wasn't comfortable with the idea of his wife's privates being stretched into something resembling the Thames Tunnel. Melissa forgave him, especially when Sanjay, whom she describes as "a soulful man who emits a distinct curry smell" (not sure if the description means she actually likes Sanjay) offered to give her cooking lessons and a month's worth of free passes to his Indian Laughter Club.

This was in exchange for Jessica's direct line. Melissa was never the best negotiator. Ian begged Melissa to forgive him because he said he wasn't the only man who had walked out. Melissa agreed, but only if he could prove that the man whom he was spending every pre-natal class with in the lobby was a stand-up guy. Ian felt this would be difficult, particularly since Sanjay's neighbors were threatening to sue him. Apparently, his habit of inviting twenty to thirty of his closest and not so close friends and acquaintances to his home to partake in laughing sessions had not caught on throughout the building. That's when Ian decided to appeal to Melissa's sense of justice and suggested that she get Jessica involved. Melissa explained that Jessica's boss charged around $400 per hour, but maybe if Sanjay gave them all free laughter club passes, then Jessica could dole out some free advice. Jessica was less than thrilled, but then again, since she had always wanted to try and practice law instead of just being a para-legal, she figured she'd go along with it.

And so, everyone was happy particularly Melissa who was now enjoying Indian cooking lessons. Sanjay's wife, who was really pregnant, was getting ill from the curry smell. So, Sanjay was happy when Melissa showed an interest, and due to her false pregnancy, could handle the smell.

Melissa was learning the pleasures of Chicken Tikka Marsala, Rogan Josh, and a variety of Naam breads, particularly those with sweet sesame and almond fillings. For weeks after meeting Sanjay, she tried to duplicate the flavorful beef and chicken dishes using stewed tomatoes and a kitchen full of spices.

I recall one of her earliest attempts: "Melissa, can I have a steak knife?"

"You don't need one. The beef will literally fall apart," she called out from the kitchen.

She came out to find me arm wrestling with my meat, struggling to win it over with nothing, but a fork to assist me. "It's supposed to be a 'succulent blend of spices washing over the tender meat,'" she recited from the Madhur Jafrey recipe book, one of the most famous of Indian cooks. "Here," she said defeated and handed me a knife that resembled a small hatchet.

She gave up Indian cooking after realizing that her secret spice blend (a combination of salt, basil, and paprika for color) didn't compare with Sanjay's own mixture of thirteen authentic seasonings. "Who has time to mix thir-teen items?" she asked rhetorically after the most recent dinner fiasco. "Much easier to go to Bombay Cafe, or a laughter club. They always bring snacks for afterwards."

Tonight was supposed promised to be a virtual feast

with everyone in the laughter club taking part in a pot-
luck. In my mind, it was the perfect night for Jessica to give
it a go.

"Are you ready?" Melissa asked.

"Jessica is coming; should be here any minute."

"She's coming tonight?"

In response, the doorbell sounded announcing Jessica's
arrival. Melissa did a little jump and ran to open the door.

"You're here!" she said with elation.

In contrast, Jessica answered, "Let's get this over with."

"I'll get my sari," Melissa announced and ran back to
her room.

"We're really doing this?" I asked.

"Apparently," Jessica answered.

Melissa came back and took note of what we were
wearing. "You know, the laughing session can really make
you work up an appetite. Maybe you two should wear
looser clothing. You know, in case your stomach
expands."

"I'm good," Jessica said referring to her black jeans and
an Ann Taylor sweater. I had to admit. She looked too
yuppie to produce even the tiniest yippie.

We got into Melissa's car and I started to relax. This
would be good, I told myself. I decided to steer clear of
jeans and wore a dress since tightness around my waist
limits my ability to fully exhale.

"This is bizarre," Jessica hissed in my ear. "I can't even
hope to find a man. I mean, imagine the type of man that
would be here. A hyena in a sari?"

"Laughter is good for you," I chastised. "Enlighten
yourself," I said and handed her a brochure touting the
benefits of the Beyond Bombay Laughter Club. The
brochure described the camaraderie established at the club
as well as Sanjay's own tell-all story. He described himself

as a man on the verge of health disaster, until laughter found him.

We pulled up to the house. Jessica was still having reservations. "How can laughter find you? It sounds like I could be minding my own business, just driving on the freeway when suddenly, laughter enters me. It grips me like a supernatural force, making me lose control of my bladder."

"Sanjay never lost control of his bladder; he just lowered his blood pressure," Melissa informed her as we walked up a rose-lined path and then entered a small house filled to the brim with smiling people.

"Here we go," mumbled Jessica.

The laughter started. At first, just a few hesitant giggles emerged. Then, a petite Japanese woman bellowed a hearty guffaw. She grabbed her nineteen inch waist with both hands and laughed so hard that she farted. Loudly. It started a chain reaction that, fortunately erupted from the more pleasing end of the guests. I heard Melissa's distinct cackle, a high-pitched noise that resembled the sound of an owl's hoot. Another woman joined in with a silent, but fierce shaking that climaxed with a splattering noise that sounded like yogurt being dropped onto tiled floor.

Jessica and I just stared at each other.

"This is too weird. Blood pressure or not, I can't do it," Jessica insisted.

"Just do it. You're making me feel self-conscious," I complained.

"It's not me."

"Well, I've never had a problem before. It must be you," I insisted.

"Did you learn that line from Ryan?," she giggled, the first time since we arrived.

I ignored her joke. It wasn't funny and it didn't make me laugh. "Let's try standing with our mouths open."

Jessica and I stood as if trying to catch flies amidst forty people who were hysterically laughing at nothing at all.

THE PEOPLE FILING OUT OF THE LAUGHTER CLUB HAD their hands pressed against their abdomens, trying to soothe achy muscles that had been stimulated from excess guffawing and chuckling. Jessica and I looked at each other and decided to do the same, although our stomachs clearly did not have a sense of humor. When we were out of view, Jessica dropped the act and asked, "Are you busy the rest of the night?"

"No. Why?"

"Good. Then you're free to join us for dinner."

"Us?"

"Well, admittedly, the last set up didn't go too well."

"You think?"

"That's because I was a third wheel. You shouldn't have invited me, but since you seem incapable of finding love on your own, I invited this guy from my office to my house for dinner and you could come and meet him."

"Tonight? Nothing like a little warning."

"You would've said 'no' if I gave you much warning. This way you don't have time to worry. It's good for you," Jessica insisted.

"Vegetables are good for me."

"And so is...Jean-Paul!" she said with a dramatic flair and a decidedly French accent.

"If he's another numerologist..."

"Don't be silly. He's French."

"But, I've kind of met someone."

"Really?"

"Don't act so surprised," I said in mock annoyance.

"The car accident guy again?"

"No. My vet. Well, he hasn't asked me out, but he has shown a distinct interest in the boys."

"That's his job." Jessica sized up the situation and then in her typical, straight-forward fashion, she gave it to me straight. "Listen, until he actually asks you out, he's just another pretty face, and someone you pay for services."

"I'm not paying for those type of services."

"He hasn't asked you out. Did I mention that Jean-Paul is a dress designer?"

My eyebrows lifted; an anorexic closet beckoned me to investigate further. "A dress designer?"

"Yes. It's a win-win, April. Even if you don't like him, you play your cards right and you get a new dress out of it."

"One can never have too many little, black dresses," I admitted. "I'll see you later tonight."

───────

SINCE RYAN MOVED OUT, I DON'T COME HOME TO MANY surprises, with the exception of Louie's cookie incident. However, I got one today: Ryan and Leandra, arguing on the front lawn, giving my neighbors their monthly installment of the news of my life.

"Why won't you introduce me to them?" Leandra wailed.

"It's not important, Leandra," Ryan answered.

I walked up the pathway leading to the house. "What's going on?" I asked.

"Nothing," Ryan responded.

"Everything!" Leandra protested.

"Is this business, because if it's not, I want you to leave," I said to Ryan. "I'm too tired. I've been laughing for the last hour and it's exhausting."

"That's not funny," Ryan said.

"This is most definitely business," Leandra added. "Ryan has his reputation to consider. If word of this gets out..." her voice trailed off.

"What? What is going on?" I insisted.

"Leandra is upset that I won't introduce her to the boys," Ryan explained.

"He treats me like the evil step-mother," Leandra complained.

And for once, I approved of Ryan's decisions. "It may be confusing to them," I said gently.

"But I want to meet them. I want to show them I care," said Leandra.

"I know, but they've been through a lot," I offered. "How about when it's more..." I struggled for the right word, "official!"

"Official?" Leandra and Ryan repeated in unison.

"Like your engagement!" I shouted gleefully.

Ryan glared. Leandra beamed.

"I couldn't get rid of them," I explained into the phone. "That is, until I suggested marriage."

"Sounds terrible and delightful all at once," Jessica said. "Can you still get here by eight to be swept off your feet by an intelligent, sophisticated, couture designer?"

"Of course," I said feeling giddy. "What house did you say he designs for?"

"I can't remember the name, but I'm sure it's a biggie."

"Jean-Paul, these are gorgeous!" Jessica squealed, looking over the sketches, and excitedly dragged her co-worker into the scheme. "Chris, don't you think April would look amazing in one of these?"

"Yeah," he said feigning interest. "Hey, you mind if I get another beer?"

"Great idea. I'll come with you," Jessica said and then winked at me as she left the room.

I had to admit, the dress designs were gorgeous and Jean-Paul was charming.

"April, you would look lovely in any of theeese," Jean-Paul said sweetly.

Accents of any type make women swoon. Suddenly, my mind went to the English guy again and I realized that another week had gone by and I still had forgotten to send him a check. I brought my mind back to what Jean-Paul was saying.

"Oui April, thees is you," he said holding up a design sketch.

I replied with the requisite hair toss and eyelash batting. "Do you really think so?"

"Oh, definitely. They would all suit you. If only they fit women like you."

Oh my God. Was he implying I wasn't of model proportions? Was he trying to say I should be shopping in the Plus Size section? Right to my face? "What do you mean, 'women like me?'"

"You know, a real woman," he said as if the meaning was perfectly clear. Unfortunately, it wasn't.

Jessica must have been eavesdropping for she jumped back into the room like a hungry flea, attempting to come to Jean-Paul's rescue and save my ego at the same time.

"April, those little waif-like models aren't even real people, let alone real women. They eat maybe once a day, probably tofu. Isn't that what you meant, Jean-Paul," she coaxed.

"Well, I'm sure all that is true. And, you are a wonderful woman, April, but that's not what I meant."

"What did you mean?" Jessica and I asked in unison.

Jean-Paul looked at us closely. "You didn't think I designed dresses for real women, did you?"

"What is this 'real women' bit?" I asked with increasing annoyance.

"Humans," he responded simply. "Women of flesh, not plastic."

An image of the film, "Lars and the Real Girl," where the man was in love with a plastic, life-sized mannequin flashed through my mind. I gave Jessica a "you've done it again" look.

Sensing that we were still confused, Jean-Paul reached into his satchel. "Maybe this will explain," he said and pulled out a doll, approximately six inches in height, with extremely disproportionate features, much like Barbie. "Meet Stay-At-Home Susie," Jean-Paul presented dramatically.

Jessica and I just stared at each other. Chris was the first to speak, "Killer legs," to which Jessica just elbowed him in the ribs.

"This is why I can't wear your designs," I said with new enlightenment.

"If only they came in your size," Jean-Paul said wistfully. "Wanna see my newest ideas?" Before waiting for an answer, he handed me a formal looking proposal titled, "Beyond Barbie: The Doll for the New Millennium." The proposal contained a long list of new Barbie titles, which included:

Street Walker Barbie - She wears the latest in sleazy, take-me-home styles and comes with an assortment of colorful, mini condoms.

Unabomber Barbie - Donned in a black cloak and sunglasses, Barbie is ready to blow up anyone who gets in her way.

Born Again Barbie - This doll is the perfect match for "Bible Bashing Barbie."

Bondage Barbie - Wearing a sleek, leather jumpsuit, this Barbie even comes with her own ties and whips.

Beatnik Barbie - With a colorful, sixties attitude, Beatnik Barbie comes with a pouch of sugar pills, which you can pretend are acid.

Binging Barbie - Just think of the food accessories!

Bulimic Barbie - She eats and she ... (portable toilet sold separately).

I was speechless. Again, my friend had attempted to set me up with a psycho.

"I'm trying these styles out for Susie," Jean-Paul informed us. "Seems like they might be a good match for her 'stay-at-home' image."

Again, Chris was the first to speak: "Does Susie have a boyfriend?"

"Actually, I was working on a prototype for a girl-friend," Jean-Paul responded with a wink.

"Oh gross," I exclaimed.

Jessica chimed in, "That's sick. Who is your target audience anyway? Little girls or little perverts?

"You sound just like those corporate types at Mattel, the ones with their ties tied too tight," said Jean-Paul. "They canceled my contract after seeing my proposal."

"Imagine that," I said.

"They said they wanted ideas to take Susie into the millennium and beyond, but they actually just wanted a rehash of the old Barbie. Just more dream houses and fancy cars. I feel I gave Susie more interesting toys," Jean-Paul said with more conviction than was necessary.

"Anyone tired," Jessica asked helpfully.

"I am," said Chris and yawned for effect.

"Me, too," I said and reached for my purse. The party broke up soon after. We watched Jean-Paul drive off with his sketches.

Chapter 16

I awoke to the sound of the boys playing tug-of-war with the rubber ring. Buster would never pull so hard as to take it away from Louie, although he was more than capable. I was pathetically jealous of my dogs' relationship. I leaned back against my pillow, closed my eyes, and wished I had something like they did--without dog breath, of course. For the second time this week, I found myself thinking of Dr. Emerson, now wondering why I didn't check to see if he wore a ring.

I was just making a mental list of reasons to pay him a visit -- vaccination boosters, flea baths, nail trims -- when Melissa screamed from her room. It was loud enough to make even the dogs stop what they were doing.

"What's wrong?" I shouted as I took off down the hall.

"Oh April, I think it's the baby," she moaned. "Oh god, the pain is so intense."

Melissa lied with her knees pulled up to her chest, her eyes shut tightly, her hands gripping the sheets. I had seen signs posted in hospitals with a series of faces ranging from smiling yellow ones to pouting, sweating red angry ones. It was the universal pain determining chart and if Melissa's behavior was any indication, I'd say she was at the maximum level.

"But honey," I said stroking her head. "You know that's impossible."

"It isn't! It feels like something is bursting inside of me."

Surely, this couldn't be happening, but something was certainly wrong. "Don't worry, help will be here soon," I said while punching my cell.

Within five minutes the paramedics had arrived.

"What are her symptoms?" the taller one asked. "She's got a fever, intense pain in her abdomen. Could it be one of those hysterical pregnancies?"

"More likely her appendix, by the sound of it," the paramedic responded. "We'll know more when we get her to E.R."

"April, I'm so scared. Will you call Ian?"

"I already did," I said squeezing her hand. "He's going to meet us at the hospital. Everything's going to be...Melissa?"

But before I could finish my thought and tell her she would be okay, she passed out and the paramedics started yelling in code.

My parents along with Ian and I paced the hospital waiting room, anxious for any news about Melissa's condition. It was a scene out of an old-fashioned film, back when women delivered babies alone. Only Melissa wasn't having a baby and deep down, we all knew it. The doctors confirmed that her appendix had burst. For an organ that has no known value to the human body, this one was certainly causing all of us to rethink our lives.

"We shouldn't have put so much pressure on them," my mom lamented.

"You were only doing your best," my father replied.

Mom wiped her eyes, her tone growing suspicious. "What do you mean 'you'? I said 'we'. We both wanted April to sort out her marriage and that's what led the girls to create this charade. You heard her," she said pointing a finger at me.

"I'm sorry," I said. "It was all my idea, my fault. I just thought if Melissa were pregnant and single, with a waiter, than that would be worse than me being divorced."

"Hey, it's not like I'm going to be a waiter my whole life," Ian snapped.

Finally, the nurse came in and asked us to keep it down. We all took our seats, thankful for the intrusion and a reason to stop speaking. Another nurse arrived shortly after to explain that Melissa must have felt something odd, but for some reason ignored the symptoms. Apparently, her bulging tummy was actually her appendix, terribly inflamed and infected. The infection spread throughout her abdomen, causing peritonitis, which could be fatal.

Finally, Ian interrupted the silence. "I just got accepted to an executive training program with Microsoft," he said softly. "I really wanted you all to be proud and not worry about us. April, you've been great letting Melissa stay at your place, and I'm there all the time too. I just want you to know that I'm getting things sorted out in my life, and we were talking about getting married." He turned toward my parents, "We were going to ask you for your blessing."

My parents both reached for Ian's hands and pulled him in close for a hug. I joined them and the four of us stood in a huddle until a doctor wearing a grave expression, interrupted us.

MELISSA HAD BEEN DISCHARGED A WEEK EARLIER. THE emergency surgery she underwent to remove her appendix and repair the tissue that lines the abdomen walls was a success, but the doctor worried about Melissa's mental state and what was occurring in her life to make her believe she was pregnant and thereby willing to ignore symptoms that were such obvious signs of an infection, not a baby.

My family agreed that we were the ones with the mental condition, not Melissa, and decided the best thing for her was to receive unconditional love and lots of rest. After leaving the hospital, she went to stay at my parent's where she could receive around-the-clock care from my mother. I had taken three days off from work when Melissa was first sent home, and as much as I'd rather stay with her, I knew it was time to return to work and the task of saving my job by way of making Ryan's celebrity meter rise.

I got to my office early, scanned the trades and looked up my horoscope. Apparently, my future still looked sketchy: *Aries-Disappointment looms in the distance. Don't worry. This too shall pass.* Perfect. Just the right amount of optimism to make me want to stay in hiding. Bebe must have tuned into my thoughts for she came tip-toeing in with a cup of coffee.

"Thanks, I need this," I said bringing the steamy cup to my lips. "How come you're in so early?"

Bebe didn't answer immediately. She just dropped a thick envelope onto my desk.

"What's this?"

"It's a proposal from The Lavin Group."

I stared at her blankly and took out the proposal. On the front cover, the bold letters appeared to be screaming at me: CAMPAIGN PROPOSAL - RYAN MONAHAN.

"No. You've got to be kidding me. When did this happen?"

"The day your sister was taken to the hospital. Ryan had it delivered that morning and told us we needed to step up our efforts or he would walk."

"At least Josh and Bruce didn't text me about it. That must mean they value me as an employee and knew that I needed time with my family and this frivolous threat could wait. Right?"

Bebe just shrugged her shoulders. "They've pretty much been brainstorming without you all week. They're worried."

"Well, I'll just have to unworry them," I said and marched down the hall to find Bruce.

I STOOD IN THE DOORWAY TO BRUCE'S OFFICE. HE WAS on the phone, looking at me with disinterest and pointing to the receiver with a "this is more important; don't bother me" look. Well, that simply wouldn't do with my job on the line. I smiled sweetly and proceeded to unbutton my top -- slowly and deliberately.

With renewed interest in me, Bruce said into the speaker, "I'm gonna have to call you back."

I buttoned myself back up and took a seat in front of him.

"Why did you do that?" indicating my now properly dressed state.

"Because I wanted you to concentrate on what I have to say and you're my boss so in order to protect my job and you from sexual harassment, I felt it was better to have this conversation fully clothed."

"Suit yourself," he said while adjusting himself in front of me.

"Charming. Now, if you're comfortable..."

"Proceed."

"You tell Ryan to give us one week. And, you give me one week of completely free reign and the staff at my disposal."

"He's going to walk, April. There's not much we can do about it and he was your biggest account so when he goes..."

"One week, Bruce."

I HAD A PLAN. FOR YEARS I HAD ENDURED COUNTLESS phone calls, lunches, networking breakfasts and mixers with other publicists. I had passed on my contacts, listened to their client woes, referred our agency's overflow to them and now, it was time to call up a few favors. The morning was starting to sound like it was on auto repeat.

"Thanks Bob, I appreciate it. That's right, I'm offering a swap of one of our agency's paid advertising spots in exchange for editorial coverage. It's a three column spot running mid-week so the editorial staff should be willing to offer a feature."

Similar phone calls occurred throughout the day. Since I was in charge of advertising purchasing for my firm, I typically bought open-ended ads that could be used by the publication when and if we decided it was appropriate. In my business, you never knew when it would be useful to run an impromptu "We love our client" type of ad. The other benefit of being the one who paid for these ads was that nobody else in the office seemed to know just how many I had stockpiled. So by late afternoon, I was assured of over fifteen feature spreads on Ryan and all I had to do was hand over a similar amount of free advertising space to publicists who over the years had said "they owe me one." So what if I was perpetuating the line from snooty reporters who complain that publicists are evil creatures who promote lies for pay? In the end, these same reporters know that without the advertising dollars, their publications would fold.

Josh and Bruce had learned about the upcoming media blitz that was expected and as a result, the atmosphere at the office had relaxed, too much so if you ask me because the next day I arrived early again only to be greeted by the sight of Josh and Bebe making out in the copy room.

I stared at them in disgust. "On the Xerox machine? Can't you get a room or something?"

"Another bad date?" Josh asked.

"How'd you know about my..." I glared at Bebe.

"I tell Joshie everything," she explained.

"Josh, may Bebe be excused?" I asked.

"Goodbye button," he said and kissed her on the nose.

I wanted to beat them both with reams of paper, but instead I escorted Bebe away from Josh's lecherous hold to brief her on the latest.

"Bebe, I want to send a pitch letter to the morning talk shows suggesting that Ryan and Leandra make an appearance as a couple."

I may need to promote Ryan to save my job, but I still needed to save my dignity. If Ryan wanted to be promoted as a sexy, leading man, he would get it. With my help, every woman between the ages of twenty and thirty would be after Ryan, and soon, even his boyfriend would question the reality of Ryan's faithfulness.

"You're actually accepting them as a couple? April, that's so mature."

"Yeah, whatever," I said.

I knew that if I didn't get Ryan some air time during this career peak, Josh and Bruce would be getting a visit from him regardless of how much print exposure he had. I also knew that if I had to promote him, it might as well be as miserable as possible for him.

I thought about what might appeal to the media while simultaneously making Ryan wish he never became an actor, let alone a born-again heterosexual. "Just draft something like, 'Love birds venture from roost. For the first time, Ryan and Leandra are ready to tell their amazing love story. Learn how they met, what Leandra makes Ryan for breakfast each morning, and how Ryan tempted Leandra to devote her life to him.'"

Bebe was scribbling furiously. "Who do I send it to?"

"I want numbers. If they have an audience share of more than two million, then they're on the list. Hold on a minute," I checked the latest Neilsen's. "Okay, 'Dr. Phil' with four million should be the first stop on his press tour. Next, the other doc, uh..."

"Dr. Oz?" Bebe asked.

"Yes! Followed by that group of women who gossip on the couch."

"That would be 'The View'," Bebe said like a walking T.V. guide. "I DVR all of these shows," she said by way of explanation.

"Great. Then go with 'Live with Regis and Kelly' but only when Regis is completely retired. I want a younger vibe to it, someone who will ask more intimate questions than Reg ever did. And round it all up with 'Kathie and Hoda' because they are sure to put him on the hot seat.

Tell each of their booking editors that this would be a soft exclusive."

"What do you mean?"

"Hopefully, they all want the interview. That means the first one on board gets the 'exclusive' on their first love encounter. We create a script for Ryan and Leandra about how they fell for each other, the hotel they did it at, etcetera. Then, the shows that follow will get the rehashed interviews. They'll already know about this stuff, so they'll probably ask the questions all over again, by which time Leandra will have the lines down pat and Ryan will be a squirming mess," I paused long enough to take a sip of burned coffee, courtesy of Bebe. "So, the show that gets the soft exclusive is actually getting the juiciest story. The others will still get Ryan and Leandra on air, but they'll talk about something benign, but of interest to mid-western housewives who watch Ryan's show."

"Something like the two of them preparing a romantic dinner while talking about the famous Los Angeles eateries they like to visit!" Bebe said with a gleam.

I felt like a proud eagle ready to let her baby eaglette fly solo. "You've got it!"

"You know what, April? I bet we might even get some new clients after all of this media we get for Ryan. Anyone would want this sort of PR treatment."

"Bebe, I think you might be right about that."

Josh popped his head into my office right about then. "You about done in here, Button?"

"April?" Bebe questioned.

"Yes, we're finished," I said and for the first time, I really felt happy for Bebe. She was going to be an excellent publicist and she truly seemed to make Josh happy.

"We're going to have lunch," she said, indicating Josh, before leaning in close to whisper, "maybe you should go for a nice one and find your wiggle again."

"My wiggle?" I said confused.

"Yeah. You used to have a wiggle in your walk, but lately it's been more of a waddle. You know, a kind of depressed walk."

"It shows?" I asked concerned. Waddle definitely sounded depressing, and probably something that would not attract many eligible men.

"Don't worry. These things tend to be temporary," Bebe said with a knowing look, before leaving with Josh on her arm.

RYAN'S ACCOUNT WAS UNDER CONTROL, AND THE others could certainly wait an afternoon. It was another unseasonally sunny day. Determined to find my wiggle, I retrieved my bathing suit from the top drawer of my desk, left behind for just such occasions, and drove to the beach to observe those unencumbered by the stresses of a job.

I headed north on Pacific Coast Highway towards El Matador. It was one of the few beaches where I didn't feel self-conscious. Rock formations and sand dunes jutted up at convenient locales scattered across the beach. In addition to being aesthetically pleasing, they provided plenty of places to sunbathe in virtual privacy. Just me and a suitably pink covered chick lit novel to pass the time.

After only five pages, the warm sun started to control my eyelids. I turned over and wiggled my butt back and forth across the blanket to create a custom-made ditch, then put my head back and closed my eyes behind my shades. It was quiet. Just the lapping of the ocean, back and forth. The hush of the wind across the rocks, in and out of the cavities. Kicking of sand across my face.

"Hey! Watch it!" I yelled.

"Sorry, my bad." I looked up to see a six-foot-tall, blue-eyed, blond-haired God carrying a surfboard in one hand and a frisbee in the other. He looked like something straight from a Frankie and Annette movie. His swimming trunks were the good kind, the ones that showed off muscles in his legs and butt, not in other places I'd rather not consider upon first introductions. He looked as if he was no doubt too young for me.

I suddenly didn't mind that he had woken me up with an abrasion of sand. Probably did me some good. The salon I go to for facials sells a tub of goo with sand already in it to pumice the skin into silky softness. The stuff costs $40, but Surfer Boy's treatment was free.

I looked around the beach to see who he had been playing frisbee with, but couldn't see anyone else.

"Were you playing frisbee by yourself?"

"I throw it toward the beach while I'm on the board and then see if the waves will get me to it in time to make the catch," he beamed with enthusiasm.

"Seriously? Isn't that kinda hard?"

"If I can throw accurately while on the board, I know there's no slippage."

I was in the midst of suggesting that the "slippage" factor would probably be less if he stood on the sand, when he interrupted with an exuberant, "Hey, don't I know your breasts from somewhere?"

"I beg your pardon! The line is, 'don't I know *you* from somewhere?' You! Not breasts."

"No, no I don't think I know you. It's your breasts that look familiar. Well, that mole actually," he said, pointing an outstretched finger at a beauty mark that resides just to the left of my cleavage. I wanted to get the thing removed a year ago, but the doctor said it was benign. In retrospect that was obviously a misguided diagnosis. "I've got it," he continued. "Yoga!"

"I don't think so," I said, and casually began to cover my chest with my arms.

"Perusha's class," he said nodding enthusiastically. "I'm going through my teacher training and helped in there. I was the one who guided you into a deep shavasana." He then proudly added, "I'm a five-year student."

I felt extremely weird. I was being recognized on virtually private beaches for my breasts. I could have taken it as flattery, but under the circumstances, I just felt exposed. I knew my bra could be seen, but now I learned that my mole was also on exhibition for the entire class to see, or at least for Blue Eyes Surfer Boy to notice. I hope he didn't look at my butt too. I think it looked large in the leggings I was wearing, and now, in a bikini, it certainly had no place to hide.

I concentrated on squeezing my butt cheeks for the duration of the conversation. "That was quite a class. Really a new experience in yoga," I said.

"You did great."

"Really?" I said feeling more comfortable.

"Yeah, the way you just let yourself relax into the positions. Even your skin seemed to hang loose," he said making the universal surfer sign with his right hand.

"Yeah," I said now squeezing my stomach along with my butt, and every other part of me that dared sneak away from my bones.

"So, what's your name?" he asked.

I might as well tell him. He was gorgeous and he already knew my breasts. "April," I answered. "Nice to meet you, again."

WHAT DOES BEBE KNOW? I RETURNED TO THE OFFICE with more than a tan. I found my wiggle thanks to the attentive conversation of Steven, my own Frankie Avalon.

"April, you're positively glowing!" Bruce said, meeting me in the entry of our building.

"It's a tan, Bruce."

"No, I think you'll find that it's a glow," he answered smugly.

He was still my boss, I reminded myself. "Okay, it's a glow."

"That's right. You're glowing for me!"

While I'm disgusted that Bruce thinks I'm glowing for him, it seems to have temporarily appeased him about moving our non-relationship forward, to a decidedly more intimate and disgusting level. I decided to let him believe whatever he pleased. It was simpler.

"By the way, I've got good news for you, he added.

"What's that?"

"Ryan stopped by and said he was pleased with the way his career is going and he's going to stick with us until at least the new year, oh and he said something about dropping the custody suit."

"He's what?" I said hardly believing my good fortune.

"He's sticking around. Great news. Good job."

"Never mind that. What about the custody suit? Tell me everything he said."

"Something about if word got out, it could harm his upward climb. Make him seem less sympathetic, you know."

Typical. He wasn't thinking about me or the boys, just his career. "Yeah, I see his point."

"He also said something about the boys not fitting into

his new lifestyle," Bruce added. "Listen, I'll see you around," he said and gave me a squeeze and a kiss on the cheek.

I was too shocked by Ryan's comment to be shocked by Bruce's action. He didn't think the boys would fit into his lifestyle. I couldn't believe that even Ryan would turn his back on his family. And with the thought of family, came another terrifying reality. Tonight was the night of my mother's weekly get-together.

Chapter 17

Melissa was always the prompt one and now with her already living at my parents, try as I might, I couldn't get there on time. Something about scheduled parental scrutiny caused me to procrastinate. Although thankfully, since Melissa's near miss, they had become much more forgiving and accepting. In fact, it was almost as if my parents were determined to let me live my life, mistakes and all, without offering any meddlesome advice.

Normally, when I would call to check in they'd ask what I was up to and then proceed to tell me what I should be doing instead. This had all changed and now I felt as if I was checking up on them. Perhaps it was reverse psychology, but lately I was the one doing the chasing. I called for only the second time and didn't particularly care for the lack of parental interest. Despite covering the mouthpiece, I could hear Dad shout, "It's April...again." I noticed that lately that nagging little adverb kept appearing after my name. I was beginning to think of it as part of me. Perhaps I would capitalize the "A" and use it as my new surname for when the divorce became final. My identity would no longer be in turmoil and I could pretend nothing has changed. "Again" had possibilities. My family was familiar with it. Easy to make sense of over the phone, which is important when making reservations. It even had a kind of rebirth quality to it. I could consider the misery I was going through was actually a religious awakening, meant to make me stronger.

Mom came on the phone, jarring me from my thoughts. "April darling, where are you? We're nearly ready to sit down."

"I'm on the San Diego Freeway. Stuck in traffic."

"Well do hurry, I've just discovered that Ian has earrings."

The connection with mom disintegrated into static and I was left to contemplate whether Melissa's beau had come bearing gifts or was blessed with additional body cavities.

***

Apparently, Melissa was growing tired of mom's constant worrying about her and wanted to move back in with me, but because mom had good reason to worry, this had to be handled with diplomacy. And in that very word, Melissa and Ian found the answer.

"Mom, did you know that Ian is planning on studying political science?"

"Oh, that's wonderful." Mom beamed at me. But her smile quickly froze into surprise when Ian took off first his leather jacket followed by his shirt to reveal an ample number of tattoos.

Ian was not your everyday tattoo-wearing bloke. His skin pictures included a pig, a canary, and the globe. It didn't take Mom but a minute to tell him that "our family comes dressed for dinner."

"Bear with me," Ian said, "these are political expressions. This will help you know me."

Melissa played diplomat by pointing out that Ian was wearing his pants. Ian further explained that his tattoos represented themes of government or society tyranny as discussed in American literature. The pig was one of the elite class of George Orwell's "Animal Farm;" the canary came from Maya Angelou's "I Know Why the Caged Bird Sings;" and, the globe was a symbol of Aldous Huxley's "Brave New World."

"I really respect that Ian is such a free-thinker," Melissa declared proudly while wrapping an arm around his neck.

"Nice earrings," I said and pointed at his lobes.

Dad looked up momentarily from his soup. I have to admit, there isn't much that will get my father agitated, especially if he's eating a meal. I have seen him angry over taxes and political battles, but even those emotions can be diminished by a tender filet.

"How nice, indeed," Mom commented, trying her best to recover from the last round. "One in each ear."

"Pass the pepper, please," Dad requested.

"Why should it be different for men?" Ian asked.

Bait taken. "Well, it just is," mom replied, and intercepted the pepper.

"That is just another attitude handed down by society and expected to be accepted by the masses."

"Mom, this is a great meal. Let's make sure and do this every weekend," Melissa said pleasantly. She and Ian shared a conspiratorial smile, and I had to stifle a giggle.

"Excuse me? The pepper?" Dad reminded.

Ian continued while Mom gripped the neck of the pepper mill. "Whether we're discussing the Orwellian messages of my chest," he said placing a hand on his breast, "or other physical acts of rebellion, the point is the same."

"Oh, and what's that, Ian," I urged, deciding to help their cause. It might have taken some getting used to having Melissa around my place at first, but I had grown used to her company, and in spite of this show, Ian was a good guy and I missed both their company.

"We're still battling equality!" Ian's voice rose. "The race issue doesn't die. Women don't get equal pay in the workplace."

"I think the only proper answer must be a completely nude society," Melissa said in between bites.

"You're absolutely right," Ian agreed. "Men's suits with those silk ties should be avoided at all costs."

"They really do only serve to show how men are strangled into accepting classist and sexist roles," I added.

Mom looked at the three of us as if we were all losing our minds and she had lost the battle.

"Fine! Eat nude, what do I care?" my father roared. "Just pass the damn pepper." And then, in his every day, gentle voice he explained, "My steak's getting cold."

For a split second I wonder if we may have taken this too far.

I IMAGINE MY ENTIRE FAMILY EATING DINNER IN THE NUDE. Yet, that's not the strange or uncomfortable part. The most awkward feeling comes when I realize that none of us think anything of this new practice.

Melissa is only concerned that the beets she spilled on her lap might stain. Mom, who has always had a remedy for everything, insists that a paste of baking soda and water will fade it.

Dad has resorted to reading the paper at dinner, using it as a cover, so there may be hope that he is uncomfortable with the concept.

I'm worried about being told off by Mom that I'm resting my breasts on the table again.

I REVIVE IN TIME TO SEE MELISSA HELP IAN RETRIEVE HIS shirt and jacket once more. I swear Mom glanced under the table to make sure his pants were still on. God knows what her reaction would have been if they weren't. The National Anthem would have made a nice conclusion to his whole equality speech. Ian would be forced to stand up, complete with a built-in flagpole. On second thought, he would have probably argued that our Founding Fathers were actually the first "old boys" network and refused.

Yet with the exception of the tattoos, earrings, and nudist tendencies, Melissa hadn't done half bad with Ian. Mom had to admit that he was a stand-up guy to stay by her side considering he was originally told she was pregnant with some other guy's baby. After dinner, Ian whipped up a batch of bananas foster for our dessert. Mom and Dad agreed that Melissa seemed healthy and ready to move out, and I agreed that the best place would be my place. It seemed like the perfect end to a great evening until Mom and Dad turned their attention to me and inquired politely about the latest with Ryan.

I tried desperately to swallow a mouthful of vanilla ice cream, but I only succeed in getting a slurpie burn and hearing my mother utter, "April, your father wants to say something to you."

"April, your mother and I have been thinking that..."

"That it might be nice for you to move back in for awhile," Mom blurted out. I think she was even beaming.

"What?! You just said that Melissa would be moving back with me!"

Dad started speaking slowly, as if I were a five-year-old.

"We know what we said aloud, but maybe it's better if you two just, you know, swap locales for awhile. After all, Melissa has Ian and you're..."

Mom finished his thought. "You're alone, dear. This will be temporary, just until you work things out. You look so thin," she explained before issuing the next flurry of questions. "Have you been eating? Ryan was such a good cook. What are you doing now?"

I could look at the upside of the conversation and be pleased that she had finally accepted the fate that I only recently accepted myself. That would be too mature.

"Mom, I don't want to move home. It would disturb the boys. They would be too confused," I reasoned. "Thanks, but I'm fine."

"Oh, of course, darling." She hissed at my dad, "Get it; give it to her."

"Here honey. We want you to have this, for emergencies," he said and handed me a Visa card. I hadn't had one of their credit cards since college.

"Dad, I don't need this. I'm an adult," I insisted, shoveling ice cream into my mouth.

"Of course, honey. It's like I said, just...in case."

I hesitated before taking the card. It was, as they said, in case. In case, Bruce cornered me in the kitchen and I accidentally threatened him with a butter knife resulting in my being fired. In case, I was put in jail and had to purchase large quantities of peanut brittle over the Internet to bribe the prison guards. In case, I regained my sanity and wanted to take a year off from work to write my memoirs.

I reached for the card feeling more like a loser than I had yesterday, if that was indeed possible.

MELISSA AND IAN DECIDED TO GO OUT FOR A DRINK after dinner. Now that she was no longer "pregnant" they were enjoying staying out late. I was too exhausted to join them and was determined to finally put the last of Ryan's belongings into boxes.

The packing was monotonous and I inadvertently found my thoughts wandering into the areas of mildly kooky, borderline psychosis, and everyday ridiculous. The worries flowed as follows:

I would never find a man as right for me as my Gay husband.

I would realize that my mother was right--about everything.

I would accept her offer, and move back home--indefinitely.

The only thought that brought me a confused sort of pleasure was the realization that as long as I kept the Visa, I could be dubbed an immature adult child and avoid the danger of becoming a responsible spinster. I put the plastic safely in my wallet and moved toward the answering machine, glowing with the number "five."

"April, this thing with Leandra has got to end," Ryan's voice said with an edge. "She's driving me nuts. Don't think that the sudden media blitz has saved your firm my account. Find me a new date for the Flamingo awards."

Asshole.

"Hi, April, it's Leandra. "Listen, I really appreciate your company buying me a new dress for the Flamingos, but it's going to look positively schleppy if I don't get some shoes to go with it. Oh, and a facial and massage would probably do me good, too. I'm sure Ryan won't mind the extra charges. I am his girlfriend, after all. Tootles."

Sap.

"Hey, Ape," it's me (Jessica calling). Listen, I'm sorry

about the whole Jean-Paul fiasco, but it could have been worse. You could have been attracted to him! Ha ha."

Amusing.

"Hello, this is Terence, uh the guy you rear-ended the other day. Listen, I haven't heard from you and I've got the quote on the bumper. It's a bit more than I expected and while you do owe me the payment, maybe we can work out something."

Interesting.

"April? This is Dr. Brent Emerson...uh, the veterinarian. (Oh my God! Like I could forget!) I just wanted to make sure that Buster was doing better after his overindulgence. Call if you need anything at all."

Sweet!

Chapter 18

"He said '*anything at all*'?" Jessica said with emphasis. "You totally know what that means."

"Hold on." I got up to close my office door and then returned to my phone call. "So, I'm not imagining it?"

"No. He likes you. You should go for it, especially since nobody else seems to float your boat."

"I also got a call from the guy I hit with my car."

"You ran over someone with your car?"

"No, the fender bender."

"Oh right. Anyway, that's boring. About the doctor..."

Jessica was right. A doctor! "I'll find a reason to call him. Listen, I have to get back to work. Call you later."

The Gods must have been smiling because not only was I being given the perfect reason to hit on the gorgeous Dr. Emerson, the office was actually quiet. For the time being, Josh and Bebe were behaving professionally. Bebe was organizing media calendars from each of the major entertainment publications, and Josh was watching footage from a recent broadcast. I might even be able to get past Bruce's office for a coffee without being noticed. I crept past his office only to find he wasn't inside. With confidence, I marched down the hall, hopeful that he was at an off-site meeting and my day would be harassment free. That's when the familiar sound reached me. Jane Fonda's command to stretch deeper. Bruce had obviously come looking for me while I was trying to avoid him and was now in my office with his Jane Fonda video. This could only mean he planned to spend an extended visit in my wing of the building.

"I see," he said into my phone while waving hello and placing his bare feet on my desk. "Well, April will be right on it." He mouthed "Ryan" while pointing at the phone. I frantically shook my head back and forth while mouthing back "I'm not in!"

"Sure, she's right here," he answered back.

I shook my head fiercely.

"Oh, sorry, Ryan. That was Bebe coming in," Bruce lamely recovered and then pointed toward his empty coffee cup.

Lazy lemming!

"Yup, right. Sure thing, Ryan," Bruce said before returning the phone to its cradle and his feet to the floor.

"Can't believe you were ever married to that guy," Bruce declared.

"Me either." For the first time I agreed with Bruce.

"You need someone more dependable," he continued.

Bruce was batting a thousand.

"I know just the guy!" he said and extended his arms to me.

Still delusional.

"April, let's go to lunch."

"It's only 9:30."

"Breakfast then."

"Can't Bruce."

"Why?"

Think. Think. Think. "New client."

"Really? Who is it?"

I answered with the obvious name -- the only one that was on my mind. "Dr. Brent Emerson!"

AS ANY WORKING, SINGLE PARENT KNOWS, FINDING quality time to spend with the children isn't easy. Dating can be looked down upon, especially if it means spending less time with the kids. What I needed was a way to make my personal life more personal -- somehow take care of my boys while dating. I needed a social club cum day care center. Someplace where the boys would be stimulated during the day while I was at work, so that when I returned home, they would be happy with quiet time. Hence, the doggie day care center was born. It was brilliant. A new account for the firm. A new boyfriend for me! I left the office, thankfully, without Bruce in tow, to grab a coffee and brainstorm.

As I sipped my Starbuck's café latté, the one with a touch of vanilla added to combat my healthy tendency to order non-fat milk, I thought about a campaign to pitch to Dr. Emerson while people watching for inspiration. Mothers explained to their children that no, they could not taste the coffee or they would remain four-feet-tall; teens poured packet after packet of sugar into their mud to dilute the taste and thus, impress their dates with their new and mature coffee-drinking habit; business people rushed; and out-of-work types meandered.

I was trying to figure out how to approach Dr. Emerson again when someone came up behind me, covered my eyes and said, "Guess who?" with way too much enthusiasm. First off, I hate when men do this, even those that I rather like. Women wouldn't dare play this stupid game because it smears mascara. "I can't guess," I said with obvious annoyance.

"It's Peter!"

Jessica's set-ups not only had the power to give me nightmares, but now were being reincarnated into my waking hours. I smiled a passive greeting and looked at the door, wondering if I could make a break for it. He sat down before I could move and to my horror he was drinking a grande cappuccino, nearly twice the size of my demure, café latté. If I had to sit here until he finished, it would take half the afternoon. I prayed he had a weak bladder and would soon excuse himself.

I RETURNED TO MY OFFICE TO LEARN THAT JESSICA HAD just called and was on hold. "Why did you tell Peter that you regularly pee on my back lawn?" she demanded.

"Who put a bee up your bottom?"

"Peter was not that bad, you know. He could've had 'it' qualities."

"He's not 'it.' I could have told him I pee on your *front* lawn," I said sheepishly. "Wouldn't that have been worse? The neighbors might see."

"No, the neighbors would not see because you don't do such things. You only pretend to do these things. Why?"

"He trapped me at Starbucks. I was praying that he would have to excuse himself, like for the restroom or something, but he never did. I was getting ready to visit my veterinarian. I needed the time alone to prepare."

"So you tell him that you urinate in public?"

I hated being interrogated. "It worked, didn't it?"

"Frankly, I'm not sure it did."

"What do you mean?" I asked worriedly.

"Obviously, Peter called to tell me about his strange encounter with you."

"Go on," I urged.

"He admitted that he was taken aback by your story, but then kept talking about how kinky you must be."

"Just what I need. Thank goodness I didn't use my reserve story."

"Which is?" she asked.

"That I sneak into friends' bedrooms to masturbate while dinner parties are being held."

"Oh April, we've talked about this. You should strive for normalcy, not lunacy."

I ignored her misplaced advice and asked if she wanted to hear about my precious vet.

WHEN THE RECEPTIONIST TOLD ME IT WAS OUR TURN, my heart leapt into my throat and Louie nearly jumped out of his fur. I needed a reason to visit. I couldn't just spring a campaign idea on someone who wasn't looking for a publicist. I'd have to lure him in so I devised a story that Louie had developed a neuroses about going outdoors, sort of agoraphobia for dogs. Quite a serious problem if you consider the bathroom consequences.

I knew Louie would play the part well. He only has to come within a block of the vet's office before he twitches and shakes. Buster would have given the game away. He loves any new place, any chance for a car ride. Worst, his excitement is contagious and always manages to calm Louie down. It was a slight doggie deception, but I was sure when I brought home a potential suitor as qualified to be their surrogate daddy as my vet, they would agree it was worth the momentary anxiety.

Louie and I were called into the same room as the night we were there with Ryan. He seemed to recognize the place and to my dismay, sat down calmly and waited.

"No, you have to pace; make your eyes dart back and forth; do something," I begged. Louie simply stared at me. I was attempting to smear Vaseline on his forehead to replicate the aftermath of his breaking out into a sweat when the vet came in.

"Bad fur day?" he asked, taking in my activities.

I nearly swallowed my own tongue trying to speak. I decided that changing the subject would be the best tact. "Louie just hasn't been himself lately," I began. "It must be depression. He won't play, barely eats..." I stopped short because to my horror Louie had found a box of dog biscuits behind the counter and was contentedly munching.

Dr. Emerson was as gorgeous today as the day Buster overindulged in cookies. He patted Louie's head who gave an appreciative wag in response. "Must be a condition of the family," he said with a smile.

I wanted to die. Was he saying that I overate too? I spent half an hour finding the right outfit that made my legs look a little longer and my thighs a little thinner. I thought I had pulled it off too.

He must have noticed that I was looking for a crack in the floor to disappear into. "I meant the furry portion of the family. Their habits certainly must not have been inherited from their mummy."

He was so sweet!

He proceeded to poke and prod Louie, until he succumbed to a more comfortable position, back against the tiled floor, feet in the air. I was ready to do the same.

"He's really taken to you," I said leaning down to be closer to the two of them.

"He seems fine. Perhaps, he's just experiencing some stress. Have there been any changes at home?"

Oh my God. I didn't want my first real conversation to include the divorce talk. The last time I was here, Ryan was with us. But if I didn't say anything, he would think we were still a couple. I quickly calculated which would be worse, to admit to the divorce, or to dream up a story about Ryan running off to be in the circus. Quick reflection made me realize that both were the same story, and frankly, it didn't matter.

"I, Louie's dad, uh..." I hated this! "We're in the midst of a divorce," I finally said.

"Oh, I'm sorry."

"I guess it has caused some confusion for Louie," I admitted. "He and Buster are both going through some adjustments, but it seems to be better when they get out of the house. You know, a change of scenery and all."

He nodded and brushed my arm. He brushed my arm! Was it accidental or premeditated? Sympathy brush or I'm interested touch? "Have you been exposed to ringworm?"

Not your usual pick-up line. "Well, he does go to the dog park. I guess you never know what you can catch there."

"Actually, Louie checks out alright, but I better give you the once over."

"BRUCE, JOSH, WE HAVE A NEW CLIENT," I BEAMED. "DR. Brent Emerson is a highly respected veterinarian. He wants to get national exposure for his practice and his new doggie play group.

"Doggie play group?" Josh asked. "Who came up with this scheme?"

"What's wrong with it," I asked, feeling insecure.

"Nothing. It's brilliant! Genius. The press will be all over it," Josh said and gave a little skip before leaving the room.

"You did it," Bruce said. "Let's celebrate the new account. My office or yours?"

"Bruce!" I said with disgust.

"What's wrong with a little congratulatory..." he said searching for a word I know I didn't want to hear.

The idea of losing my job just as I was finally going to have a chance to get to know Dr. Emerson was not appealing. And while Bruce was even less appealing, he was the owner of a rather peculiar firm, which I owed my job to. "Bruce, how 'bout a hand massage. It's all the rage in Europe," I lied. It was the only way to pacify him.

"Does it end with the hand?" he asked.

"Yes, but it's very sensual," I assured him and reached for my ringworm cream.

Chapter 19

Melissa was beginning to remind me more of my mother. She had developed an innate talent for being over-protective, which coming from my baby sister, who was just starting to get back on her own two feet, frankly seemed a bit misplaced.

"I thought you would be happy. I've got a sort of date and I'm happy," I said.

"Exactly. This isn't a real date. You're merely going for him because of your idea of what makes for a good partner. I'm worried about you. You're still living life through the dogs. It's the strangest case of needing to cut the umbilical cord that I've ever witnessed."

"There's nothing strange about it. Consider it a common interest, or something. He's a vet," I explained. "He's gorgeous. Louie and Buster love him. Josh will get off my case for at least a week or so, since I'm bringing in a new account."

"So what's next?" she goaded.

"Make him love me, too. What else?"

"At least Mom will stop crying about the dissolution of

your marriage. Didn't she always want you to marry a doctor?"

"You see?" I gleamed, "It's perfect. I only have one problem."

"Yes?" she questioned.

"I sort of accepted a date with Steven, the guy from the beach, and I'm not in the mood anymore for a new date experience. Can you go in my place?"

"You're forgetting that I'm in a committed relationship now."

"What if I get Ian to say it's okay?" I begged.

"No way. Besides, dating isn't that bad. It's like a litmus test for what Mr. Right should be. If you have a bad time with Steven, then you can tell yourself that there's even more potential with your vet. If it's a good date, then you need to reevaluate your desire to hook up with someone else."

I thought for a minute and couldn't come up with a reasonable comeback. "Anything else?"

"Yeah, even if the date is bad, you still get free food," she reasoned.

———

STEVEN, A.K.A. SURFER BOY, SUGGESTED STAYING CLOSE to his "office," the beach, so we decided to meet at Duke's Restaurant in Malibu. Steven had one thing going for him, the most beautiful eyes I had ever seen. Unfortunately, that's all he had going for him. After the effect of staring into his eyes wore off, I tried to focus on his plan to make it big.

Steven was a small-town boy from the Midwest who had watched the same beach movies growing up as I had. A star football player in high school, he attracted the attention of college recruiters and earned himself a scholarship and a ticket to sunny, Southern California.

"Just didn't have it in me," Steven said with a shrug.

"How could you let an opportunity like that just slip away?" I asked, wondering if perhaps, there was still a chance for him to go back and learn to speak in complete sentences.

"Wasn't ever college material...good at the game, but not the studying part. Don't get me wrong, there was plenty of stuff about college that was cool. But all those tests and classes...that was as bad as high school."

"That's kind of the point."

"What do you mean?"

"It's kind of tough to get what you want without putting in effort."

"I agree. That's why I'm down at the beach almost every day. I've got to stay close to where the action is. I'm doing some R&D right now." He leaned over the table, cocked his head, and said, "That stands for research and development."

"Ahh," I said smiling and nodding and wondering when I would come to my senses.

"You see, Allison,"

"April."

"Huh?"

"My name is April."

"Oh sorry, I meet so many people each day it's hard to keep all the names straight. That's what I was getting around to telling you, April," he said flashing his baby blues. "I'm out there interviewing people like me, the boys on the boards, to find out what makes them stick."

"You mean tick?"

"No baby, stick, stick to the board. You know, for my wax. It's got to be something unique. I want the label to read, "Special Formula," or something like that, make it sound like it was created in a laboratory. Know what I mean? Forget that 'sex wax' brand. That was an eighties kind of product. Now we're into family values. Much better that I stick to laboratories. That's where the test tube families are born. Right?"

"Sure," I said simply, letting him have the floor.

"There's no telling how far it can go. I think after my product catches on I can hit the talk show circuit. Maybe even meet Oprah and be the next celebrity chef to introduce a diet to her."

"Steven, you have to be a chef, to be a celebrity chef."

"Well, that'll come," he said with a toothy grin. I had to admit, he was so darn cute, but that shouldn't have been enough reason to have accepted this date. My ability to find the right man was so obviously impaired.

Something resting on Steven's shoulder caught my eye. "What's that?"

"What?" he asked between mouthfuls of Ono, Steven's favorite fish he informed me, not because of the taste, but because he liked saying its name and could easily spell it.

"That," I said pointing.

He adjusted himself, "Just a strap."

"What's it doing on your shoulder?"

"It could be worse," he laughed.

I thought for a moment, decided a strap attached to a garter belt was indeed kinkier than one coming off his shoulder, but still relished the end of the evening now knowing he was not only naive, but also strange as well as stupid. Hardly the perfect man to bring home to mother. I could only imagine what Melissa would say about the strap in light of what mom put Ian through due to his politically correct tattoos. That was a meeting that would never happen.

The waitress came with the check, and asked if we wanted dessert before she left it behind. Steven said a quick no for both of us. I couldn't help feeling sorry for Steven, and decided to pay my own way.

Buster and Louie were waiting up for me, each taking turns shaking Mr. Noisy. The sound of Mr. Noisy's squeaking and the dogs clickity clack nails on the wood floors echoed in the empty entryway, but rather than feel lonely, for the first time in months I felt hopeful. Melissa was right. I had to go through a series of bad dates to see the potential of the good one in front of me. I got ready for bed and actually looked forward to getting to work tomorrow where I could start a plan for Dr. Emerson's campaign.

Chapter 20

"April, I'm plum tired of root vegetables," Bebe complained.

"It's a temporary assignment," I assured her. "Here," I said, handing her another stack of cookbooks. "We have to find some edible rutabaga recipes before our next meeting with Farmer Joe. Just be happy we don't have to do a taste test."

The phone provided a temporary reprieve. "April, line two. It's a Doctor Emerson. "You sick?" asked Bebe with more curiosity than concern.

"I'm fine," I said feeling suddenly light-headed, and then answered the phone in my sexiest business voice.

"April, how are you?" my dream doctor said cheerily.

"Fine...Brent." It was the first time I had tested out his name. Prior, it had always been Dr. Emerson, but I was determined to take our professional relationship to a decidedly more personal level.

"Good. Listen, I've got a little problem with this afternoon," he began.

No. No. No. He cannot cancel our meeting. I had the

proposal together and Buster and Louie were ready to be his first enrollees in the doggie play group. I crossed my fingers and legs, cradled the phone in my neck and then crossed my arms into yoga eagle pose too. Bebe walked by my desk and handed me a cold washcloth. "Thought you could use this," she whispered. I waved her off frantically, afraid that my wonderful doctor could see my distress.

"I've got an appointment that had to reschedule, so could you stop by, say at two o'clock? I'd rather have lunch with you, but I've got no choice."

Relief. I let out a bigger sigh than if I had just had the most awesome orgasm in the world.

"April?" he asked.

"Sorry about that. Yes, that's okay. I'll see you then."

I hung up the phone and looked at the clock. Eleven o'clock. Three more hours. I suddenly panicked. "Bebe, what are you doing at lunch?" I must be insane.

"Nothing important? Do you need something," she asked with clipboard in hand. I looked at her outfit: tight grey sweater, short black skirt, long black socks that came up to her thighs and revealed a two-inch patch of skin, which peeked out between the lace tops of the stockings and the bottom of her mini. No wonder Josh couldn't keep his mind on business. "Yeah, I need your help in picking a new outfit."

"Ooh, my type of assignment," she replied giddily.

I ARRIVED AT BRENT'S OFFICE WEARING SOMETHING decidedly more sexy than when I left the house that morning. Bruce would have given me a new employment contract on the spot, had he seen me in my new black pencil skirt with black high-heeled boots and fitted top. As I walked into Brent's office, I felt giddy.

"Do you have an appointment?" asked Snooty Receptionist.

"Yes, I do." She wouldn't intimidate me.

"And your dog's name?"

"They're at home. The appointment's for me."

"Oh, and what seems to be the trouble?" she asked sarcastically.

I'm sure she was being nosy, because last time I checked, Dr. Emerson was still a veterinarian. "Nothing's wrong. Could you tell him I'm here."

"Of course. Who are you?"

She knew my name. It was just her way of having power over me. I decided to play it up, and simply handed her my card. Make it look professional and all that. No point in letting on that I was here because I hoped to get the good doctor in my pants.

"And you say you have an appointment?"

"Yes! I have an appointment."

"Well, he's not quite ready for you. Do you care to wait?" she said snippily.

"How do you know? You haven't even told him I'm here. Maybe you could check."

"He's busy."

"It's lunch time and you're closed. There isn't a dog or cat around!" I screamed.

Then the lunatic really confused me. She smiled sweetly and said, "You know, you're probably right. Why don't you just pop your head into the first room on the right. That is, if he's expecting you."

"Of course he is," I said huffily and walked through the reception area. I proudly marched down the hall, found the door, and opened it. No dog inside, just Ryan sitting on the examining table having a chat with my doctor!

Why was Ryan with my doctor? I was taking care of the boys. He didn't even have a hamster! What's more, I recognized that look in his eyes. It was the same one he used to use on me. The one he flashed at the camera. The look that made women think he was God's gift to them. They're all foolish idiots. He wasn't a gift from anyone, and he offered a terrible return policy. But the worst part about this scene was the look on Brent's face. I had seen that look plenty of times...on Leandra's face, in Matthew's eyes...I wanted to scream, "Don't fall for him, Brent. He'll dump you, too!" Unfortunately, I couldn't be so sure that was true.

"What are you doing here?" I blurted out.

"Hello to you, April," he replied calmly. I hated when he did that, but remembered to keep my poise in front of Brent.

"Hello, Ryan. Of all the places, I never expected to run into you here."

Brent to the rescue: "April, we were just talking about you."

I feared the worst. "Oh?"

"I was telling Ryan about the campaign you're launching for me. He's been kind enough to offer me some voice lessons. You know, for all those upcoming interviews."

"How kind," I grimaced. "Well, speaking of the campaign," I hinted, feeling like I'd rather run than stay for lunch. My sexy skirt was now clinging suspiciously around my thighs. I felt that my cleavage looked saggy, if that was indeed possible. Worst, I feared that Ryan was having a better hair day than myself.

"Yeah Brent, you and April better get at it. We can

continue this later. I'll meet you at your office in an hour. That should give you two enough time," he said and gave my doctor a buddy-like punch in the arm. Hah! Male bonding arm punches! My physical contact involved applying ringworm cream. I imagined whether Brent would be impressed by a right-hook to Ryan's jaw.

THE PRISTINE, TILED FLOOR OF BRENT'S EXAMINATION ROOM was gone and in its place was a small wading pool filled with warm oil. Ryan was already in the pool, looking seductively slimy. An oxymoron if I had ever heard of one, but still, the look worked.

He taunted me, "Afraid of what might lurk underneath," he said while doing the breast stroke with his strong arms.

"Not a chance," I countered.

"Come on in, then. The oil's lovely."

I wasn't sure about the whole scene. Ryan in a tub of oil, wearing only a teeny brief. Myself, feeling highly conspicuous in a thong bikini. I've no idea how the thing got in my wardrobe, let alone on my body.

Brent was watching us. He leaned casually against the door of the examining room, as if daring me to walk out. "Go on, April. Let's see a real media-worthy event."

What could I do? Once again, I tested the oil by sticking in my big toe, carefully. It was futile. Ryan grabbed my calf and yanked. I fell into the pool causing my bikini thong to edge up even higher between my cheeks, if that was possible. My right breast started to protrude from the triangular top that was holding it captive. Ryan saw what was happening and undid the tie from behind my neck while my hands were busy trying to put myself back in place. My efforts were lost as the top came falling down to my waist. Brent whistled from the doorway.

I appeared awkward in my half-dressed condition, carrying with me the drowned rat look due to oil seepage into my hair. I glared at

Ryan, who flashed his most innocent smile. With one move, I removed my top, fished under the oil and grabbed for Ryan's briefs. Triumphant, I found the bit of material and pulled them off, throwing them striptease style to where Brent was standing.

The show continued as I dove through the oil and slicked back my hair in a sexy, French twist, and stared at Ryan. "Give me your best shot," I glowered. He reached around my head with his right arm, pulling me in closer until our lips met. My tongue darted into his mouth and my hands reached down beneath the oil.

My thoughts were lost with the comforting return of Ryan's hands, yet not so far that I didn't notice that Brent had also climbed into the pool. He stood in the corner, fully-clothed, in a business suit and tie, but watching our every move. "Don't just stand there," Ryan called after him. Although Ryan's back was to Brent, he must have sensed his presence. Brent obliged the request and came closer. Ryan and I had stopped kissing long enough to watch Brent peel off his clothes, which I must admit was no easy task. We waited to see who he would approach first.

MY TIME WITH BRENT FLEW PAST AND I REALIZED THAT this was a real guy, someone who was responsible, kind and who I hoped saw something in me besides a way to increase his public worth, but I couldn't be sure. When I returned to my office, Ryan was waiting in the conference room.

"So, how'd your meeting go?" he asked.

"None of your business," I said, perhaps too hastily.

"Hmm, trouble with a client--how unusual," he replied sarcastically.

"Speaking of clients, as your publicist I advise you to end your relationship with Brent."

He rolled his eyes and answered, "That sounds like the words of a jealous woman, not a professional."

"My relationship with Brent is professional."

"Bet you wish it wasn't," he said like a child.

"Listen to you. You're so misguided. Besides, I thought you were with Matthew?"

Ryan stuck to his story, "Sure am. Like I said, I'm just Brent's voice coach."

"I don't buy it. Why are you hitting on my veterinarian?"

"He's Buster and Louie's vet."

"So stay away. I can take Buster and Louie to the vet. You don't need to offer your services to me or Brent."

Ryan looked at me smugly. "April, I wasn't going to tell you this, but I can see that I have no choice. Brent called me."

Chapter 21

"He's after my vet," I huffed hysterically at Jessica during our power walk session. I was hyper-ventilating, more likely from my current mental state than the aerobic activity.

"I'd let him have the vet. Who needs someone tracking cat hair and dog smells into their home?"

"He smells clean," I insisted. "Like antiseptic."

"That's appealing," she replied. "Turn him over."

"Ryan will mess up his career."

"Oh, I see, you only have his best interest at heart?"

"His and mine," I said honestly. "Brent is my ideal man; he loves animals."

"That's your criteria? Peter has a goldfish."

"You're still going on about Peter. Peter is a boring freak," I explained patiently, "And fish don't count as cuddly animals."

"April, maybe you should just let life take its course. Do your job, but if Ryan doesn't listen and your vet prefers him over you, let it be. Besides, I can't imagine why you would consider a man who might be considering your ex."

"It's not like that. Ryan is very convincing. His demographic polls say that he is as appealing to men as women and I feel like he's trying to prove that."

"By stealing your potential date? There has to be some interest on the part of your vet for Ryan to have a chance," Jessica explained patiently. "April, for me, why don't you try, just for a day, to lead a normal life."

"I just don't know how" I said defeatedly.

"Honey," she said giving me a hug. "It's okay. In truth, peculiarity kind of works for you."

ARIES: RELATIONS FORM NEW RELATIONS; TAKE COMFORT IN the continuum of change. What to make of that? It seemed benign enough to let it stand alone without interference from any of the other signs. What with the planets pulling this way and that, I was tempted to leave fate alone. I was hoping that the "relations" referred to Ryan, and he was going to settle down with Matthew and leave Brent to me. Maybe this was God's plan to make me accept his relationship with Matthew, even if dumping Leandra was bad for his career and the fact that what's bad for his career ends up costing me mine. Keeping up with the love life of my ex along with his string of ex girlfriends and boyfriends was quite simply -- exhausting.

I set down the paper and put on my best, dress-for-success outfit. Pitching the media around-the-clock about the doggie play group had paid off and a news crew was scheduled to make a visit to see the pooches in person. I had called Melissa and Mom, who in turn, had called Aunt Brenda, to tell them that Buster and Louie would be on the six o'clock news.

I was nearly out the door when Aunt Brenda phoned. "Hello Honey, do you have a minute?"

"Actually, I was just out the door. Today's the day for Buster and Louie," I added.

"I know, dear, that's why I'm calling," Brenda continued. "It'll just take a minute and it's extremely important."

"What is it?" I asked worried. "Is Mom okay?"

"She's fine, it's you I'm worried about. Your career could be in jeopardy."

"Mom told you about Bebe!" I said getting worried. "You think she's after my job? I knew this would happen. She's screwing my boss and she'll probably end up with my job instead of being my assistant. Sure, she seems nice and all, but I'm convinced that one morning I'll find them on my desk, going at it from the night before."

"I don't know anything about that, dear," Brenda interrupted. "I just think you should postpone your news conference to seven o'clock."

"Why?"

"Because at six o'clock the news is presented by that woman who left Markie a broken man," she replied. "Honoria Vitale."

"She gave Mark a disease?" I said shocked. Mark was Brenda's son. Melissa and I used to have to play with him when we were little. He was the only boy in the neighborhood who would play dress-up with us. Who would have imagined he would end up the press advisor to the Governor of California?

"Honoria," she repeated.

"Oh. I thought you said..."

"Never mind," she interrupted. "She's an awful woman with an even worse name," Brenda insisted. "She dated Mark long enough to get an interview with the governor and then dumped him the moment it was finished. You don't want that woman introducing your doggie play group. She'll make a mockery of it."

Brenda could be so naive. "Thanks for the warning, but it's not up to me. The assignment and planning editors will determine when the news crew comes out and when the story gets on the air. Frankly, as long as it's on, I'll be happy."

"Oh April, you can be so naive," she said and wished me luck.

WHEN I ARRIVED AT THE OFFICE THE NEXT MORNING, MY desk was completely clean. Ordinarily, this would be a good sign. Today, it was a disaster, and as I saw Josh creeping past my office, I decided to let him know.

"Josh, where have you put Bebe?"

"What's the problem?"

"Nothing has been done!" I screamed only to find that he was trying his best to sneak back down the hall. "Okay, come back." I took a deep breath, closed my eyes, placed my hands in prayer and uttered a single "namaste."

"Better?"

"Much," I admitted. "Now Josh, this...this thing between the two of you...isn't it about time that the attraction has grown old and you're ready to focus on your business again?"

"Nah."

"But Josh, I've had it. I asked her to do the press kits and where are they? You're going to have to do something."

"Maybe a spanking," he said lecherously.

"Stop it!"

"I'm sorry, April. You're right."

"So, you'll take care of it?" I asked suspiciously.

"No. I don't think it's necessary to upset Bebe. She had a late night."

Gross. I didn't want to hear any more. "What am I going to do?"

"I'll help you. It'll be just like the old days when I actually had to do work -- I mean, that sort of work."

As I collated, Josh stuffed. Bebe arrived in time to help, sort of.

"Good you're here," I said.

"Right on schedule, Pookie," she said to Josh. I wanted to vomit. Josh immediately got up from his chair and lay down on the floor.

"Oh, no. Not in here. I'll be sick," I threatened.

"Don't worry, April. I use completely natural, odorless products," Bebe reported and got down next to Josh.

"What about the press kits?" I asked feebly, trying to stop what was about to begin.

"Nearly finished," Josh reported. "You'll be fine, April. Why don't you take a seat and we'll run through the press conference as Bebe gets on with her work." He motioned to Bebe, "That's right, darling. You can get started," he said and started to remove his shoes.

"Wait!" I shouted. "This is obscene!"

Josh and Bebe stared at me.

"You okay, April?" Bebe asked.

"I always thought I had rather nice feet," Josh declared.

From his supine position on the conference room floor, Josh started to spew advice and Bebe proceeded to give him a pedicure, part of her new work assignment, they informed me. "Now then, April," Josh started. "Try to steer the camera crew away from the vet and onto the dogs."

"Why? Brent is the client," I answered.

"Yes, but people like cute, furry things. Is Brent furry?"

"Not that I'm aware of," I answered.

"Well then. Dogs it is. If we're lucky, the news people will have a busy day and they won't even run the story as part of the line-up."

"What?" I exclaimed.

"April, you've been hanging around our clients too much. They've polluted your mind, probably convinced you that they really deserve to be on the six o'clock news."

"Don't they?" I asked weakly.

"Well, they've paid us enough, but that's not the point. If you get that camera crew to take lots of nice doggie shots, we can then suggest they run them at the end of the broadcast, over the credits. It's a much longer play time and in the end, your client will be happier. More play, more pay!"

"And that makes you happy," I said glumly.

"Cheer up. It pays your bills too," he added and turned over for his back rub.

I DROVE TO BRENT'S OFFICE WITH BUSTER AND LOUIE IN the back seat and repeated Josh's mantra. "To keep the client happy, find a baby in a nappy." Josh's way of saying that clients don't know what's good for them. They think they'll be happy plastered over the news, but in reality, they'll get more business with a simple shot of a baby. I hoped Buster and Louie would do the trick, and Brent wouldn't be too unhappy. But worse than arriving at my office to the press kits not being compiled was what I found at Brent's office.

I EXPECTED TO FIND HIM FEELING A BIT ANXIOUS AND IN NEED of a gentle touch and a soothing reminder that it was normal to be nervous before a big event. I was supposed to be the one to comfort him. I had planned it for days and my mind knew the scenario by heart.

"How are you?" I would ask.

"Okay, I guess."

"Nervous of a few cameras? A few thousand viewers?" I joked. He just laughed and put his hands up to his temples.

"Let me help," I suggested and without waiting for an answer, I moved toward him. "There, how's that?"

"Much better. I can't think of how I would get through this without you," he said.

"You don't have to say that. Maybe I shouldn't have insisted we try this."

"April, don't be silly. I'll be famous after today and it will all be because of you."

We smiled at each other, declared our love, and kissed! We promised each other that the fame and fortune wouldn't affect our love for each other and that we would marry and have at least four puppies in the next year!

It would have been beautiful...

IF ONLY BRENT HAD READ MY MIND SCRIPT. HE DIDN'T, however, and apparently, neither did Ryan who was holding Brent in his arms.

"Oh my God!" I screamed.

"April!" they answered in unison.

Ryan spoke next. "April, it's not what you think. It's just voice lessons. You know, for the interview," he stammered.

"Interesting tactic. You helping him with his tonsils as well?"

"April, we should talk," Brent interrupted.

"I can't. Remember to tell people how they can find out more about the doggie play group. I see you have the eye contact and voice thing down pat," I said and ran from the room, dragging Buster and Louie with me.

"April, please, just one minute," Brent yelled out.

It all happened so quickly, kind of in the cliché style of a Doris Day movie. One minute I was running from the arms and entanglement of Brent and Ryan, and the next moment, I saw tails and teeth. True, it would have been more romantic to run from one room with two men kissing into another with a man waiting to be kissed, but that just didn't happen.

I left Brent's office and ran with Buster and Louie into the waiting room without the "all clear" signal from the receptionist. What I didn't know was that an agitated German Shepard was waiting for an appointment. I assumed that any dog in the waiting room on this partic- ular day would have been screened for news crews and the doggie play group, but this one, an enormous specimen, slipped past with some excuse of illness.

In one deliberate leap, the Shepard was air bound, her mouth poised for landing on Louie's throat. Buster saw her first and mistook her intentions as kind. He began to shake and shimmy, wagging and wiggling with frenetic energy in an attempt to win her over and start a game. Louie knew the game and started to jump, becoming tangled in the leash. Holding an armful of press kits as well as Buster at my left side and Louie at my right, I became a maypole wrapped in their leashes, until I lost my balance and lay face down on the tiled, waiting room floor, inhaling the scent of animal urine mixed with cleaning solution. The press kits went flying. Fortunately, a handful were flung at the Shepard, which gave her enough of a scare to allow her owner to gain control. And that's when I heard his familiar voice.

"I've left you half a dozen messages."

I pulled myself up to a seating position, gathered my press kits and untangled the dogs' leashes.

"Oh shoot."

The handsome English man from the traffic accident motioned to my skirt. "You're skirt, it's..."

I looked down and saw that my skirt had slid up. I tugged downwards best as I could given the fact that it was far too narrow for my thighs and Louie wasn't helping matters by taunting the Shepherd who appeared to want him as an afternoon snack.

"Thanks. I haven't been trying to avoid your call. I'm just a bit overwhelmed with life at the moment."

"Maybe I can help?"

"But you don't even know me. And, I hit your car."

"I've listened to your voice on answer mail enough times that I feel like I know you. Also, I spoke with your assistant about ten times. She told me some pretty interesting details."

"Really?"

"She's a gem," he laughed. "And, she did say on a few occasions that you were in crisis mode so I figured you didn't need the added stress of taking care of my bumper. Consider us even. Besides, I slammed on the brakes that day."

Wow. I was looking at a real man. A nice honest to goodness good guy who was attractive and kind and didn't even cause my mind to daydream into a different scenario. The one I was living was actually preferable. But as they say, all good things must come to an end, especially as Brent had just come through the door looking for me.

"April, let me explain," he said.

I looked over at English guy sitting before me. "I'm sorry, but I have to go. I'm actually working. I'll try and call you so that we can resolve everything."

"Like I said, you don't have to."

I smiled my goodbye and then followed Brent. The receptionist decided that Buster and Louie were no threat to the cats and allowed us to go to the other side of her desk in the area designated as Feline Waiting. Buster and Louie didn't seem to mind, although I took mild offense to her comment that "due to their emasculated nature they could wait with the kitties."

The four of us sat in a huddle on the bench. On one side of us was a woman with a Persian cat. Following true to the perception that people begin to resemble their animals, (or is it the other way around?) her cat had a runny eye problem and she had a clumpy mascara and droopy black eyeliner look going for her. Across from the Persian sat a woman with two identical Tabby cats. The only difference is that one would meow while the other hissed at the dogs. Louie and Buster looked up at me, ready to leave. The seeds of embarrassment were beginning to settle into their psyche.

"Is Ryan still here?"

"No," Brent said simply.

I just nodded. I never saw Ryan leave. I assumed he snuck through the back with his own tail between his legs.

"I'm sorry," he said.

"Let's just get this over with," I said referring to the press conference.

"I never meant for it to happen. I was interested in you as well," he said feebly.

"Gee, thanks, but you chose him? What has he got that I don't have except a penis?"

"I understand what he's going through...because I feel it too."

"Great. Maybe I should post a warning sign on my back, 'Straight Men Beware. Extreme Risk of Homosexuality Could Develop!'"

"It's not your fault. It has nothing to do with you," he said gently.

I took a deep breath, "I know. Hey, you know what will make me feel better? Seeing us on the six o'clock news. Are you ready?"

"Just have to see to a Shepard. I'll meet you in the play room in fifteen minutes."

"BEBE, CAN YOU TAKE BUSTER AND LOUIE FOR A WALK? Ryan and I have a meeting with Josh and Bruce." I leaned in closer and whispered, "I wouldn't want them to hear us," I explained.

Josh and Bruce were already in the conference room. They knew something was serious because I immediately went to shut off Bruce's Jane Fonda video and on my way back to the table, I grabbed Josh's foot pumice stone from him.

"I called this meeting to simply ask to be removed from Ryan's account. It is going to be impossible to get him positive publicity with his blatant galavanting."

"Galavanting! Listen to you, April. I just want to live my life."

"You don't have a life of your own," I reminded him. "You are an actor. I am your publicist. That means we create the life that the public wants you to have."

"Bruce, Josh," Ryan said hopefully, "explain to April what my account means to your firm. All I want is a life outside the shadows and someone who can handle the media properly. Is that too much to ask for?"

"Well," Bruce started, "I hear the vet chose you over April. While I'm thrilled about this chain of events, I must say that I'm worried how your lover might react. Does Matthew know?"

Before Ryan answered Josh spoke: "Hey, you can't go back to Matthew. If we're not careful the vet might blackmail you in the media."

"You know none of this would be an issue if Ryan had left Brent alone," I stated.

"I was only going for voice lessons," Ryan said. "He approached me."

I was losing my mind because at that moment I only wanted Ryan to remain with the man who stole him away from me. "What about Matthew?"

"He's still in the picture," Ryan replied.

"What about Brent?" I asked.

"April, he's not your type. Trust me," Ryan said evenly.

"What's that supposed to mean?" I asked. "Isn't time that we let Ryan's account go?" I said to Bruce and Josh.

"No!" Bruce and Josh shouted together.

Ryan merely smiled and I wondered if I was destined to chase gay men while running from the peculiar straight ones who inhabited my life.

Chapter 22

"Hurry," I shouted into the kitchen, "they'll be on next."

I had thrown a celebration-cum-sympathy party for myself. The celebration was the fact that the doggie play group had made it on the six o'clock news. The sympathy part was for what was going on in my personal life. Mom shared in my misery when she learned that I probably wouldn't become a doctor's wife.

"Shh," I hissed. "It's on,"

A brassy blonde with too many teeth and an Armani jacket filled the screen. "It seems children's play groups have gone to the dogs," she said coyly.

"What kind of an opening is that?" I asked aloud, my anger seething. "Who is this woman?"

"That's Honoria!" Brenda wailed. "I told you she's horrible."

The newscast continued: "In Westwood, local veterinarian Dr. Brent Emerson has initiated a new service for his furry clientele. Known simply as 'The Doggie Play

Group,' this new promotion allows dogs to do what they do best."

The camera cut from Honoria to show footage of a Maltese trying to hump Buster's back leg. "That's not fair!" I screamed. "That was the little fluff ball's first day at the play group. He was just trying to fit in."

Melissa added her opinion, "Too bad they show such a little thing dominating Buster. Kind of embarrassing, huh?"

I covered one eye and peered out between my fingers while Honoria's voice continued over the footage, "Here at the play group, dogs whose owners are too busy at work to spend time with them need not be cooped up all day."

"Not a bad plug," Mom offered.

"Yeah," I agreed, "But, she makes it sound like we're a group of selfish parents who want to cast off our fur children. Why doesn't she mention that it builds their independence and self-esteem?"

The footage continued to show two dogs rolling on the ground together, another one playing with a pen of tennis balls, and ending with Louie walking straight toward the camera. The newscast cut back to Honoria who said to her robotic co-anchor, "As you can see, the Doggie Play Group is open to all sorts." She smiled directly back to the audience and delivered her usual close, "This is Honoria Vitale--coming at you again soon." Teeth. Smile. Hair Toss.

I flipped off the television with an angry push of the button. "What did she mean by that?"

"What?" Mom asked.

"That bit about 'all sorts' when the camera was aimed at Louie. Made him sound like he's a different sort of sort."

"Different is good," Melissa chimed in. "That's what you're always trying to convince us."

"She probably didn't mean anything by it," Mom added. "After all, Louie is a rather unusual dog."

"See what I mean by her?" Brenda asked. "If it wasn't for you, April, I would never watch her. It's simply unbearable to hear her say how she's going to come at me. Honoria coming to get me--what a thought," she said and grimaced.

At that moment, Buster also grimaced, a loud, soulful moan, which made us all turn and catch our breath at the sight. His nose was swollen beyond recognition, making him look rather camel-like and not at all like a pedigree Golden Retriever.

"Thank God he didn't look like this on film," Melissa said. "You know how the camera adds ten pounds."

"Buster, what's happened to you?" I said reaching to stroke his head. He only whimpered and made an awful snorting sound as I reached for the leash.

"HE LOOKS DIFFERENT," THE RECEPTIONIST NOTED WITH a cock of her head.

"He's having a reaction," I said barely believing the inadequacies of her perceptive abilities.

"No, him," she said pointing at Louie. "I would never have recognized him from the newscast," she said and smiled eagerly. "Really great coverage, huh?"

"Great. But about Buster, this one," I said and pointed dramatically at his nose. "He's having trouble breathing. We need to see Brent right away."

She came around the desk and patted Buster on the head, then reached down to stroke his chest. Buster immediately dropped to the floor, rolled over on his back to give her easy access to his stomach, and wagged happily. "We'll get him in as soon as possible, but as you can see, we have other emergency cases tonight, and he seems pretty happy. Why don't you take a seat and I'll see what I can do."

I looked past the emergency office and into the main waiting room. A Beagle wrapped in a blanket shook fiercely and made crying noises as his owner, a woman in her forties with bird-like features, sang "Hush, Little Baby."

The receptionist returned, "We have another case already with the doctor. It'll just be another minute."

"I'm sure it's just an allergy to all those cats earlier today. Buster isn't used to feline dander," I added.

She glanced down once more: "He certainly is swelled beyond Retriever recognition," she added. "Let me see if the doctor will allow a quick cortisone shot." She left again with a swish of her uniformed, polyester pants. Within minutes, I saw Brent's face peering through the window in the door separating us from the examining rooms. He waved his latex glove covered hands and smiled brightly. The gesture appeared more frantic than friendly, but that impression was no doubt left behind by the tension that had developed between us.

The door half opened and he peeked his head out, a move that reminded me of a soldier peering out from behind a rock to wave the white flag. I decided that Buster's health depended on me breaking the ice. "I won't bite, and I don't think Buster is capable of doing so." I motioned to Buster, "Take a look."

"Ahh," he said in a very doctorly manner. "Your diagnosis seems to be correct. Let's give him a quick shot and see if the problem corrects itself. Did he eat anything unusual?"

"No. Actually, I think he's allergic to cats."

"You may be right," he said, and then as an afterthought added, "You can't be too careful who you have contact with."

We smiled. "How is everything with my ex?" I asked.

"We're going to give it a try."

"Were you ever interested in his acting advice?"

"I was a little nervous about the camera," he hedged.

I looked at his gorgeous face, trying to imagine it leaning in to kiss me, or perhaps, sleeping on the pillow next to mine. I couldn't.

"I'm glad he was able to give you the advice you needed."

As Brent led the way into the examining room I knew that I had no right to be upset. We hadn't even had one date. I had played out a fairytale relationship in my mind simply because I had a messed up marriage and then reverted back to my mother's antiquated notion that if I had been with a doctor things would have been different. The truth was that I'm the only person who can change the course of my life.

"So, shall we see how we can help Buster?" Brent asked hesitantly.

"Lead the way, doctor," I replied without any trace of hidden agenda or animosity.

Brent took Buster into the examining room for his shot and then observation afterward. Louie was feeling highly superior at getting out of the vet's office without a poke, and was quite more relaxed as we approached the waiting room. I peeked through the window to see what might still be waiting at this hour of the evening.

The German Shepard was back. It sat next to its owner, the two of them, side-by-side, on the couch meant for humans. "Be good," I warned Louie. It was a futile attempt for the moment I opened the door, he decided to regain his dominance and tried his damnedest to pull my shoulder out of its socket.

If Louie and I were having an arm wrestle, he was definitely ahead, pulling me toward the dog, despite my efforts. "I see you couldn't stay away from me," he replied.

"You've got my number!" I joked.

"Funny. Little good it's done me. I do better to meet you at the vet's office."

I allowed Louie to approach the dog. He stood at the base of the couch, staring up at her, three feet above him, due to both her height and the advantage of being on top of the couch. "So, you know my name, where I work, that my life is in crisis. Care to spill anything about yourself?"

"Nope."

"Well that's not good enough," I said and sat down next to him. Oh my, he even smelled good.

"This is Misty," he said indicating his dog, and then he held out his hand. "I'm Terence."

I took his hand and he squeezed mine gently, not releasing immediately. We were like that when Brent came into the waiting area and smiled when he saw us.

"April, Buster's fine, but no more cat visits for him," he said at me. "Terence, give Misty one of these in the morning and evening. They should make her more comfortable. You can both call me if you need anything."

Brent left us alone and to my delight, Terence, the Shepherd's owner, didn't immediately stand to leave. Buster, always the passive one, was lying on his back, feet in the air, while Misty sniffed under his tail and Louie jumped happily back and forth over his head.

"What was wrong with her?" I asked while watching the dogs romp.

"She's been scratching and chewing her leg. The doctor said it was a hot spot."

"You came to emergency for a hot spot?"

"It was keeping me up at night."

I laughed.

"What's so funny?" he asked.

"It's just that most people would say that it was keeping their dog up at night."

"Well, I guess I'm not like most people."

Imagine that. I had met a man in a vet's office who loved his dog and admitted that he wasn't like most people.

———

Chapter 23

"Congratulations, April," Bruce said as I entered the office. "Great coverage."

"Thanks. Brent seemed pleased with it, although that nasty Honoria made a couple of quips."

"Well, that's to be expected. The public won't remember the negative, just the coverage. But I must say," he said with a smile as he edged closer, "the boys certainly don't take after their beautiful mommy." I wanted to bite him.

Before I could respond, with or without teeth barred, Bebe announced the latest office catastrophe. I was expecting something along the lines of a client threatening to walk if we didn't get coverage immediately, or a retraction needing to be run due to a sloppy reporter. Instead, I learned that the latest crisis was of a more personal nature.

"Josh suggested the most vile thing, April," she wailed. Considering that I have walked in on them making out on the Xerox, massaging in the conference room, and sloughing dead feet cells in any available cubby, I feared the worst.

"Leather? Chains?" I asked with mild curiosity.

"Rutabagas!" she announced.

I couldn't bear to imagine it. "I don't want to know any more," I said.

"But you have to help me," Bebe continued. "He suggested a rutabaga cake for my birthday just to get on Farmer Joe's good side. What about my good side?"

"Not a bad idea," Bruce agreed. "April, you should have thought of it," he said in mock scolding and walked away.

Bebe just looked at me hopefully. "Well, everyone likes carrot cake. How bad could a root vegetable cake be?" I asked weakly.

LEANDRA HAD LEFT ANOTHER MESSAGE ON MY VOICE mail inquiring about her dress for the Flamingos. I had yet to figure out what I should wear, let alone Leandra.

"Leandra?" I said into the phone. "Buy whatever you want. It will be on Ryan's account and he's insisted that nothing, but the best should be worn by you."

"Ooh, goodie! What color should I wear? Basic black?"

"Oh no! Someone like you should be noticed," I said. "How about electric blue or ravaging red?"

"Ravaging red? I like it!"

"It's sure to be picked up by all the camera crews," I reminded.

"Red it is!"

The firm was purchasing a table for the event. Ryan and Leandra, Josh and Bebe, Farmer Joe and Dr. Emerson, as well as Bruce and myself would be together. With Leandra set to hit the boutiques of Rodeo Drive, I fingered the Visa given to me by my parents and wondered if I could justify using it one time.

"So, we'll finally have our date," Bruce announced at the door of my office.

"Bruce," I protested.

"Shh. Don't say anything, April. Just anticipate the evening," he said before leaving.

One crazy was replaced by the next as Bebe and Josh walked in. "April, no need to rent a stretch limo. Bebe and I are going to take our own car since we're staying overnight at the hotel," Josh said, snuggling into Bebe's neck as she squealed with delight.

"I take it you rectified the birthday cake dilemma?"

"Yes. It inspired our first make-up sex session," Bebe declared.

"Glad to hear it," I said.

Sometimes exhaustion breeds a sense of rejuvenation. I was so tired of going along with Bruce's delusions, helping to create my own set of fantasies in the press, and waiting for Josh and Bebe to fall off their cloud that I didn't pay attention to my own reality.

"It's time to get real," I said aloud and to nobody but myself. With that declaration, I reached into the top drawer of my desk, pulled out the scissors, and with one, efficient snip, cut the Visa in half. I had some serious shopping to do, but it would be done on my own.

Chapter 24

R yan, who didn't normally drink, was making up for it tonight. Neither his nerves, nor Matthew wanted to be ignored. Matthew had gotten wind that Ryan was involved in helping Brent prepare for his media conference and in spite of the fact that Matthew and Ryan had reconciled, he was still feeling somewhat cast aside since Ryan was now seated with Leandra. I had done my best to arrange for Matthew to be at a nearby table, but the atmosphere remained high intensity.

Ryan was nervous about his award and whether he would actually receive it. Josh and Bruce knew that if he didn't, they might lose their biggest account. Leandra knew that Ryan had a wandering eye that may or may not have included two different men as well as the fact that tonight of all nights, Ryan only seemed to be appeased by my presence.

"You need to stop drinking," I said under my breath.

"I'm nervous. It's helping."

"Ryan, que sera sera...whatever will be will be."

"Easy for you to say. Your life is perfect."

I stared at him with my mouth open. This was the man who had ended our marriage, decided that he preferred men, acknowledged that he had been cheating on me, then decided to pursue the one guy I may have been interested in because as an actor, he is extremely insecure, which is probably what caused half my battles at work.

"Perfect?" I repeated, hardly believing my ears. "How?"

"April, you are the strongest person I know. If you fail, you just get back up. You don't care what people say about you. And if they ever do say anything negative, you prove them wrong. Let's face it; I'm a screw up. Even with all the good publicity you've gotten for me, I'm no farther along in my career. So what if I'm up for a Flamingo? It's for a fucking soap opera."

I stared at Ryan. He was right. I had nothing to complain about. If I looked deep inside, my life was still pretty good. And Ryan quite possibly did me a favor. I mean, what if we had human children and then he came to the realization that he was gay? At least, he saved me that heartache. It wasn't his fault that he didn't realize things sooner, and I guess I was pretty lucky that we were still somewhat friends.

"Ryan, everything's going to be okay. But, I need you to trust me. Can you do that?"

"Of course I do, but what are talking about?"

"Just trust me. It'll be okay." And then the moment we had been waiting for arrived.

The emcee announced, "Now for the winner of the Best Daytime Actor Category." Four other names were read along with Ryan's. We all sat in silence, waiting.

Finola Anderson, last year's best actress winner, spoke next: "And the winner is...," she said while ripping the envelope. "Ryan Monahan!"

Our table was located in a prime location, just a few feet from the steps leading to the podium. The cameras were trained on all of us, gauging our reaction. Ryan broke out into his practiced smile and accepted congratulations from colleagues seated at nearby tables. He shook hands and patted backs, walked slowly around the table ensuring that the cameras caught his soon-to-be even more famous face. He was too busy to notice that I had also left my seat and was making my way up the stairs.

"Uh, accepting on behalf of Ryan will be...," Finola struggled to figure out who I was.

"April Monahan," I said distinctly into the microphone. "...Ryan's soon to be ex-wife and his highly-talented publicist."

Bruce and Josh were already making their way up the stairs. I was surprised they weren't carrying a net with them in hopes of hauling me off. I didn't have much time. "In a perfect world, tomorrow's headlines would read, 'Bum rap for Hollywood heart throb,'" I continued, "for as far as I'm concerned, Ryan is a contender for an Emmy. This beautiful, sensual, homosexual man has not been recognized until now for the true depth of his perfor-mance. I'm here to tell you, that his acting the part of the Hollywood heartthrob was his best role to date."

"April, sit down!" Josh insisted.

"Come back to the table," Bruce was pleading.

Bebe followed us to the stage: "April, stop shouting or you'll get worry lines."

I looked over the crowded room to see the faces staring in surprise. Bruce, Josh, and Bebe became frozen, realizing that they were also on display. Ryan stared at me from a distance, a small smile forming on his lips.

He turned around in his seat, searching until he found the person who he most wanted to share this moment with.

Matthew. I wasn't the only one who caught the glimpses between them. The cameras followed Ryan's gaze and filmed every minute. Leandra was now sobbing over the reality that she would never become the next Mrs. Ryan Monahan, but Matthew was beaming with pride.

"I thank you for this award," I say holding the Flamingo. "I created your image of Ryan, and so, I believe this award is mine." And with that, I left the massive room, waving the majestic bird at all of them.

Chapter 25

I waited two hours before the day extended into an hour reasonable enough to phone Jessica.

"What made you do it?" she asked.

I rolled onto my side, still cradling the phone in my neck while massaging my temples. "I was in a bad mood?" I said into the phone, but was smiling the most genuine smile that had graced my face in months.

"You've got that right. Call it a temper-tantrum, or hypoglycemic fit. Maybe a nervous break-down. Whatever you want to claim as the reason for the outburst, was it worth it?"

"You know what? When I left the room, my heart was pounding with the reality of what I'd done. I mean, my god, I outed Ryan in front of everyone! But then, as I drove home, the elation started to fade and I was, of course, faced with what I had done. I started worrying about law suits from every direction, Ryan, my work, even his lover." Wow. That was good. I should start writing speeches as part of my PR services.

"You know how to make friends and influence people," Jessica stated.

I gave a feeble, little laugh. "You've got that right. And you know what? I'd do it all again."

I ARRIVED AT RYAN'S APARTMENT NOT SURE OF WHAT OR whom I might find. Leandra would no doubt be lurking nearby. The press was probably ready to pounce. I knocked timidly on the door, clutching the Flamingo statuette in my free hand.

A bleary-eyed Ryan opened the door. "Hey, I'm glad to see you. You haven't come here to hit me over the head with that thing?" he asked, pointing to the award.

"I came to return it," I said humbly. "It's your award. You deserve it."

He took the award from my hands, carefully turning it over to examine it from all angles. He handled it gently, lovingly, like it was a baby to be cradled, rather than a piece of cold metal, which would eventually end up on a shelf.

"April?"

"Yes"

"You deserve it, too," he said and smiled. "I realize that I've never thanked you for all your work."

"Well, maybe you shouldn't. My work, as you say, has now outed you in Hollywood. I don't have to tell you what that might do to your career."

"You're right," he said cooly. I feared the lawsuit talk would come next. "You never told me it would be the best thing for me," he said with a huge smile.

I looked around, wondering if I was experiencing one of my daydreams, but the room was as it had been a moment before. Ryan was still standing in the same position, and I was coherent! "Excuse me?" I asked.

"You heard me. Half the press believes you; the other half doesn't. The 'is he, isn't he' buzz around town is getting me a lot of free publicity and the producer of "Setting Sun" called to congratulate me on the award and renew my contract!"

"What about Matthew?"

"Are you kidding? This was the best thing for us! Matthew always wanted me to be upfront, but I thought I would lose everything. The only thing I lost was Leandra and that, as you know, is a blessing!" he said and laughed. "So I have to ask you something."

"What is it?"

"Why'd you do it, April? You're too good of a publicist to not know that this was the best thing anyone could've done for me. But I've been such an enormous jerk."

"I did it for us," I said simply and without any trace of wanting. "I started as your publicist and in retrospect, it probably should've stayed professional between us. I figured it could end the way it began...me as your publicist, you as a terrific client."

"You think I could get back to that status?"

"Yeah, I do."

We smiled at each other and pulled each other in for a hug. It felt better than good. It felt right.

"WHAT'S GOING ON?" I ASKED, WITNESSING TOTAL chaos in the office. Junior publicists seemed to be scrambling faster than usual. The phones sounded incessantly and Bebe was perpetual motion answering them. She placed the calls on hold long enough to utter, "Josh is in his office. Wants to see you."

I expected the worst as I walked down the hall, and then timidly opened his door a crack.

"Bebe?"

"No, it's April."

Josh beckoned me in, but before saying anything, he called for Bebe on the intercom. "Why do you want Bebe here?"

"Because she has a lot to do with what I'm about to say," Josh said simply. I knew it, they wanted to sue me and Bebe was supposed to be a witness to what was about to happen.

"Josh, I regret my outburst," I began.

"Hold on, April," he said as Bebe came into the office. "Come here, darling," he said to her. How inappropriate! Right in front of me!

"April, I realize that your meltdown..."

"Outburst," I corrected."

"Well, call it whatever you like. In my book, you went bonkers." I felt mildly insulted, but not enough to risk arguing. "As I was saying," Josh continued, "You put things in perspective for me last night."

"I did?"

"Yes. We all need support from each other. It's obvious that you didn't have sufficient support from this office or in your personal life. I want to correct that immediately."

"It's really not necessary..." I started to say.

"That's why I've asked Bebe to be my wife!"

My mouth dropped and an image of Bebe walking down the aisle, donned in white with an enormous, protruding stomach entered my mind. "She's pregnant!"

"Of course not!" said Josh. "We're in love."

Bebe moved in closer and Josh pulled her onto his lap.

I watched in horror as she sat on his lap, arms wrapped around his head. My worst fear had been realized. My secretary was marrying my boss. However, I couldn't argue with how happy they each looked.

"Congratulations," I said to them, and to my surprise, I actually meant it.

I LEFT BEBE BEHIND IN JOSH'S OFFICE TO DO WHATEVER it is she normally does, and found Bruce waiting for me in the hall.

"Can we talk a moment?" he said and motioned to the conference room.

"Sure," I said uncomfortably. "I wouldn't want to leave you out."

He gave me a funny look, but continued nonetheless. "April, as senior partner, it's my job to make sure our office is run efficiently and profitably. You know how fond I am of you," he said copping a feel for my arm.

"Bruce," I said inching away. "I can't date you."

"Of course not," he agreed — finally! "You'll be away."

"Away?" I asked.

"You are going to seek help," he said more as a statement than a question. "I'll hold your job open while you undergo treatment."

I felt strong. "Bruce, I'm fine. I won't be needing psychiatric treatment. And, while I appreciate your offer to keep my position open, I won't be needing that either."

"You're angry?"

"Not at all," I said and kissed him lightly on the cheek. "I'm opening my own firm and I was hoping that you would send your overflow to me. I learned so much from you, but I want to try and make a go of doing things my way."

THERE WAS ONLY ONE FILE I BOTHERED TO TAKE FROM my desk. I left the office and headed down Pacific Coast Highway, taking in the late afternoon glow of the sun shining on the ocean. Surfers dotted the waves and I smiled wondering if one of them was trying out a new surf wax. Girls that looked like Barbie watched the guys from afar, and I smiled thinking of them being the next proto-types for Jean-Paul's designs. I had my own business ideas. Perhaps, I would call Peter because in business one always needs a good accountant.

The plan started small, just a local hangout where owners could leave their pets for a few hours, but my idea was to grow it into a national franchise. The doggie play group would include fitness and diet experts, groomers, and special equipment such as wading pools and tread-mills. I was even thinking of hiring a chef to create unique treats that could be branded and marketed to an even bigger cross-section of my demographic. As I arrived home, I felt excited to enter the test market phase of my plan starting in Orange County, Los Angeles, and Santa Barbara before branching out to Northern California and beyond. Buster and Louie were anxious to help.

Epilogue

A *ries: "Move cautiously while moon is in Venus. Ram's sunny exterior has taken cover."*

I read my horoscope twice, taking in its negativity, and then, without bothering to find another reading more to my liking, crumpled up the paper and through it in the recycling bin. I would make my own future and in my opinion, it looked bright.

Josh and Bruce wished me the best and made me promise to call them if I needed any help getting started. Bebe even offered to spend a few weekend hours helping me get my filing system in place. With everything falling into place, I drafted a proposal for Brent to serve on the advisory board of the doggie play group in order to find investors. I suggested incorporating the name "Doggie and Me," and basing the idea off the popular mother/child play groups that have already swept the country. With venture capital funding and my public relations expertise, I was convinced we had a winner.

Two months after opening our charter location in Beverly Hills, Buster and Louie had twenty-five playmates, who regularly used my newest exercise facilities and took great enjoyment in partaking at a doggie walk-up bar.

The press was all over it. Brent and I were great business partners and I had learned from previous experience not to want for more. However, one particular client had caught my attention.

"Misty's hot spot trouble seems to be under control," I said to Terence.

"Indeed. She bounces back quickly. You've been busy."

"Yes, but things are settling down now."

"Do you think Buster and Louie be opposed to having a play date outside of Doggie and Me?"

"What did Misty have in mind?" I asked coyly.

"Perhaps a gourmet doggie meat loaf for the kids and something more upscale for us?"

My heart suddenly was pounding so loudly I was sure he could hear it too. Terence waited for my answer, looking at me with an expression of hope. It was the same look that I had found myself wearing before, but this time I was actually sharing it with someone else. "We'd love to."

And then, without any warning, Terence showed me how a man acts when he's really interested in a woman. He pulled me in close, tipped his head down to meet mine and stared into my eyes.

"You are a beautiful person. I knew it the night we spent here."

I just stared at him. Our faces were so close I could feel his soft breath near my ear as he whispered to me. There were no voices in my head, only his in my ear.

"April, you are an original."

He let his lips touch my ear and then trail across my cheek toward my lips. Oh my god, he was going to kiss me.

A real heart-pounding kiss, not the kind that lurks in my imagination, but one with intention and purpose and based in reality. It was all a bit too much to take in and nerves got the better of me.

I interrupted the kiss that I so desperately wanted. "An original what?"

He smiled and brushed the side of my cheek with his fingertips. "I'm not sure. But I know this, I can't wait to find out."

"I'm sorry I interrupted what you were about to do."

"Was I about to do something?"

"I think, maybe."

"I think you're right," he said before tilting my chin upwards and allowing his lips to find their way to mine. It was perfect.

Thank you for taking time to read "Alert the Media."

If you enjoyed it, please consider telling your friends or posting a short review. Word of mouth is an author's best friend and much appreciated.

Thank you, Mia.

About the Author

Mia Fox is a Los Angeles-based novelist who writes across varied genres including Contemporary and Paranormal Romance, Chick Lit, and Satire. She received her Bachelor of Arts Degree in Communications from U.S.C. and a Master's Degree in Professional Writing, also from U.S.C.

Before writing full time, she worked as an entertainment publicist, a career she chronicles in her novel, "Alert the Media." However, she is happy to leave that world behind her, preferring that any drama in her life is only that which she creates for her characters.

She lives in Los Angeles with her husband, three children, and their fur children, Oliver and Bean.

Stay in touch with Mia…
www.miafox.net

www.ingramcontent.com/pod-product-compliance
Lightning Source LLC
Chambersburg PA
CBHW030319200626
46816CB00006BA/1848